TO SAVE A HIGHLAND SINNER

LORI ANN BAILEY

OLD WORLD MEDIA, LLC

For Gunner,
whose boundless energy,
and kind heart are the greatest of treasures.

CHAPTER 1

berdeen, Scotland
July 1811

Although born Katherine Mitchell, Kate went by many names.

Today, she'd be taking on the persona of a wealthy merchant's sister. But in actuality, the name she would be assuming belonged to a twelve-year-old girl who lived in the city apartment rented by her adoptive family of rejects. None of whom knew of her plan or the danger she'd be facing.

Her family was about to lose that home, affectionately called Camelot. The circumstances leading to the imminent catastrophe were all her fault, so she was on her way to rectify the situation.

She stepped out of the carriage she'd been riding in and could finally fill her lungs. If she could have arrived by horseback or hackney, she would have, but the task she'd set for herself this time required that she appear to be a lady who enjoyed refined things. She dreaded getting back in that box, even if only for the short ride remaining to reach the Earl of Stonehaven's estate.

Soon, she would be someone else. But for the next few

minutes, she could just be Kate—a person even she no longer recognized. Kate was a woman who few had ever met, and she planned on keeping it that way.

"Thank ye. I'll only be a couple of minutes," she said to her coachman, who she'd hired weeks ago, but only met up with this morning.

She trusted the driver because he sometimes did jobs for her brother, Will Douglas, leader of their motley crew. Will was feared and known as the King of the Streets. She laughed at the nickname, which seemed ridiculous to her—but there was another man in the city who had been given the moniker the King of the Docks, so she guessed it was appropriate for both men to stake out their territory.

The coachman could be trusted to keep her secret safe because no one wanted to invite Will's ire upon themselves. No one except for the King of the Docks had ever challenged Will.

She slipped off her shoes and removed her stockings before dipping her toes into the cool creek beside the road. The stop had been spontaneous, but as she'd neared her destination, the confines of the coach and the pressure she'd placed on herself had her heart racing. A bead of sweat trailed down her temple.

The gurgling sound of the water, the fresh light air of the afternoon, and the warmth of the sun enveloped her and eased the nausea in her belly. She wasn't nervous about the task in front of her. It was so easy to fool others. Most people didn't know how to sway unsuspecting souls to their cause. She did. The trick was being honest about everything you could but lying when necessary.

No, the ache in her belly had to do with the damned box she had to get back into to make her appearance at the house party where the game would begin.

As she waded out into the stream, the cold of the brook covered her feet and gave her clarity. This was the most carefully planned ruse she'd ever crafted. But still, she had to be able to recall the lessons she'd learned over the years, so she went over the list she knew by heart.

Flatter your mark. Everyone loves to hear about themselves and how accomplished and special they are. A flattered fool will like you because they think you have things in common and you have good taste.

Make them think you're on the same side. Whenever you can, try to team up with them to solve problems or have them help you with one. When speaking with your opponent, using *we* and *us* helps your mark associate with you because they think you both wish for the same outcome.

Use your target's name. People like hearing their name, and this makes your relationship personal, adding value to your presence. They'll be more likely to keep you by their side and continue talking.

Mimic the posture of those whose trust you seek. The more they think you are similar to them, the faster they will open up.

Let the mark think they are winning. Doesn't everyone love to win? This puts them in a favorable mood and more likely to agree with your suggestions.

Set an urgent deadline. When pressure is applied, one's reasoning is often diminished. Take advantage of a flustered target.

Your flaws can be a strength. Make yourself sympathetic. Why would people trust someone who couldn't appear vulnerable?

This one she had down to an art. Being a woman helped, but also, she had some serious failings that made her appear fragile.

Promise whatever you need to. Promise a meeting with the prince or another businessman. You won't be around to follow through, but they don't know that yet.

Hoof beats pounded on the ground and reached her ears.

She ignored the lucky bastard—instead of riding wild and free on the back of a steed, she would be forced to return to her torture chamber. She held her face up to the sun and waited for the stranger to pass as she focused on the sounds of the gurgling stream and the nearby chirps of birds.

If she could have a place to call home, it would be near a stream. The pleasant sounds had calmed her nerves and had her wishing she'd found a way to take a nap.

She was becoming weary of moving from location to location and never finding out who she could be if she didn't have to be someone else. Sure, she could stay at Camelot, but the only person who knew her there was Will. As soon as the others did, they would either want her gone, or they'd leave themselves.

Perhaps after this ruse, she would even purchase a horse as a companion. She'd heard they live a long time. She'd seen people heartbroken when they'd lost their domesticated cats and dogs. She would not set herself up for that kind of pain. A mount might stay around for a nice long time.

Dreams could wait. She needed to focus on the plan at hand. It had taken months of careful planning, and now the moment was at hand. She turned and strolled back to the carriage, picking up her stockings and shoes along the way.

It was time.

All the pieces were in place and going according to plan. Now, she turned her focus to getting the job done.

∽

Gavin Davidson had never attended a house party before. He hoped never to again. Even now, he'd snuck away to race his steed down the road—anything to wake him from the boredom of sitting around and being still.

As a constable in the City of Glasgow Police, he was accustomed to breaking up brawls and tracking down criminals. Danger had a way of finding him, and he had his ways of dealing with the strain by keeping a strict moral code.

Gray areas didn't exist.

There was only black and white, wrong or right, unlawful or innocent. He never strayed from this belief. This was what kept him going and prevented him from sinking into moral dilemmas, and questioning his reactions, when judgement calls could mean the difference between life and death.

Of course, he spent some days doing menial tasks involving street maintenance, lighting, and occasionally refuse disposal. All of those were preferable to sitting in a room and attempting to look polite by not dunking biscuits into his tea. He liked a challenge, but so far, the biggest one at the Stonehaven estate was which style of eggs to choose from the sideboard.

While he liked the guests well enough that he'd met so far, this event seemed like a huge waste of his time. He'd only come to the Earl of Stonehaven's estate to catch a criminal. One who he had on good authority would be here, but so far, there was no sign of the villain.

Lazing around a house and playing games didn't come naturally to him. He'd been working since an early age, and having idle hands while he waited was driving him mad. He'd only arrived late last night, but today the activity was walking around the grounds.

He would have joined the others to examine the layout of the lands, but they'd set out just as he'd returned from his morning run. He'd seen a small portion of the grounds during his exercises but would take the time later to learn more. Even so, he didn't suspect the person he was looking for would wander far from the drawing room.

Especially since he'd learned there would be no children around for the deviant to target.

As he galloped down the road, he came across a carriage pulled over. He slowed his pace to see what could be going on. He imagined some robbery he needed to assist with, but all seemed well as the coachman casually waved and smiled at him.

He pulled his horse up short. He'd even taken to daydreaming, which was something he'd not done since he'd been a young lad. For instance, right now, he wished to place his hands around the waist of the lovely lass striding into the stream. She looked genuine, void of deception—the picture of a good, honest woman who would make some man a proud husband one day if she hadn't already.

Her carriage, and the style of her red gown, indicated she was a lady of some means, but he'd never known a woman of such status to give up her pretense of refined culture and be her true self. He wanted a woman like her, one who was sincere and honest.

But he was too rough around the edges for such a lass . . . his world too dark.

He scared off any lass that came near him, and he couldn't help but be direct with them about who he was. He was not an easy man to take, and he might never be husband material. He didn't know how to be gentle.

Still, if he could be such, he'd want a woman like that one.

A woman who knew how to be herself and was comfortable with it.

He abhorred dishonesty.

And that was why he found himself at a country estate not far out of Aberdeen. He had a crime to solve. Since the usual miscreants seemed to be taking a vacation in Glasgow, his superior had allowed him to pursue this case. Then, he'd move on to the one in the city of Aberdeen he'd been preparing for what felt like an eternity. The assailants he was tracking had perpetrated injustices committed in his city, one recent, one over a decade ago.

Both had left a muddy footprint on his soul and had the darkest part of him crying out for justice.

Aye. He was accustomed to dealing with hardened criminals, those who hurt children. He wouldn't know how to treat a refined lady.

The lass seemed to sigh as she gazed toward the heavens. Her obscured face took in the lovely day. He almost wished she'd turn his way so he could see what color her eyes were. Her hair gleamed a coppery red in the rays of the sun. Gentle hands held her skirts aloft as the water sped past her bare ankles, her shapely calves just visible.

He readjusted himself in the seat, then started back toward the estate.

He should be scoping out his new environment, not dreaming of a lass who wouldn't be able to handle his dark side.

CHAPTER 2

*K*ate's coachman, Donnie, turned from the main road onto one lined with ancient oaks, their trunks strong and thicker than the largest barrels she'd seen rolled off ships in Aberdeen. Massive limbs stretched from either side and reached far across the top of the well-trodden path, shading it from the mid-day rays of light that battled to peek through the canopy.

There was something magical about the way they draped the span, as sun-dappled shadows brought to mind the tales of fae that her brother, Bran, liked to tell. It was cooler here, and a soft breeze blew through the windows, easing the heat of confinement. The air carried with it the scent of earth and wilderness, age and wisdom.

She had the urge to tell the coach driver to stop one more time so that she could alight from the carriage and touch one, run her fingers along its rough white-and-gray speckled bark. Some of the bases had a smattering of greening moss on the sides, which remained hidden from the light of day.

As the tunnel of trees opened up, golden rays once again beat down on the smooth gravel path flanked by hedges and matching gardens of colorful wildflowers. She craned her neck through the opening to stare at the beauty, then to see the estate as it came into view.

The formidable building looked more like a palace than a house. The walls were made of the same gray stones that lined Aberdeen's streets, but these stones were polished and cleaned and almost gleamed with reflected light. Large windows symmetrically lined the two main floors, and smaller ones complimented them from the ground level and the attic.

Kate said a quick prayer that the rooms would be as large as they appeared and the windows would easily open to the air.

The estate was a magnificent work of art. She had never stayed at a place so grand.

Donnie drew the carriage to a stop in the circular drive. He jumped down and pulled open the door, then held out his hand. "We have arrived."

She stepped out and took a deep, soothing breath. Anything was better than being stuck in that carriage. She was dreading the completion of the mission because it meant she would have to ride in the box again . . . possibly with her mark.

She shivered.

"And so it begins. They should take good care of ye, and if all goes as planned, ye can relax the next few days until we need to return to Aberdeen," she said.

"Good luck, my lady." Donnie winked as someone rushed down the steps of the house to greet her.

The man stood before her, bowed, then smiled in welcome. "Good morning. Would you be Miss Reid?"

Aye . . . she was now. "I am. Do ye have someone who can help my coachman with my trunk and instruct him as to where the stable is?"

"Yes, my lady. I'll send someone out straight away."

"That would be lovely."

"Can I show you inside?" the man asked.

"Please." She held her shoulders high and effectuated a sophisticated air.

"Lord and Lady Stonehaven are showing guests around the estate. I expect them back soon. I can show you to the drawing room until your room is prepared."

"Thank ye."

The reception hall was as magnificent as the exterior of the palatial home. Shining marbled floors, with black and gold squares, were lined with white and gave way to warm wood-paneled walls. A vase sitting on an intricately carved side table overflowed with flowers in a rainbow of colors as the sweet scent of gardenias wrapped her in comfort.

"Would you like some refreshment while you wait?" the butler asked as he whisked her straight through.

"No, thank ye," she said.

The man bowed and left the room. The drawing room was large, but she still craved open space after being in the carriage. She bypassed studying the chamber and darted directly for an expansive opening that led onto a terrace.

She stopped in the doorway and breathed in, then glanced around the back lawn to enjoy the beauty, thankful for the spare seconds to collect her thoughts and prepare herself for the coming machinations.

Once she'd had her fill of fresh air, she turned to take in her workspace.

She jumped.

A man sat in the far corner of the room watching her. His hair was dark as coal. He leaned back as if relaxed, but it was a deception because his gaze was watchful, predatory. Every muscle in his body appeared to be on guard, and she thought he could hurdle to attention faster than she could call for assistance. She only knew two other men who'd inspired spikes of fear to flush through her body: her brother, Will, and Drostan Webster, the King of the Docks.

This man was pure danger.

He stood, and she swallowed. His lazy gate was deceptively casual as his interest remained rooted to her, scrutinizing and assessing. He moved closer. And even though his gaze never left hers, it still felt as if it had scanned her and learned more than what she'd wanted to give away in the few moments that she'd thought she was alone.

She only let his purposeful regard distract her for an instant. Straightening her shoulders, she drew her them back but relaxed into the posture with practiced ease. She reminded herself it was good to show vulnerability.

"Ye startled me. I was led to believe I was alone." She didn't fight it and let the blush color her complexion as the thought struck her that he had examined her as a man might a woman he was interested in bedding.

"I like the way ye look when ye think no one is watching. It's refreshing."

She'd been right, and now the flush on her skin heated. His voice was deep and masculine, making her feel small. Despite her average height, this man stood at least a head above her, and she had to tilt her face to stay focused on his eyes, which were the shade of blue matching that on a jay's wings. They were a startling contrast to the darkness of the rest of him.

She'd only been in the room a few moments, but she felt as if he'd had too much time to study her. How had he known her true self was different?

"Thank ye, kind sir," she purposely flattered. "Are ye here for the house party?"

In all her months of preparations, she had imagined every situation she could encounter, but her preparations had not readied her for this man. Why was he here? And why did her body spring to life as if he presented peril that both frightened and excited her?

"Aye. I am."

Then who the bloody hell was he?

"Then 'twould seem we will be spending quite a bit of time together." She batted her lashes, a slow, seductive blink that she'd learned had a strong effect on the opposite sex. If possible, his granite form grew still, and she knew that even though he didn't let on so, he'd taken the subconscious clue. He was aware of what she was doing.

She continued, "I'm Allison Reid. 'Tis a pleasure to meet ye."

A shock of suspicion flashed in his eyes, but he hid it well. If she weren't good at reading people, she would have missed it. How could he not believe her? No one here should know Allie. Who was this man?

"I'm Gavin Davidson. Where are ye from, Miss Reid?"

His shoulders had tightened, and he deliberately lowered his head to inspect her closer. His set jaw led her to believe something in their short conversation had turned her into prey. She held back the shiver that wanted to slide down her spine. Now his interest was not on her as a woman but possibly as a wooden puzzle box that he intended to bend and contort until he knew every inch of her.

She swallowed, took a deep breath, and continued with her ruse. "I'm from Stirling. My brother is a merchant there."

"Interesting," he said as his tone flattened.

Why did he doubt her?

"And will yer brother be joining us?" he continued.

"Nae. He is away on business." She gave a longing smile to make it appear as if she was sad that he couldn't be present.

"What's yer brother's name? Perhaps I've heard of him." Mr. Davidson moved closer, his large frame making her feel as if he was one of the immovable oaks from the drive, strong, weather-worn, and all-seeing.

"Oh, aye. He's quite the self-made man. His name is Joseph."

"Joseph Reid." He seemed to roll the words over in his

mind as he spoke them. His brow crinkled slightly, then straightened as his gaze became darker. "And ye say yer name is Allison."

"Aye." Her heart began to flutter. She should take offense to his casual use of a name that wasn't truly hers, but she couldn't muster the outrage as something more akin to fear flowed in her veins.

"I'd like to hear more about yer brother's business."

"Oh there is plenty of time for that and it bores me to tears. I wish to hear about ye." She hedged and hoped to turn the conversation back to flattery. "What do ye do, Mr. Davidson?"

"I'm a constable." His predatory gaze pinned her, and one eyebrow rose as if he expected her to flee at the declaration.

Ice pumped through her blood, and she rubbed the gooseflesh that spread across her arms. She hoped he didn't notice, but his eyes seemed to take in everything.

Well, he was correct. He was a man of the law. If she didn't have to be here, his presence alone would send her running for the safety of the carriage she dreaded.

Charm him, then avoid him. It was all she could do in the circumstance.

She smiled. When she leaned in, her gaze traveled from his eyes to take in the span of his chest. A trace of fresh woods and bergamot filled her nostrils, refreshing and all male. The scent was heady and dizzying. She deeply inhaled as nerves fired in her body, surprising her. The smell of men never called to her in this way.

Perhaps her fear was causing her senses to misfire because she didn't have to feign the desire to see what he looked like without his shirt. Her deep intake of breath as she imagined touching his chest astonished her.

Once her eyes returned to him, she was pleased to discover the move had garnered his interest. He looked like a man who thought he could save a woman in distress. Now that she had his attention, it might be time to show him how vulnerable she could be.

Let him think he's in control.

The best deceptions had truth to them.

~

Gavin was no longer bored.

Sure, his jaw ticked, and his blood boiled at the lass's deception. But he was intrigued. She played with him, but a part of him wished the dilation in her eyes as she'd moved closer had been a real reaction to him.

This woman was blatantly lying to him and doing it with an ease that rivaled an experienced English lady serving tea. He suppressed the urge to accuse her outright. He had the belief she would retreat if pressed on the topic and then she might run, and he'd never know her agenda.

He needed more time to study her, learn who she was, and then swoop in and . . . what? She'd committed no offense in Glasgow. She might be impersonating someone, but he didn't have the authority to drag her back to his city and charge her with such a minor crime. He'd never let a bonny face distract him from his mission, but damn if his mind didn't go back to seeing her in that creek when he'd thought her genuine.

Analyzing her now, he was struck by the beauty and inconsistency of her eyes. They were brown near her pupils, then bled into a bright green ringed by a color that could almost be called blue. They were quite appealing, like the rest of her.

He'd seen hesitation in her eyes when she'd discovered he was a man of the law. She was right not to think he'd go along willingly with her ruse, but for now, he needed to expose what she was up to, and her pleading a headache and running off to her room wouldn't do.

"Shall we take in some air? I regret not joining the others on touring the estate." He deliberately lightened his tone and attempted to put her at ease.

Her eyes softened slightly, but he could tell she wanted to flee, to hide away and try to decipher what had tipped her hand. He wouldn't let her escape that easily, and she'd never figure out how he knew she was fabricating a great number of things.

"Come. Ye have paled. The bonny sun will do ye some good."

He didn't give her an option to bow out gracefully. He took the crook of her arm, firmly but gently, in his hand and drew her toward the large, windowed door that opened onto the terrace.

Sparks sizzled and ignited as their bare flesh touched. He tamped down the sudden thrill that pulsed in his veins. She was a deceiver, and nothing about her could be trusted. So, why did he find her so damned fascinating?

"Ye have strong hands, Constable Davidson," she cooed in a lovely voice that teased but also bordered on being sultry.

Flattery or truth, he wondered.

"That sounds so formal." She pouted, drawing attention to her full, luscious lips. "I believe, due to the nature of this party, we will get to ken each other well. What do yer friends call ye?" She fished for more information on him.

"We've only had moments to become acquainted, Miss Reid. I barely ken yer name."

He knew for sure it wasn't Allison Reid, and she didn't have a brother named Joseph. The real Allie did, but not this imposter. His research had been meticulous, and he knew everyone that stayed at the house William Douglas called home. But how did this lass have knowledge of the children who resided with the man referred to as the King of the Streets in Aberdeen?

Her smile was delightful and aimed at him as if she

understood how to wield it as a weapon. She kept the bonny expression, even though a flash in her eyes told him that she was aware he was on to her.

A slight breeze blew on the terrace as the sun shone down. A whiff of oranges with a seductive blend of spice and gardenias. She was intoxicating, and he understood that she was confident in her deceptions because she knew the effect she had on men. He'd trained himself to be good at reading others and picking up on the signs their bodies offered when telling an untruth.

But her tale was so subtle that even he could barely pick it out.

Two blinks, but instead of the action of being subconscious, she'd trained herself to give the signal as a sign of innocence. Damn, she was good. He should be furious at her ruse, but he was intrigued.

She was a challenge, and he was good at puzzles.

"Let's remedy that. What brings ye to the Stonehaven's estate?" she asked.

"Pursuit of justice."

They took the steps down, and he guided them toward the manicured gardens.

"Do ye always follow such noble causes?" Her eyes teased as her chin tilted up to meet his stare.

"'Tis what I live for." He stopped their progression and met her gaze straight on.

"Ye are well suited to the occupation, with yer dark, brooding eyes and strong build." She laughed. She'd been honest with him and intended to flatter him at the same time.

Her voice was husky and overly familiar. A tactic to draw him in, he thought. And it was working because he had to shake away the lust that ignited in his breast.

He began walking again, drawing her with him at a comfortable pace. "What brings ye here, Miss Reid?"

"Business," she stated, then took a short breath and quickly continued, "But I have to say that I love this country air. I shall savor the visit if the days are like this one. Do ye live in the city or out in the country?"

She had told the truth again. He knew by the way she'd held her head up to the sun like when he'd spied her earlier, and by the way that her eyes sparkled. As they strolled through the grass, her eyes appeared greener than they had in the light of the drawing room

She'd also deftly changed the conversation.

"I have a small cottage just outside of Glasgow."

He guided them toward the symmetrical rows of roses of all shades, and blue, white, and orange flowers he couldn't name. They were surrounded by plants and bushes that had been cut into shapes. The effect was lovely, but they didn't catch his eye the way the lass at his side did as she took in the magnificence of the grounds.

"Tell me about yer family, Constable Davidson. Do they miss ye?"

"I have no family."

"That's why ye can sneak away for so long. No' even a wife?"

"Nae."

She was fishing. He wished not to volunteer any more personal information—time for her to answer a couple of questions.

"I ken ye have a brother, but any other family?"

"Nae. 'Tis just us." She froze and wiggled her fingers from his grasp to inspect a rose. He suspected it was another diversion, but he wasn't certain this time. She leaned down to inspect it and inhaled.

A movement to the right caught his attention as guests emerged from behind a row of tall hedges that formed some barrier. He guessed the configuration might hide a manmade maze. The group seemed to have spied them and were headed in their direction.

He was about to lose his time with her. Certain she'd use any excuse available to escape his scrutiny, he took her arm again and guided her toward the path that led away from the people she'd not spied yet.

Her eyes lit, and she halted their progress. He attempted to pull her along, but she said, "Look." Then she pointed to the small grassy area between the tall row of triangular and round bushes he'd steered them towards and a large pond on the far end of the property. Rabbits dotted the green space.

"They scare easily," she whispered.

He glanced over his shoulder as murmurs began to reach his ears. He had more questions, but he had the sense she was like one of those creatures and would flee if provoked. It went against his nature to not probe. If they were in Glasgow, he could detain her, but he didn't want her to run before he could find out how she was connected to the man he'd be going after as soon as his mission here was accomplished.

So, he stood there, waiting for the interruptions as she watched the small brown animals hop and feed. Perhaps the presence of others would ease her concerns, and she'd give away some helpful information.

"I've never seen so many in one place. They don't do this in the city."

At least he'd learned she truly was from a highly-populated area. However, he knew she'd not come from a home in Stirling, because she came to the party from the north, the direction of Aberdeen and William Douglas. His jaw clenched at the thought of the wretched excuse of a human being.

Some of the party guests broke off and headed for the house, while Lady Stonehaven and her friend who managed a theatre in London, Mrs. Bartrom, continued toward them.

Gavin relaxed, though, because he may have just been dealt the winning hand with this lass who must know his next investigation's target. She could give him the upper hand if he could squeeze the information that he needed from her.

In a gesture meant to reassure her and tempt her to resist the urge to flee, he released his hold on her arm and took her hand in his. She blinked, surprised by his move as he drew her hand to his lips. He let his mouth linger on her sensitive flesh a little longer than necessary. A lovely tint of rose-colored her cheeks, and her lips fell open.

Spiced oranges and gardenias enveloped him—not the gardens, but the alluring aroma of the so-called Miss Reid.

She was successfully flustered.

His head rose, then he let go of her hand as his lips began to tingle.

"It seems our time alone is coming to a close. I look forward to having yer attention to myself again."

"Are ye trying to disarm me, Constable Davidson?" Her breathy question told him he'd succeeded.

"Is it working?"

"I believe it is." She didn't blink. She seemed surprised by her reaction to him.

An older voice, Lady Stonehaven's, reached his ears. "It appears ye have found our latest arrival, Constable Davidson. It's a pleasure to see you again. So thrilled you could take the time to join us."

"I have had the pleasure of her company but only a few moments."

"How was yer journey, dear? Did you and your brother finish his business in Edinburgh?" Lady Stonehaven asked.

"Aye. We did. He was most successful, and I'm sorry I missed the chance to introduce ye." The supposed Miss Reid blinked two times.

"At least we have you for now. I'm thrilled you were able to change your plans and join us." Lady Stonehaven beamed.

"I'm pleased to be here. Thank ye, Lady Stonehaven. What I've seen of yer estate is breathtaking."

"If we were able, we'd come more often. This atmosphere gives us a chance to throw away all the strictures of society and enjoy ourselves for a little while."

He'd sought out Lord Stonehaven when he'd heard the man he was investigating would be here for a week or so. They'd had drinks in a tavern, and Gavin had told him of the man's depravity and the need to bring him to justice. Lord Stonehaven, who was English peerage, agreed to let him come and investigate the man.

In the talk, he'd heard that Lady Stonehaven had once been a famous singer and daughter of a merchant. While they enjoyed a happy, fulfilled marriage, she sometimes craved gatherings of people where she didn't have to guard every word she said. Being a member of the ton was like a job, and she occasionally needed time off.

They were very much in love, and Lord Stonehaven had confided that he relished seeing his wife blossom back into the self she had to hide from society. So, it was a quite unconventional crowd she'd invited to join them. He glanced at the woman still by his side.

He would wager he knew Miss Reid better than their hosts.

"Our butler will be preparing some refreshments. Would you like to join us in the drawing room?"

"That would be lovely," Miss Reid said.

He strolled behind them, giving the ladies a chance to catch up, listening for clues.

As he did, the curve of Miss Reid's graceful neck caught his attention. Masses of curls were pinned up into an attractively casual pile, secured with red ribbons that matched her gown. She'd left a select few of her loosely woven ringlets dangle at the front of her temples. He wondered if she had a maid or if she'd done it herself. Perhaps if she had someone else with her, he could question them. Sometimes servants were the best informants.

She glanced over her shoulder and gave him a sly smile. She most likely knew his thoughts hadn't wavered from his inspection of her.

As they crossed the threshold into the drawing room, she covertly scanned their surroundings. What was she up to?

Lady Stonehaven said, "The refreshments will be ready at half-past the hour. Your room has been prepared."

"Thank ye. I'd like to get settled and will return shortly." Miss Reid smiled at their host.

"Jenny will show ye the way."

The lass followed the maid. As soon as they'd exited the room, he excused himself and trailed at a discreet pace. At the top of the stairs, they turned toward the wing of rooms where he'd been given a chamber. He assumed the other direction led to the family's private apartments.

The maid guided Miss Reid to the first door on the right. They disappeared inside. His room was two more down on the left-hand side of the hall.

He popped into his room, which was graciously furnished with a large wooden desk where he had the paperwork he'd brought with him. Placing the information on this case aside, he retrieved the intricate details he'd gathered on William Douglas. Spreading it out, he studied the names of the people who lived at the flat they called Camelot.

He ticked off the names of the females to see if somehow, he'd missed something. Flora was the oldest at approximately twenty-one years of age, then came Peggy at around nineteen. But he had descriptions for both of them, and they didn't match the lass who was here. The rest of the girls were too young to be the mystery woman.

His finger ran over Allison Reid, called Allie, age twelve.

Legitimate brother Joseph, age nine. His memory had not failed him, and he was confident the fake Miss Reid had something to do with the bastard he'd been chasing for years, even if her name hadn't been collected.

Was she William's lover? The thought made him angrier than believing she was one of the people living with him and perpetuating his intolerable behavior.

Either way, she was a link to William Douglas, and she could be the key to taking him down. He stacked the papers, set them neatly in the left corner of the desk, exited, locked his door, and then moved back to the drawing room to wait on Miss Reid's return.

CHAPTER 3

$\mathcal{K}$ ate's room was plush and massive, but instead of studying it, she swept toward the window and flung it open. She took a deep breath of the fresh air. Gazing out into the expanse of land, she savored a view of the gardens and a large pond.

The rows of bonny flowers and bushes were the area where she had been strolling with the dark, dangerous constable. The man was playing games with her. Currently, she seemed to be in control, but she didn't think she would like to lose to the man. He honestly scared her. The watchman in Aberdeen was a friend to William's crew, but this man was unpredictable.

If her family didn't need her, she'd be running right now. She couldn't, though, and she'd spent way too much time planning this. And although her mark was delayed in his arrival, she had to see this through to the end.

She'd never met someone who could pick her untruths from her like fruit on a low hanging branch. But something about how he was skirting around accusing her gave her hope that he'd not expose her lies.

Although she thought she could handle the man, something was unsettling about the way her body sprang to life when he touched her. His lips on her hand had ignited a curiosity somewhere deep inside. Her heart pounded even now as she thought about the tingles that had lingered long after his mouth had receded.

She inhaled the scent of the fresh blooms and wilderness, which wafted in from across the pond just visible beyond the garden. The Stonehavens had given her a room larger than any she was accustomed to, but she still craved the feel of knowing she wasn't closed in. It didn't matter where she lay her head at night as long as the windows were open.

Here, with this space, she should sleep better than she had in months. Inhaling a final soothing breath, she turned, checked herself in the mirror, and once again became Allison Reid. She opened the door and headed back down the front stairs.

As she took the steps, she reminded herself that she should avoid the constable at all costs.

There was no sight of the lawman when she strolled back into the room. Sighing internally, she made her way to the Bartroms. They were the lovely couple she had made contact with to secure an invitation to this event. Staunch friends of the Stonehavens, they ran a theatre in London, so it wasn't hard to strike up a conversation with them about their shared admiration of the arts.

Mr. Charles Bartrom was a jovial man with gray hair and rosy cheeks that made him always appear happy. His wife, Irene, was a tall, thin woman with dark-ebony tresses. Her locks were sprinkled with silver, and it made her appear worldly instead of old. The woman was elegant, but at the same time, gave off an aura of approachability.

Kate had charmed them, but it had been easy because she truly fancied their company. The next day when she'd purposely come across them in the hotel lobby, they had invited her to tea with the Stonehavens.

Claire and James Moore, the Earl and Countess of Stonehaven, were slightly older than the Bartroms, but they'd held a fast friendship for many years, dating back to Lady Stonehaven's time as a celebrated singer.

The earl was a tall man with engaging eyes and brown hair that hadn't changed with age. He was lean and still retained a ruggedly handsome appearance. She'd bet when he was younger, he could have had any woman he chose, but he'd settled on Claire, who his family hadn't approved of. Lady Stonehaven was a good head and half shorter than her husband, but she was slender, and her silver hair brought out dazzling blue eyes. She was witty and personable. They gazed upon each other as if the love they'd felt when they defied society, and the earl's family, was stronger now than it had been back then.

When she'd married Lord Stonehaven, she'd had to give up her career and concentrate on becoming a proper lady for the ton. She'd managed it and after years of diligence, she had been accepted by the peers in London. The pair of them still came to Scotland to escape and be themselves without stressing society's rules. Kate had taken an instant liking to them as well.

As they enjoyed the afternoon together, she had mentioned her brother, a wealthy merchant looking to procure property in Aberdeen soon. He'd been called away on business, and she'd have to make the journey all on her own. It was terrifying because she didn't know anyone in the area and might have to stay on her own for a couple of weeks.

Did they know of any reputable place to stay where she would feel safe? It had been too easy; she'd almost experienced remorse because the group of them were so delightful.

Camelot was at stake, though, so she'd persisted in the endeavor.

They'd pounced on the opportunity to invite the sister of a well-to-do man, then brought up their single niece and nephew, who would already be at the estate for a visit from London.

Kate strolled up to Charles and Irene, just as the Stone-havens entered the room.

"The weather is lovely today. I wish I'd arrived earlier to inspect the rest of the grounds," Kate said.

"There will be plenty of chances for that. I'm sure the constable would like to explore them too, so we can schedule another tour." Lady Stonehaven's eyes twinkled as if she thought the constable had an interest in Kate. He did, but it wasn't what her host was thinking.

She wasn't certain she should take the Stonehavens up on that particular offer.

"Speak of the devil." Lord Stonehaven laughed and nodded toward the door.

She glanced over as the tall, dark, and menacing man who could read her appeared in the room. His scrutiny was focused on her. She wondered how long he'd been watching.

Lady Stonehaven interjected, "I think Archie may be too late if he wishes to catch yer eye. I do believe the constable finds ye to his liking."

"I dinnae ken that I'd call it that." A nervous giggle bubbled to the surface. It sounded like something a shy lass might let escape. No one but her knew it was laced with fear.

The constable came up beside her as her hosts and the Bartroms began a conversation about horticulture. The words skidded over her as the perilous man seemed to keep his focus on her.

"That reminds me. I have something you must see," Lord Stonehaven said.

Before she could feign interest in their topic, her hosts had pulled away from the group, taking the Bartroms with them to examine some book. She was left alone with the constable.

"Are ye running from me?" Constable Davidson leaned in. Any pretense that he didn't have some idea she wasn't who she said was gone. His eyes were stormy and determined. The scent of bergamot and masculinity mingled in an intoxicating combination that wrapped her in fear and fascination.

He was all business. The constable's take-charge demeanor said he was accustomed to people breaking under his interrogation. And he seemed determined to learn her secrets. She imagined if they were in his jurisdiction, he would have placed her in a cell and probed her for answers. She flushed that her thought had a double meaning and that her mind had gone there.

Good, blushing made her look vulnerable.

"Ye have to admit that yer a wee bit intimidating, and perhaps overbearing." She glanced down at the hand clasped around her arm as he once again steered her in the direction he wanted. *Let him think he's in charge.*

A blur rushed toward her before she had time to react— arms wrapped around her, thwarting the constable's attempt to guide her away from the other guests. The embrace was warm and welcome, familiar. Flora.

A tall, well-dressed man sauntered up beside her sister from Camelot. The constable's piercing blue eyes analyzed both the newcomers with the contemplation of a man who was jaded into thinking the world was against him. He looked like a man about to do battle and willing to use any means necessary to win.

Flora finally let go. Her eyes filled with moisture.

"Where have ye been? I've been so worried." Argh, Flora was going to jeopardize everything.

Kate was sure the panic shown in her eyes, but she recovered quickly. "Flora, 'tis so nice to see ye. Let me introduce ye to my new acquaintance." Although they'd pulled apart, she kept her hand in Flora's and gave her a tight squeeze.

Flora winced.

"This is Gavin Davidson. He's a constable . . ." Kate paused, meeting the man's gaze, and smiling before glancing back to Flora. She turned her lips up farther, her eyelids expanding and accentuating the whites of her eyes with the overly enthusiastic announcement that she hoped the constable couldn't see. "Here all the way from Glasgow."

She turned back to discover his face had tightened, his lips not showing any sign of pleasure at meeting Flora; in fact, his irises had darkened, and he rubbed at the small scar that ran across his left temple.

"Nice to make yer acquaintance, Mr. Davidson. I'm Flora." Flora blinked, then her gaze skimmed to the handsome man she was with, who seemed to be as threatened by the constable as everyone else.

The lawman's intense scrutiny shifted back and forth between her and Flora, ignoring the man altogether.

"And this is Isaac," Flora said.

The man with Flora held out his hand and said, "Nathaniel Isaac Hamilton, Earl of Dunbridge."

"So nice to meet ye, sir, I hope ye are taking care of my dear Flora." Kate smiled, then said, "I'm Allison Reid."

Flora's head tilted as she took in the words. Her sister stared, confused. She had a right to be, but Kate couldn't explain that here.

The constable held out his hand. "And Flora, what is yer surname?"

Kate shook her head in warning, but Flora didn't notice as she volunteered, "MacGregor."

He scowled, although she'd not thought it possible for the man to look more predatory. "Are ye from close by?"

"Oh, aye. I'm from Aberdeen." Flora plucked one of the treats from a nearby tray and took a small bite, oblivious to the interest in the subtle questioning.

The man continued, knowing Flora was not as adept at deception as Kate was. "Tell me, Miss MacGregor, what is it that yer family does in Aberdeen?"

All color drained from Flora's face as she caught on to his intentions. Her casual acceptance of him faltered as she stiffened.

"Ah, so glad you could make it, Nate." Lady Stonehaven's voice cut in as she rejoined the group.

Now it was Kate's turn to be confused because she thought Lord Dunbridge's name was Isaac.

"Ah, Lady Stonehaven," he took her hand and gave a short bow. "We did finally arrive. Thank you for the invitation. You do remember Flora MacGregor?"

"Of course I do, boy. I invited you this weekend, so I could learn if your mother would approve of the company you are keeping." She laughed, high-pitched but light at the same time.

Kate stepped in, not caring what the constable thought when her sister's honor was in question. "Lady Stonehaven, I can vouch for Miss MacGregor. I have had a long acquaintance with her, and I ken she comes from a family of good reputation."

The woman paused briefly as her stare darted to the lawman, who had latched onto her arm again and whose visage had darkened farther. Kate couldn't stop; after all, if it hadn't been for Flora, Bran, and Will, she wouldn't have survived her childhood. "She is a saint, who feeds the poor and shelters the needy. You could have no better guest in your home."

"You know with my past, I'm not judging, but if the gal needs some advice on how to manage with the ton, I'm the one she needs to speak to." Lady Stonehaven winked at Flora.

Kate should have known that Lady Stonehaven wouldn't hold Flora's past against her, but the man at her side had her questioning everything.

Another young lady came up to stand beside Lady Stonehaven. Her spine was stiff; she was a proper young English lady. This must be Miss Eleanor Clarke, her hosts' niece. The lass's hair was a perfect coiffure and her manners impeccable.

The large drawing room shrank. The sensation of being suffocated shrouded her.

"Lady Stonehaven, may I have the honor of being introduced to your other guests?" Kate asked, steering the conversation to safer topics.

"Oh, of course, my dear." Lady Stonehaven introduced her to the men first, possibly interested in making a match for the lass. "Lord Dunbridge, Constable Davidson, this is my niece, Miss Eleanor Clarke. She'll be having a season in London this year, but I'm sure some lucky gentleman will beat the rest of the ton to her." The older woman's green eyes held a bit of mischief, and although the lady studied both men with interest, her eyebrows rose in the direction of Flora's companion.

Thankful for the distraction, Kate struggled to come up with a reason for knowing Flora as the constable's glare remained fixed on her.

Gavin strolled out onto the terrace, holding onto the little liar. After the newly arrived earl and Miss MacGregor promenaded out the window and toward the gardens, he'd managed to extricate Miss Reid from the group. He'd decided to follow them.

His rage was so hot that it bubbled over and ate at his

insides, but he remained calm on the outside. It wouldn't do for Miss Reid to know how affected he was by her callous disregard of the truth.

She had intimate knowledge of William Douglas's family. Of course, she would be incapable of telling him the facts if she had anything to do with that man.

He remembered a time when William had gone by a different surname . . . a time before the man had destroyed everything Gavin had held dear. That was why it had taken him years to find the man's location. And why he had to pursue him at any cost. If he let this opportunity slide and William discovered Gavin was on his trail, he could disappear again, and Gavin might never find him.

He couldn't get back what William had stolen from him, but he could bring the man to justice for the crimes he'd committed in the process. And if the woman by his side continued to lie to him, he might not even be able to do that.

He had to be in control.

"Can ye slow a bit? Yer legs are longer than mine."

He continued but shortened his stride as he drove onward without speaking to the lass at his side. He watched the pair ahead of them head toward the pond. Flora MacGregor was one of the women who lived at Camelot. He spared a glance at the woman by his side, the one who was not Allison Reid.

"Is something amiss?" she asked in a lovely, confused voice.

"Aye. Ye are no' being honest with me."

How could she be the same woman he'd thought so perfect this morning?

"But we barely ken each other," she protested.

She was right. After he deciphered what Miss MacGregor was up to, he'd turn his attention back to Miss Reid.

"Agreed. I have many questions for ye."

"Yer cheeks become an attractive shade red when ye are angry," she replied. Was it amusement in her voice?

He'd been following the other couple and not noticed if she had blinked. But when he glanced at her now, she was smiling at him. Did the wee wench want him flustered?

He paused behind a row of hedges where they would go unnoticed. Lord Dunbridge and Miss MacGregor were just on the other side of the trees, tossing rocks into the pond.

"Ye have nae idea how furious I am." But oddly, looking into her eyes had a way of negating some of the rage.

"I can tell ye that yer face darkens as if storm clouds are roiling inside, but you seem to be calm and in control."

She looked nervous but appeared to be trying to acknowledge his anger and compliment him simultaneously.

"How do ye ken Miss MacGregor?" he prodded.

"Is this an interrogation?" One side of her mouth quirked up.

"If it needs to be, but I was hoping ye would find a way to be honest with me."

"I have visited Aberdeen on many occasions, and each time Flora has been the most gracious, selfless person I have ever kenned. There is nae reason for ye to mistrust her." She was telling the truth.

"She is an associate of William Douglas," he stated, but perhaps she wasn't aware of the man's criminal activities.

"Yer eyes have turned the color of an angry sea, but it's quite appealing." She deflected the question with enticing words. She didn't blink.

He pushed her seemingly genuine accolade aside. "Ye relish making me angry."

She pulled free and set her hands on her hips. "I'm attempting to lighten the mood."

"Ye can start by telling me yer name."

She drew her shoulders back. He had to give her credit

because she looked bonny and innocent in the late afternoon sun. "Allison Reid." She blinked twice.

A breeze blew her spicy, alluring scent his way, and he found himself seeking it out, as an undisciplined man craved the taste of whisky. The smell of her was overpowering and alluring. He wrapped his arm around her waist and drew her close.

He'd not wanted a woman like this . . . ever.

He chided himself for letting her get to him. But it was not her appealing face with the barely discernable smattering of freckles, or the shapely form that molded to him like a soft, fitted glove. It was the conundrum she presented.

He liked the challenge.

He was in total control, and he'd cut her defenses down. They had a couple of weeks together for him to learn all about her and if she had a connection to the King of the Streets.

"Ye are going to lose this game." His voice was taut, and he wasn't certain if it was from irritation or the desire that had exploded in his loins as he held her near.

"What do ye mean?" she asked.

She didn't look scared. She looked alive, and interested, and like a beautiful, unattainable horse waiting to be broken.

"It means I dinnae play fair, lass."

"Neither do I." She tilted her chin so that their eyes locked.

Every muscle in his body tightened. He wanted to kiss her. Take her lips on his and punish her with the hunger she was purposely stoking in his breast. Most women looked the other way when they saw him; she met his challenge and defied him.

Her tongue darted out and swept across her bow-shaped lip. She didn't blink; she didn't move. She wanted him to claim her mouth. The knowledge emboldened him, and he was about to dip his head when he caught movement from the side of his eye. Flora MacGregor and her companion had fallen, and they seemed to be lost in an embrace.

His attention returned to the woman at his side. Her pupils were dilated, and the rim around her green irises had turned a deep blue. A thrill rushed through him. He liked this look on her.

Perhaps his anger wasn't the way to sway her. And if he continued to badger her, she might flee and warn William that he was onto the arse. He'd seen many criminals retreat when confronted. So far, this lass was meeting him head-on. Perhaps a different tactic. One he had never tried; one he'd never thought to use.

Seduction.

It was tempting, but no, he wouldn't purposely set out to take advantage of anyone. It wasn't in him to use such deceitful tactics.

The lass had worked her charm on him, and he was falling for it. She was not the innocent lass he'd glimpsed this morning. He'd have to recognize when she was trying to turn the tables on him. He shook his head and released his hold on her.

Glancing toward the pond, he noticed Miss MacGregor and Lord Dunbridge were on their feet and moving swiftly toward the house. He'd have to track down and question the lass later. He knew of no crimes she'd committed, only rumors that she picketed pockets—but in his book, she was guilty by association.

He guided Miss Reid back toward the house with the intent of becoming more casually acquainted with her. He might not want to seduce her, but he couldn't remove the thirst to taste her. And perhaps if he did so, he could catch her off guard.

He swallowed. "I suggest we move to a topic we can agree on for now."

"I like that idea," she said.

He nodded.

"What are yer thoughts on the canal that's being built near Glasgow?" she asked.

He was impressed with her interest in the endeavor.

"If it's managed properly, I think 'twill be a good thing."

"I've heard that the funds to keep up the expansion are running low."

"Ye keep up with events in Glasgow?"

"I tend to do my research when I'm interested in a project."

He wondered what project would have brought her to Glasgow. "Now that our portion is complete, the amount of crime in our area has decreased."

"Is that why ye can take time off?"

"I didnae say I wasn't here on business."

"Do ye ever do anything for pleasure then?" The tone in her voice was wistful.

The word "pleasure" evoked images of the two of them tangled in covers. He glanced away before she could read his thoughts.

Clearing his throat, he said, "I enjoy my work."

She nodded and volunteered, "I find the project interesting because I would like to ride on a boat one day. It must be freeing with all that open space and no walls to close in on ye."

She closed her eyes and glanced up to the sky as a breeze played with the strands of hair cascading from her temples. She looked to be imagining being out over the water. A peace washed over her that hadn't been there since they'd met in the drawing room. It was like she was again the lady he'd desired on the side of the road.

"Next time ye visit Glasgow, if ye wish, I could secure tickets for a short passage." He didn't know why he volunteered, other than he liked glancing upon her when she was relaxed and being her true self.

"I should like that." Her smile was genuine.

He enjoyed her company when they weren't arguing. Perhaps this gentler approach with her was the way to go. When they reached the house, he almost regretted that their time alone would be at an end for this afternoon.

CHAPTER 4

$\mathcal{B}$ack in the drawing room, Kate was thankful that Flora wasn't present. Actually, by the time she and the constable had finished touring the grounds, everyone had retired to their rooms for a rest and to prepare for the evening meal.

She'd have to keep him away from her sister. Flora didn't know how to tell an untruth. She was genuine and caring and didn't deserve the attention of a constable who might wish to lock her away. Thankfully, Flora was well-known in Aberdeen, and there wasn't a soul around who didn't adore or respect her.

Flora's reputation had made it easy to claim an acquaintance without sharing details of their family.

She'd savored their leisurely return to the estate and the constable's attempt to diffuse his anger. She'd also liked the way he'd watched her as if he knew the real her and still wanted to kiss her. She was accustomed to men attempting to gain physical contact with her, but none of them knew her, and she'd always found a way to rebuff their attention graciously.

With the constable, she didn't want to.

There was something illicit about him knowing there was more to her. She'd grown heated, and her heart rate had increased when he'd drawn her into his body. Even now, the thought melted her core, like a fire.

He was dangerous. She had to stop thinking like this.

"It appears we find ourselves where we started."

He grinned. "I'll walk ye to yer room. We dinnae want to be late preparing for the meal. I dinnae ken how these house parties work, but I've heard the English take the structure seriously."

"I've thought the same, but it appears Lady Stonehaven is different. She enjoys an opportunity to indulge in relaxed rules."

"And do ye?"

"Aye, I dinnae like rules at all," she jested.

He gave her a disapproving glare and stated, "And I live by them, but these, I'm afraid I will nae know."

"I think that if we but ask, we will find the answers."

"Do ye ken the Stonehavens well?"

"Nae. We but met last week in Edinburgh."

He stopped in front of her door. Chills erupted down her spine—he'd been doing some research of his own. Had he spied on her for the few minutes she'd excused herself earlier?

"I will see ye at dinner."

She couldn't resist teasing him again before they parted. "If we unknowingly break the rules, ye can blame me. I don't mind being the villain when my service is needed." She smiled and winked at him.

He took her hand, raised it toward his lips. The blue of his eyes was darker in the dwindling light of the hall.

He looked like a predator—as if he was waiting for the right moment to strike, and she knew he hadn't forgotten whatever he was after. A shudder ran down her back. She inhaled audibly and caught a whiff of bergamot and fresh woods. The scent roped its way around her core and coiled there. The smell mixed with danger was heady and left her swaying.

She expected his mouth to linger on her skin again, but this time the caress was too quick, as if he'd been aware of what she was thinking and wanted to keep her guessing. He continued to hold her fingers in his, though.

"Do ye play chess?" he asked.

"Nae. I never liked it. I do better with games of instinct rather than strategy."

"Then, lovely lass, ye are already at a disadvantage." His husky words wrapped around her as the dark of the night.

She tilted her head . . . confused. He was trying to throw her off guard. When her mouth fell open, but words failed her, he gave a cocky grin that reached into her chest and sent an odd thrill coursing through her.

"Let the games begin," he said, his mouth curving up in a devastating and dangerous smile.

He dropped her hand and walked to a room two doors past hers and on the opposite side of the hall. Taking out a key, he placed it in the door and twisted. He pushed in the door and then glanced back to give her one more smile before disappearing.

After shutting her door, Kate plopped down on the bed to analyze her current situation. She'd only known the constable a few hours, but he'd crawled inside her and claimed all her thoughts. She'd even wanted to kiss him.

What was wrong with her? She was supposed to be charming him, not the other way around.

Sure, he was dark and brooding and intense, but the danger and intrigue surrounding him drew her in like a puppy seeking out a larger dog that would only pounce on it. She was being foolish. And she had to get herself together.

She rose, took a few calming breaths, then changed for the evening. Once she'd reapplied her perfume, a dash of confidence had returned, and she felt ready to meet the challenge.

Yes, he might have strategy on his side, but she was adept at reading others, and he wasn't immune to her. Intrigue reflected in his gaze as surely as it did in hers. The curiosity in his stare did odd things to her . . . things that made her want to spend more time with him. Still, once she found out what he was doing here, she needed to stay as far from him as possible.

She couldn't help but think, perhaps, with this man, she was in over her head.

~

Gavin sponged off with a basin of water that had been left in his room. He dressed quickly, then made his way back down the steps. He was entirely too eager to pry information from Miss Reid, especially now that he'd turned it into a challenge.

The arse he was after wouldn't be here for a few days, and the mission with Will could wait a little longer. He'd waited more than a decade already. That left his time free to focus on the mystery of Miss Reid.

He'd thrown her off balance, and he liked the dazed look it had left in her gaze. She was both terrified and thrilled by his proclamation. He would bet she'd never been caught at her game and would be overconfident.

When he reached the drawing room, Lord Stonehaven and his wife were already there, waiting for their guests to reemerge.

"Constable. Would you care to join me in the study for a drink?"

"Aye. I would be pleased to."

He followed his host down the hall. When they reached

the room, Lord Stonehaven opened the door, motioned him in, then shut the door and locked it behind him.

"Whisky?" Lord Stonehaven asked.

"Aye. Thank ye." A few seconds later he had a glass with a generous serving.

Lord Stonehaven let out a breath. "I've had word from the Fordices. They won't arrive until late next week."

"Hmm. I was hoping to be done with this business sooner."

"The one yer concerned with, Thomas, has come down with some illness, and the wife will be staying at home with him until he recovers. They will join Mr. Fordice and his eldest at a later date."

"That may mean I'll have to extend my stay. Are ye comfortable with me staying until all of them arrive?"

"Yes. My wife is quite enjoying your presence, but I haven't told her the true nature of your visit, or that we might be welcoming a depraved criminal into our home."

"Dinnae worry. I will be certain nothing untoward happens here, and yer reputation is my deepest concern."

Lord Stonehaven held up the decanter. "Would ye like another?"

"Aye," he said.

The pair stayed and drank a few minutes longer, talking about the business of the day, the Prince Regent, and the Scottish countryside.

Lord Stonehaven looked at the clock. "Good heavens. Claire's going to be furious. I'm holding up our meal."

He stood, and Gavin followed.

When they reached the drawing room, Lord Stonehaven split off toward his wife. Gavin paused in the doorway to watch his little liar. Her hair was still pinned in the same fashion as earlier, and while the other ladies had added pearls and ribbons and shiny baubles to their coiffeurs, Miss Reid had left hers plain. She had changed her gown; this one was mostly white with what appeared to be tiny flowers embroidered on the cloth, but he wasn't close enough to be certain.

What he was sure of was that the bodice was too small. Her amble breasts seemed to be ready to spring from the confines of the restricting material.

She was latched onto Flora MacGregor and appeared to be pleading for something. Miss MacGregor nodded, but she didn't look pleased with whatever Miss Reid was saying.

He smiled. He'd knocked the little deceiver off balance.

She was bound to make a mistake now.

CHAPTER 5

*O*nce Kate returned to the drawing room, it was to find that neither the constable nor Flora were present. Breathing a sigh of relief that she wasn't too late to keep the two of them separated, she stepped over to the window to glance out upon the terrace.

Twilight had claimed the day. She took in the splendor of the open spaces and the deepened colors of the flowers as shadows elongated over the gardens. Two deer dashed from the area where she'd been walking with the constable earlier today and bounded toward the tall row of hedges that she guessed might be a labyrinth.

They disappeared towards the woods. It dawned on her that while the area might be their home, that was also where a hunter would lie in wait for them. The innocent animals weren't aware when danger lurked in their midst.

Flora might be compared to one of those creatures with her beauty and simple grace, but Kate wasn't going to be like the deer. She was more like a squirrel. It wasn't in her to wait for trouble to find her; she wanted to know who was stalking her and prod and taunt the beast to destroy his equilibrium. It was imperative that she discover why the constable was so interested in her and Flora. And the only way to do that would be to learn more about him.

She needed to get into the constable's chamber.

Decision made, she moved back into the room and approached Miss Eleanor Clarke. She spent the next bit of time listening to Miss Clarke talk about herself and fret over some man her parents were considering forcing her to wed. As Kate listened, her mind wandered, and fear and desperation returned and began to swirl in the depths of her gut for the first time in years.

She'd always had the upper hand on her schemes. How was it a man who didn't know her had so easily thrown her world onto its side? She had to find out what he had discovered because he was ahead of her, and she wouldn't win if she couldn't see what was coming.

It was almost time for the meal when Flora and the Earl of Dunbridge strolled into the room. The man seemed enthralled with her. Kate was getting worried that perhaps, Flora was barely keeping her head above the waves that were prepared to crash down on her.

Kate drew her close and leaned in, whispering in Flora's ear, "I need yer help."

She hated asking for assistance. And she'd never asked Flora for anything before, but she had a unique talent that could help her find the truth about the constable.

Swiveling back to Lord Dunbridge at her side, Flora pleaded, "I only need a moment." He was reluctant to let the lass go, but when he did, Kate led her several steps away.

"The constable is too interested in our family," she said.

"What?" Flora shuddered.

Her sister knew all too well a man of the law looking into Will's activities could lead to them losing him.

"Ye have to stay away from him," she warned as she pulled Flora farther across the room and into a private corner.

"Ye're going too fast. Why would he have any interest in us?" Flora asked.

"He kens who ye are. He kens I'm not who I've said, but that's all he kens about me."

"That still doesnae explain . . ."

Kate cut her off. "I need ye to pick his pocket."

"Why?" Flora's gaze glossed over as fear took root.

Guilt exploded in Kate's gut. She'd not ask it, except Will might be in danger, and she didn't possess the skill to do it herself. Camelot would survive without the rest of them, but all those kids depended on their brother.

"I need the key to his room. He has something on Will, on ye. I dinnae ken, but I have to discover what he's doing."

"Oh, God, Kate. Do ye ken what ye are asking me to do?"

The tremble in Flora's voice and fingers forced another round of regret to wash over her. Perhaps if she'd been more careful in Glasgow, they wouldn't be going through this right now.

Kate straightened. "Aye, I'm asking ye to protect the family."

Her eyes stung, guilt knifing into her gut, as she used the only words that she knew would sway Flora to do something so risky. But she wouldn't let Flora get caught, and if she did, Kate would take the blame. She'd never let anything happen to her sister.

"I'll get ye the key, but what are ye going to do with it? Ye arenae a thief. Ye dinnae intend to go into his room. What happens if he catches ye?"

"Let me worry with that, but I don't stand a chance at stopping him if I dinnae ken what he has. But ye have to be careful. After the deed is done, dinnae go near him again."

"Ye dinnae need to get mixed up with a constable," Flora pleaded.

"I have to do this. I wouldnae be alive if it weren't for ye and Will. I ken I havenae always been here for ye, but I can stop him." She hoped she sounded more confident than she was currently feeling.

Flora nodded. "Aye. Where does he keep it?"

"'Twill be so simple for ye. 'Tis in a pocket sewn inside his jacket, on his left side." She had seen him put it there when he'd walked into his room earlier.

"Ye may need to provide a distraction."

"I can take care of that," Kate reassured.

"Will ye tell me what he's up to when ye figure it out?"

A faint tingling reached her ears.

"Och, I'll see ye after the meal." Kate shot across the room, hoping to claim a position anywhere at the table but by the man she couldn't erase from her thoughts.

No luck.

The constable stood in the doorway, waiting for her. She reluctantly admitted to herself that at least Flora wouldn't have to converse with him throughout the meal, and his appearance made her heart thud a little faster. His stare met hers, and she flushed.

He'd changed into a formal jacket that fit snuggly at his chest, emphasizing the power beneath the fabric. The material was dark, almost as black and sensual as the thick, lazy curls that landed just below his ears. She had the urge to run her fingers through his hair to feel the silky strands.

As her gaze trailed down, her eyes caught on a tartan kilt. Her heart skipped a beat. The garments had been outlawed some time ago, and although the proscription had been reversed, not many men still wore them. His plaid combined deep hues of green and ebony with bright blue stripes interspersed into a pleasing weave in the fabric. The sapphire color accentuated his eyes as his mesmerizing irises focused on her.

Her mouth watered.

"Shall I escort ye to the table, *Miss Reid*?" He emphasized the last to let her know he still didn't believe her.

"Aye. That would be lovely."

She threaded her hand through the crook of his elbow and held onto his forearm. Shocks of electricity sizzled at the sinewy muscle her fingers had curled upon. He guided her in as she thought about how she might pursue an affair with him if circumstances were different.

The table was long and could have accommodated more people, but the settings were placed, and chairs set to match their exact number. By the time they entered the room, only two chairs remained. The constable pulled out her seat, then smiled. After she'd eased into the chair, he took his.

The Stonehavens' niece, Miss Clarke, was seated to his left. Once everyone entered, she noticed she'd been incorrect. No one had taken the seat on the end, which meant she didn't have anyone to shield her from the attentions of the constable.

She wondered who was missing. Ticking off the names of the guests who she knew were supposed to be here, she came to one she'd not seen as of yet, the Stonehavens' nephew, Archie.

Flora sat directly opposite her, and while she could have talked loudly across the table to her, she wanted to keep the lawman's attention off of her sister, so she resigned herself to command absolute control of his regard. Later, she'd have to find out how long Flora would be in attendance because she needed a plan for shielding her.

Time to turn on the charm and divert the constable.

"How did ye meet the Stonehavens?"

"On business." His curt reply meant he was hiding something.

She was about to form a response when he glanced across the table to scrutinize Flora. "Miss MacGregor," he called.

Kate's heart fell into her belly.

The constable continued, "Can ye tell us more about what life is like for ye in Aberdeen?"

Flora gaped. "Aberdeen is a wonderful city, and it's known for its shipping industry."

The constable was about to step up his interrogation when Kate cut in, "Aberdeen is one of my favorite places to discuss. What do ye want to know?"

She looked directly at him as she placed her hand on his leg under the table. A raw awareness of the heat and strength beneath her palm slammed into her, and she drew her hand back quickly, but the motion succeeded in pulling his attention from Flora.

The constable's eyes focused on her, darkened, and he inhaled sharply. He blinked, let out his breath, then dismissed Kate.

Ignoring her question, he glanced back toward Flora, who was being pulled into a conversation by Lord Perry, a single man from the southwest of England who owned a small bit of land and a family title.

Kate surmised that Lady Stonehaven had invited both Lord Perry and Flora's earl as potential matches for her niece, Miss Clarke. Although both prospects were currently more interested in her sister, Miss Clarke didn't seem to notice as she carried on a conversation with Lord Dunbridge.

The constable opened his mouth to call across the table. Kate struggled with the best way to deflect his efforts.

"Aberdeen is beautiful this time of year." He attempted to snag Flora's attention, but she ignored him and kept talking to Lord Perry.

Good girl, Kate thought.

The constable was about to try again when Kate replaced her hand high on his thigh. Her fingers curled into the strength of his leg.

He stilled. But he wasn't the only one affected by the gesture. An odd thrumming started in her body, one that made her aware of how intimate her touch was. His head turned toward hers, and he tilted closer to her to whisper something, but as he did, Lord Stonehaven stood and began to welcome them with a speech.

She withdrew her hand, but before it could hit her lap, he was grasping it and placing it back on his thigh, holding it there for the remainder of the speech. A yearning ignited in her core.

Once the meal began, she removed her fingers without protest, and they spoke of menial things such as weather and food preferences and of the inventor Robert Fulton. He had produced a working submarine and developed steamboats that were operating in the Americas. Although he'd not completely taken his attentions from Flora, the conversations flowed, and Kate had successfully distracted the constable.

When the guests were done, they rose in unison to leave the room. It was time to put Flora in position.

As they filed into the drawing room, Miss Clarke began asking her questions about Kate's fake wealthy merchant brother. While encouraging the conversation, Kate was able to skirt to the opposite side of the constable.

Kate saw her chance when Lord Perry and Flora strolled into the room. Luckily, she caught Flora's attention and winked, then tripped and knocked into Lord Perry. The collision bumped Flora into the constable. Kate smiled as her sister easily slid her hand into the man's pocket, so quick, only one watching for it would know it was happening.

Flora had done it. Rushing to her side, Kate reached out to her as if to steady her. "Oh my. Are ye all right, Miss MacGregor? I'm so sorry."

Her sister deftly placed her hand in Kate's, dropping the key into her waiting palm. "I'm all right."

Kate turned her attention to Lord Perry and then the constable. "Pardon me, gentlemen. My shoe became stuck on the hem of my dress. I must see that I haven't ripped it."

Bounding up the stairs, she rounded the corner and inserted the key into the constable's door with shaking fingers. Once unlocked, she pushed it in, standing on the other side. Every inch of her trembled as her gaze adjusted to the dark of the room.

It was a clear night, but the moon was on the other side of the house, so she received no light from it. Deeming it too risky to ignite a candle, she moved over to the desk to study a stack of papers that lay on the table. It was too dim to read the words.

Grabbing the papers, she hurried toward the window to take advantage of the late evening glow of the summer sky. She scanned the first page. It was a list of recent crimes in Glasgow and his status in examining the cases. The second page was more of the same.

When she reached the third page, she gasped at the list of names . . . her family. William Douglas was on top, followed by a detailed description of what he looked like, places he frequented, and crimes he was thought to have committed. Bran's name was next, then Flora's, followed by everyone who had been living at Camelot for the past few months, including Isobel, who was here at the estate acting as a lady's maid for Flora. Even Allison and Joseph Reid were scrolled at the bottom.

That was how he'd know she wasn't Allie, but it also explained why he didn't know her true identity. She'd not stayed at Camelot in at least six months, so perhaps that was how she'd escaped the notice of whoever put the information together. Her fingers shook, and the papers rattled in her hands.

The next page was more about her family, and interviews conducted by people in Aberdeen regarding their crew. Her stomach lurched.

A clock gonged from somewhere out in the hall. She flinched. How long had she been in here?

She wanted to look through more, but she'd already been gone too long. Could he toss her in prison for breaking into his room? She doubted it, but they weren't in Glasgow, and she wasn't sure of his authority. He might be able to detain her and derail her mission.

She stacked the papers back in the middle of the desk as neatly as her trembling hands would allow. Dashing for the door, she opened it and peeked out into the hall. The way was clear. She locked the door, moved away from it, then took several calming breaths before descending the stairs.

When she re-entered the drawing room, Flora was nowhere in sight. Kate would have to return the key on her own. Dread filled her, and a drop of sweat slid down the base of her back. She had to get close to him.

She swallowed to remove the lump in her throat and made her way to the constable, who was conversing with Miss Clarke and Lord Perry. Their hosts' niece seemed to be monopolizing the conversation and had her focus set on the titled Englishman, so Kate glanced at her intended target.

"Constable Davidson, I could use some air. Will ye walk with me out on the terrace?"

Suspicion spread across his face. He was too deft at reading her. She offered her left arm because the key still rested hot and heavy in her right hand.

"I'd be delighted." His eyes narrowed, but he took her arm and moved toward the windowed doors, which were now mostly closed because the temperature had dropped to a chill.

"What did ye think of the fish?" she began.

"It was delicious."

She sighed as an invigorating breeze blew over her. She never minded a cool wind because it meant she was out in the open and alive. Fresh air always gave her peace.

Pianoforte music drifted out from the music room, which

was adjacent to the drawing-room. She wondered who was playing. "The music is lovely."

"Aye. It is." The lawman's interest seemed to be more on her than the melody drifting toward them.

"Do ye play an instrument, Constable?"

"Nae. I spent most of my youth in an orphanage, and we didn't have such luxuries."

"That's a shame."

"What about ye? Where were ye raised?"

He was fishing again. Did the man ever relent? She drew free from him to add a little distance.

"I always moved about and never stayed in one place." It was as close to the truth as she could offer him, especially after what she'd seen in his room.

"Ye and yer brother?" he asked.

"Aye." She blinked up at him, and he scowled, picking her falsehood as easily as one would swipe a biscuit from a proffered platter.

She shivered. "'Tis colder out than I imagined."

"Would ye like to head back in?"

"Nae. I prefer the outdoors when possible." She made a show of rubbing her arms as she glanced up and took in the wide expanse of stars dotting the sky.

"'Tis a bonny night."

"A fitting end to a beautiful day." She hugged herself.

"If ye insist on staying out here, will ye let me share my jacket with ye?"

"I would like that."

Yes, thank heavens, she had thought she would have to physically reach out and pretend to be interested in the material or his chest. Well, technically, her interest wouldn't be completely feigned.

But Flora was the pickpocket of their group. Kate was good at other things, like persuasion.

He unfastened the buttons, pulled the coat free, then

stepped behind her to place it over her shoulders. She was enveloped in warmth as the aroma of fresh wood and bergamot surrounded her in its aromatic embrace. She closed her eyes and brought the sleeves around her, luxuriating in the comfort it brought.

They both seemed to be in a trance. Time stood still, with his hands not leaving the fabric as his touch seared through to her arms. He cleared his throat and stepped back.

Her senses returned, and she slipped the key into the pocket from which her sister had swiped it. The pace of her heart began to settle.

She turned toward him, knowing she had to continue to converse with him a little while longer. She'd been the one to invite him out onto the terrace. If she weren't who she was, and he were not a man of the law, she'd like to get to know him better.

"What do ye do when ye're no' tracking down criminals?" She settled on a question.

"I like to go for walks on my land," he said casually.

"That's lovely. Do ye have a decent parcel?"

"Aye. It will do." His eyes lit, and she knew it must be grander than he let on.

"Does a stream run through it?" Why had she asked such a thing? He was a constable, and she lied for a living. She would never see his land.

"Aye. 'Tis a bonny one. Wide enough to wade into, but no' so deep that the current will carry ye away." He smiled as if he held a secret that she wasn't privy to, but it was fitting because it was his land, and her imagination probably wouldn't do it justice.

She'd never have a place like that, but she was glad he did. Even if he was investigating her family and she'd known him but a day, she knew people, and despite his rough edges, he was a good man.

"Why have ye no' married?"

He shrugged. "I've never taken the time."

"Ye should."

"Why?" His eyes sparkled, and he leaned in closer, waiting for her response.

"Because I think ye would be a good provider, and ye would be a pleasing sight to see strolling through the door at night."

"Ye are only trying to charm me again."

She ignored his words and continued, "Look at ye now, like a dark pirate who wouldn't let anything stand between him and what belongs to him." She laughed, but when her gaze landed on his, she swallowed.

His eyes were dilated and focused on her. She'd been telling the truth. If she weren't exactly the wrong person for him, she might be tempted to ask him to kiss her. Hell, she wanted the knowledge of what his mouth would feel like on hers. The smell of him on his coat was doing odd things to her. Her lips were suddenly dry, so her tongue darted out to wet them.

"Why are ye no' wed?"

A bitter laugh escaped as he turned the question on her. "Because nae one would want me for that long."

"I dinnae think that's true. Ye are a bonny lass, and while ye're infuriatingly intriguing, there is something almost empathetic and compassionate about ye."

No one had ever seen her so clearly. She experienced others' emotions so completely that she'd always been able to conform to what people wished to see. He could read beyond that.

She wanted to kiss him and to know what it was like to have his body melded next to hers. Her lips parted as she studied his mouth.

A rumble came from somewhere deep in his chest. "Dinnae make me want ye, lass."

"And what would be so wrong with being desired by ye?"

She'd lost her mind. The danger was a vice her body was craving.

"I always get what I want," he said as his penetrating eyes studied her.

She swallowed.

"And that won't end well for either of us," he growled.

He took her hand, which had just returned the key, brought it to his nose, and inhaled her perfume. His lips parted as he kept firm eye contact with her. She heated at the warmth of his breath on her wrist.

"I think ye'll find I'm no' as easy to tame as other lasses," she managed.

"Who said I wanted to cage ye in? I want to release the wild creature inside." He breathed in again as she fought the tingles expanding down her arm as the tip of his nose caressed the pulse point.

"You are quite bold for a man who has known me for but a day."

"I would wager that I'm the only man who has ever truly seen ye." His head rose, and he stood tall, but he didn't release his grasp on her.

She took in a deep breath. He was right. How did he know her so well? Fear, and a strange sense of wanting to lean into the threat, flooded the blood pumping through her. She needed to escape or risk giving into a desire she'd never had before.

She backed up and pulled free from his grasp. His slow grin suggested he was pleased that he'd once again thrown her off balance.

"Thank ye for the air, Constable. 'Tis been a long day, and I fear I am in need of some rest."

"I can escort ye to yer chamber."

"Nae," she replied too quickly. Taking a breath, she continued, "I ken my way, and I'm sure the other guests would like to enjoy yer company."

His dark smile unnerved her. It matched the shadows of the night—unending, filled with peril and hidden delights. Pulling from the comfort of his jacket, she handed it to him.

She turned and attempted to control her stride as she walked toward the door.

"Sleep well, *Miss Reid*." His deep voice reached her ears as she fled, a promise that his efforts to discover who she was would continue tomorrow.

She dashed for the security of her room.

If Kate could leave this party now, she would. She couldn't, though, because her family would be on the streets if she gave in to the fear.

The Fordices would be here within a few days. She could avoid the constable, even if she couldn't squash the pattering of her heart when he glanced her way.

She had to.

Gavin couldn't remember the last time he'd felt so alive. As he watched the imposter retreat, a flutter started in his chest. She was rattled. He had the upper hand, and she was about to crumble right into his grasp.

As he donned his jacket, he wondered what game had she been playing with him to invite and entice him out here on the terrace? And during the meal as she'd placed her soft hand on his leg. He'd known the gesture was to distract him from questioning Miss MacGregor, but he'd relished it. He was certain she didn't know what had sprung to life or what beast she was awakening with her hungry eyes, and he'd silently willed her fingers to move closer.

She was his puzzle to solve, and he wasn't going to let her retreat. He thought about following her, but as he strolled back into the drawing room, he was pulled into a conversation with Lord Stonehaven and Charles Bartrom, the theater man from London.

Before he knew it, he'd had two more servings of whisky and had barely won a game of cards. He was eager to sleep off the effects and get a fresh start tomorrow. He crested the steps, then reached into his pocket and withdrew the key.

Unlocking the door, he walked in and noticed straight away that something was wrong. The papers on his desk had been moved. Someone had been in his room. He'd have to find out from Lord Stonehaven who else had a key.

He picked up the stack and held it to his forehead as he chided himself for leaving it out in the open. Spiced orange and gardenia wafted from the papers . . . Miss Reid.

How had she done it?

He thought back through the evening. Miss MacGregor bumping into him, and then the imposter's desire to get him alone on the terrace. Her efforts had not been to seduce him but to return the key she'd taken. The little wench had orchestrated the whole affair.

Anger exploded in the back of his head. He slapped the papers down, let himself back out, and stomped down the hall.

He turned the knob, and her door opened straight away. She'd not thought to lock it. The room was dark, save the moon shining in through the open window. Along with it came a cold breeze. He shivered at the temperature difference between the hall and her chamber as he entered and closed the exit.

He'd been ready to confront her about her duplicity and not thought of the time. Moving deeper into the room, he noticed her body's curves under the covers on the bed. He moved to stand over her.

The night was clear, and the light that drifted in allowed him to see her hair free, draped across the pillow. Her expression was peaceful. How had she not woken?

His regard drifted to a long object prone on the bed beside her, a wooden club with different objects and symbols carved into it. He blinked to make certain he saw it correctly. Why would she feel it necessary to sleep with such a weapon?

This woman was full of surprises.

His attention returned to the lass sleeping on her side facing the baton, his gaze rested on her gently curved fingertips, which rested on top of the blankets. He followed the curving slope of her arm up to a creamy bare shoulder.

She slept in the nude.

Breath lodged in his throat. He swallowed as every muscle in his body became alert and tense. He backed away as desire tightened its grip on him.

He should not want this deceiver. He should not wish to see desire for him in her ever-changing eyes.

But he did want her.

He thought back to her words, "Because nae one would want me for that long." She'd thought she had been speaking the truth. She believed someone would willingly toss her aside. She was one of the bonniest and wittiest lasses he'd ever met.

Perhaps the worst untruths she told were the ones she said to herself.

He retreated farther so that he wouldn't be tempted to reach out and caress her soft, exposed flesh. Why had she left the door unlatched? Had she known he'd come in here? What if it had been someone else to invade her space and find her in such a vulnerable position?

A sudden jolt of aggravation washed over him that she would be so careless. He wouldn't wake her, but he'd damn well let her know she'd had a visitor during the night. She'd gone through his things.

It was his turn.

Heading toward the barren desk in her room, he rifled

through the drawers. They were all empty. He glanced over to see she still slept soundly.

He moved to the dressing table and found nothing of interest, except the enticing scent she wore. He picked up the bottle and inhaled sharply, memorizing the fragrance he would now always associate with her.

Next, he checked her wardrobe and the chest on the floor. He found gowns and necessities, but nothing of a personal nature. Nothing that said anything about who she was. It seemed the only item of significance was that strange wooden club.

He shivered, then glanced toward the open window. He drifted toward it, then slowly drew it closed and secured the latch. Next, he navigated back to the armoire and pulled out a gown of his favorite color, a deep shade of blue, and draped it across the chair at her dressing table.

Smiling, he glanced at her one more time. She'd not moved. He ducked out the door pulling it closed behind him, then drifted back to his room as he thought of her surprise when she awoke.

Tomorrow she'd learn that he was the one in control.

CHAPTER 6

*K*ate jolted awake to a weight pressing on her chest. She couldn't explain the foreign sensation until she sat up and discovered her window was closed. Odd, she always left the window open when she went to sleep, even if just a little. She needed a constant flow of air about her.

She rose and raced over to fling it open, leaned out, and inhaled the early morning air. When she turned back to the room, she froze. One of her gowns rested draped across the back of her chair. For a moment, she was perplexed. Then, she realized the truth.

He knew.

The constable had been in her room. She closed her eyes as a flush crept over her bare flesh. She ran for her wardrobe and pulled her only nightdress out and drew it over her head. What had he seen?

Several breaths later, she decided it was a good sign he'd not immediately taken her into custody. If he'd planned on detaining her for trespassing, he would have done it last night. The man was toying with her.

And he was enjoying it.

She dressed, paying close attention to her appearance. He hadn't attempted to hide that he harbored an attraction for her. It was time to use the knowledge to her advantage. Perhaps she savored the challenge as well.

She'd never had a lady's maid to help her, nor did she want one. She'd learned how to do everything she needed on her own. She found the ribbons that matched the gown he'd picked and deftly threaded them through the braids she'd used to pin up the remainder of her hair. She also made certain to pull down just enough of her relaxed curls at her temples to soften her face.

Lastly, she applied her perfume. She'd seen his eyes close in appreciation when he'd smelled her wrist yesterday. He was underestimating her knowledge, and one thing she knew was that he wanted her in the way a man desired a woman. She was going to exploit it.

If he were going to treat this as one of his strategy games, she would rise to the challenge. Maybe instead of avoiding him, she should meet him directly. Last night had shown her that he wasn't looking to lock her away. He was on some mission to take down Will, but she'd never betray the man who had saved her life.

Let the constable think her a weak animal caught in a predator's lair. She knew he wanted to be the one in control. She was going to allow him to believe he possessed it.

By the time she reached the breakfast room, most of the other guests were present, including the constable, who was already ensconced in a conversation with their host and Lord Perry.

She prepared a plate from the sideboard and slid up to the table, next to the only man she'd not yet met. Of course, she knew who he was. The man who had been missing from the table last night, the Stonehavens' nephew, Archie. He was known for his roguish ways and carefree attitude. He'd probably been off with a woman last night.

Settling into the seat next to him, she looked his way and smiled.

His bleary, but attractive, brown eyes lit with appreciation.

"No lady has the right to smell so incredibly delicious." His voice was a purr meant to entice.

The giggle that escaped was genuine. He was going to be a pleasant diversion.

"Thank ye."

"And who might you be? My aunt and uncle didn't say they'd invited Venus herself to join us."

"I'm Allison Reid."

"Pleased to make your acquaintance, Allison Reid."

She knew he was about to introduce himself, but she delighted in doing it for him. "Ye must be Archie Clarke. Ye ken, ye are too late, I've been warned about yer rakish ways." She laughed openly. She'd heard the only thing he took seriously was pursuing fun. He was just the kind of ally she needed.

"I thought Claire and James didn't know how to relax, but so far, this is the best estate party I've ever attended."

"This is my first." She confessed as she let her gaze drift for a brief instant down the table.

The constable's eyes were darker than usual. His stare pinned the unaware Mr. Clarke with tight scrutiny. She returned her attention to Mr. Clarke before the lawman could tell she'd spied his examination of the Stonehavens' nephew.

"Well then. I'm at your service and will teach you how to enjoy a house party to its fullest. Will you be riding this morning?"

"I would be, but I fear given yer reputation, I must warn ye upfront that the constable is trying to gain my affections. I believe he thinks me a challenge."

"Then I must be upfront, my lady. Are you interested in his pursuit?"

She paused but a moment. It served the constable right if he had to work to gain her attention. She now thought she might be holding the winning hand.

"Aye, but I dinnae wish for him to ken it yet."

She hadn't realized until she'd said it, but yes, she did want his attention on her. When the constable's blue eyes were focused solely on her, she felt alive and desired. She'd never wanted a man's consideration when it hadn't involved furthering whatever scheme she'd planned, but he made her insides quake with a desire to get closer to him.

"I like ye. We shall prove to him that you are a prize worthy of the stiffest competition, and he will have to fight for you."

"I like that idea."

"Then, dear Miss Reid, you have a willing participant in your plot. I am at your service."

"I thank ye, kind sir."

They laughed their way through the rest of their meal as he shared the tales of his friends and what he did in his spare time.

She told him of how different life was in Scotland versus England, and in the end, he decided, he liked the less rigid environment of the north. And she agreed, he was suited to it.

"I will make it a point to venture to Scotland more often," he said.

When all the guests rose, Lord Stonehaven announced, "The ride begins in half an hour."

"I must return to my room to get my riding habit."

"I believe the plan is to meet in the hall and walk to the stables as a group. If ye meet me in the kitchens, we can sneak out ahead of everyone. That should drive the man mad with jealousy."

"So be it. We shall meet in the kitchen."

She fled the room for her own, not giving the constable the chance to seek her out.

A little while later, she met Mr. Clarke in the kitchens. Then they made their way to the stables. When the others arrived, they'd already mounted and were ready for the tour. Archie and Kate rode side by side, talking and laughing the whole time.

The few times she'd risked acknowledging the constable, he was either speaking with Lord Stonehaven or studying the landscape. She was disappointed her plan didn't seem to be working. Perhaps she'd misjudged his interest in her.

Once they'd returned to the house, she sponged off the dirt from the ride and once again made herself presentable for the drawing room.

As soon as she breeched the doorway, the constable strode up, took her arm in his, and led her out the door.

He was staking a claim before she had time to reach Mr. Clarke. He had been affected by her lack of devotion.

Gavin had finally secured Miss Reid's attention, pulling her from the drawing room. Relief washed over him as the warmth of her hand pressed into the crook of his arm.

He guessed she was attempting to make him jealous or trying to avoid him, but he wasn't going to play into her hands and acknowledge her interaction with Archie Clarke. Although it had bothered him, and he wasn't quite sure why.

Every time he'd let his gaze wander her way this morning, she'd been deeply ensconced in conversation and not concerned about his presence at all. He planned on changing that.

"Ye look lovely today."

"Do ye like the dress?" she asked.

"Aye. 'Tis my favorite color, and it makes that lovely ring of blue around yer eyes stand out."

She blushed, glancing down but for an instant before her shy, innocent gaze returned to his. "Did ye like what ye saw last night?"

Was she openly trifling with him? He stopped at the small enclave under the front stairs, spun her around, and drew her into his body. She melted into him.

"I like what I see now."

Her lips parted slightly as her eyes took on a dreamy, pleading quality. She wanted him to kiss her. He lingered a moment, attempting to decide if it was too soon. If he kissed her now, would it be giving in to her plan? Because once their lips met, he would brand her lips, and any pretense of trying to make him jealous with the Stonehavens' rogue of a nephew would have to go.

He was spared the decision by arguing coming from the hall. They weren't alone, and when he gave in to the temptation to taste her, he wanted all the time to delight in her surrender.

The angry, sharp shrill of a woman's voice bounced off the wall. He drew back and guided his quarry toward the hall and the dispute. The sound was the prickly voice of Miss Eleanor Clarke as she lit into Miss MacGregor.

Miss Clarke stepped forward and said, "You should leave now before you embarrass yourself even further, or worse yet, embarrass Nate. You are nothing but a whore. Now that you've warmed his bed, let him marry someone of his station."

Miss Reid's hand tightened on his arm.

Miss MacGregor backed up and shook her head. She then saw his companion and latched onto Miss Reid, pulling her toward the front door. He didn't protest, because although he knew the lass to be an associate of William Douglas's, she was still a person who should be treated with a modicum of decency.

He was left alone with Miss Clarke.

"That was an awful thing to say." Gavin couldn't believe he was defending a member of the Camelot Crew.

He knew Miss MacGregor was not of the same social class as the Stonehavens' niece, but what she'd said was cruel and intended to hurt. He couldn't abide anyone acting in such a fashion.

Returning to the drawing room, he conversed with the other guests for a while before heading to his room for a short reprieve. Not long after, voices from the hall caught his attention. He cracked his door enough to find Miss Reid arguing with the Lord Dunbridge over Miss MacGregor, who had apparently fled the estate.

There was something about a box and ships, and then he clearly heard Lord Dunbridge say, "She stole them, Kate."

"Kate," Gavin mouthed, his body tensed.

"How does one steal a ship?" Kate laughed as if she didn't believe the man, but as she did, a thrill shot through him.

Her name was Kate. It wasn't much to go on, but it was a start.

Kate and Lord Dunbridge's words became muffled as the pair headed below. He counted to ten, then followed.

By the time he'd reached the bottom of the stairs, Archie Clarke was escorting Miss Clarke, Lord Dunbridge, and Kate down a couple of doors to the study.

He trailed them into the room and shut the door.

Lord Dunbridge questioned Miss Clarke, who admitted to purposely misleading Miss MacGregor into thinking that Lord Dunbridge thought her beneath him. Lord Dunbridge looked at Mr. Clarke. "We have to leave straight away. I have to get to her."

"I'll have the horses readied," Mr. Clarke said.

Lord Dunbridge met Gavin's gaze. "I have someone to discuss with you. Will you walk us to the stables?"

"Aye. I can." Gavin nodded to the lass at his side, Kate. Her name was Kate. "Please excuse us."

Kate nodded as he hurried after the two men, leaving Miss Clarke to Kate's displeasure.

As they walked out the door, the Lord Dunbridge asked, "Have you ever heard of the crime lord of Edinburgh? A man named Alastair."

Gavin had, so they talked at length on the man and some of his recent activities. Somehow the MacGregor lass had earned Alastair's displeasure, and Lord Dunbridge was keen to see that no harm came to the woman as a result of it.

After their talk, Gavin made his way back to the house. He was looking forward to letting Kate know he'd once again gained the upper hand. Her distractions were gone, and he was going to let her know she no longer had anyone to hide behind.

CHAPTER 7

*K*ate paced the study floor as she fretted over what had occurred between Lord Dunbridge and her sister. Flora was one of the reasons there was a Camelot, and without that, Kate would have been forced into servitude, or God knows what else by now.

She shuddered.

If that earl didn't make her happy, she might track him down and, well, she wasn't a violent person. Instead, she'd send Will and Bran after him. And what on earth had Bran done to put Flora in danger, to begin with? She had so many questions for her family. Perhaps she'd been gone too long.

Lord Dunbridge had asked the constable to join him in the stables. She had no idea why because they'd been staring daggers at each other the past two days. It was as if Lord Dunbridge had known the constable was a threat to Flora and protected her. She liked the man more because of it. He also seemed to be smitten with her sister, so she held out hope that Flora might find a happy ending. No one deserved it more.

She, on the other hand, would never have that. No one ever accepted the real her. As long as she was someone else, the world adored her, but as soon as she confessed the truth, they were out the door or selling her to the highest bidder. She tucked those memories away and straightened her shoulders.

Back in the drawing room, she conversed with the Bartroms for a while. She liked their company.

"Dear, we would like yer help," Irene Bartrom began.

"I'd be happy to. What do ye need?"

"We thought that one rainy day, we could come up with some indoor games to play."

"I think that's a marvelous idea," she said.

They spent the next couple hours plotting, but she was aware the constable had returned. His steady, penetrating gaze openly watched her. He wasn't even trying to hide his interest in her.

Quite some time later, Mrs. Bartrom yawned. "Let's finish planning tomorrow. I feel as if I need a rest."

They were rising to go when she glanced over to find the constable was watching them prepare to make their exit.

"I believe ye have an admirer." Irene Bartrom laughed.

She blushed, not knowing how to respond.

"Ye two would make a great match. I'm sure yer brother would approve. Do ye think we will get to meet him?"

"I'm no' certain. Perhaps when I join him in Aberdeen, I can suggest he return with us," she said, knowing it would never happen.

"We will see ye at dinner."

"Enjoy yer rest."

Mrs. Bartrom had barely left her side when the man who had been openly eyeing her excused himself from Lord Perry and Miss Clarke's company and made his way toward her. They didn't seem to mind, as the pair continued in a deep conversation.

"We were interrupted before. Would ye take a walk with

me? I havenae been to the gallery and would like to stroll through it."

She smiled and rose. "I'd like that."

She was playing with fire. She had no one to hide behind, yet she didn't want to retreat. She looked forward to sparring with him.

They walked in silence for a moment until they came to the gallery. It was a long room with bench sofas strategically placed around the perimeter to admire the artwork on the walls.

As they strolled, the light sounds of music filtered down the hall as someone began strumming on the pianoforte. It was most likely Miss Clarke, who had been the one to play last night. The melody was slow and steady, a relaxing tempo to meander to.

"It appears most of these are of the Stonehaven family," he said.

"Aye. I see the resemblance."

They'd made it about halfway through the space when the constable's hand reached for hers. The sizzle was immediate as currents shot through her.

She peeked up at his eyes, and for the first time, they weren't dark and suspicious of her—they held kindness and understanding. And for a second, she was jealous of the person she couldn't be, the one who could have had a relationship with this man.

A lady would be lucky to claim his heart one day, but it couldn't be her.

As soon as he truly knew who she was, he'd be gone.

Still, she couldn't pull free. And he knew it. He was playing with her again. Was it his strategy to have her fall for him then press her for all the answers he desired? What he didn't understand was that the closer he got, the harder she would guard her secrets because once told, he'd leave, and she wouldn't set herself up for the consequences.

She was damaged, and she would be the one to leave first.

"I like this one." He pointed to a painting with a man in full Highland regalia on a proud steed, overlooking a captured stag.

She laughed. "Of course ye would."

"And which one is yer favorite?"

"This one." She nodded to the piece that depicted a couple dancing, surrounded by musicians. It was most likely a marriage, which she could look past because they were out in the open.

"I supposed that one is nice." He winked.

They reached the end of the gallery and hooked to the left, crossed the hall, and entered a large ballroom. He guided her a few steps in, then turned to her. "Dance with me."

Soft strains of music still reached them. The notes had been joined by a lovely voice singing in a language that must be Italian. She guessed the beautiful sound was Lady Stonehaven.

She nodded and turned toward him. The constable's free arm coiled around her waist and drew her near. She felt as if she were headed straight for a wreck, an accident she wouldn't recover from, but the thrill of being desired by this strong, dark, and dangerous man was intoxicating.

And she let go. She was no longer Allison Reid. She was just a girl dancing with a man who was giving her all his attention, a man who desired her for who she was and not the person she pretended to be. She relaxed into the rhythm and let him carry her around the dance floor.

Suddenly, the music no longer drifted through the room, and the constable stopped. The comforting weight of his hand on her waist slackened, and he caressed her cheek with his fingers. His head tilted close, and she thought he might kiss her.

Her breath caught.

"Ye are so lovely." His gaze penetrated hers, burning hot

with a yearning that matched her own. The hand in hers let go and curled around her side. He pulled her flush to his tight frame, and she nearly moaned as tension wound tight in her body, recognizing the need in his.

"I like this side of ye." His face was next to hers, then he dipped his mouth to her ear and whispered, "Kate."

Icy fear froze her to the spot. What did he know?

$\sim$

Gavin knew Kate was her true name because the change in her posture and demeanor was immediate. He'd been tempted to continue to swirl her around the floor, despite the disappearance of the melody that had been lightly drifting in. She'd been pliant and playful until he revealed his hand.

But with his words, the mood had shifted, and it was as if a hot kettle had burned her. He hadn't known what to expect, but fear wasn't what he'd anticipated. He'd thought she would bat her lashes and light-heartedly let another untruth fall from her pretty pink lips.

He missed the moment they'd just shared. Instant regret crushed something inside as the ease between them vanished.

She became as skittish as the rabbits they'd spied on the lawn. He drew away to analyze the tightness that had gripped her. He'd not intended to frighten her, but the emotion that poured from her gaze was sheer panic.

"'Tis all right. I didnae mean to scare ye."

She tried to pull free. He held on, reluctant to see her flee. She shook her head.

"How?" she asked. Her eyes held a sheen he'd not seen before, as if she were on the verge of tears.

He'd meant to hold the knowledge a while longer, but he'd been so taken with how she'd let herself go, how she'd become that lass he'd seen yesterday morning. He'd been lost in how he wanted her. How he'd wanted Kate . . . not the imposter.

"It doesnae matter. 'Tis just a name. I willnae give yer secret away."

His hand cupped around the back of her neck. She stopped her struggles but still turned from his grasp.

"I wish to go to my room," she whispered, unable to meet his eyes.

He loosened his hold, knowing he would have to let her retreat. He'd played his hand too soon. She needed time to realize he meant her no harm, then return to thinking she'd once again regained her power over him.

"I'll walk ye there. This way will be faster." He tilted his head toward the back of the room.

She nodded, and he released her, but unwilling to break the connection completely, he took her hand in his. He guided her toward the stairs at the rear of the house, knowing they would come out at the opposite end of the hall from where they typically entered the next level.

They walked the distance to her room on the other end of the passageway. He caught her trembling fingers as they began to turn the nob. She closed her eyes, and he couldn't tell if it was to keep him out.

"I promise I am not here to harm ye."

She opened her eyes and met his gaze straight on. "I'd like to have some privacy, Constable."

"Call me Gavin," he pleaded.

She nodded.

"I will see ye at the evening meal, Gavin."

He released her hand, and she turned the knob, entered, and shut the door. He waited to hear the click of a lock, but none came. He needed to have a talk with her about securing the room when she was inside. Although the company here was safe until the Fordices arrived, it was a habit everyone should develop.

Walking to his room, he sat at the desk and penned two letters. One to his contact in Aberdeen, asking the man to discover what he could about a woman named Kate, who associated with the Camelot Crew. The other was to a man he knew in Edinburgh, requesting information be delivered to his home in Glasgow on the crime lord known as Alastair Sinclair. He had too much going on here to focus on a new case, but Lord Dunbridge from England had requested he look into the man, so he would.

Once the missives were complete, he dressed, then descended the stairs and found the Stonehavens' butler to request his letters be delivered. Then he waited for the others to arrive and the evening meal to start.

When Kate strode into the room with a smile on her face, and her shoulders held high, the sour mood that had claimed him vanished. She'd put her mask back on, and while he liked the real Kate, he had to acknowledge that something about her deception still held true to who she was. There was a hidden strength to her.

She was again the sister of a wealthy businessman. He wondered why she'd chosen that and what had brought her here. There was some reasoning behind her presence, and it was more than having fun or a free place to live for a couple of weeks. There were high stakes here for her, and the proof was that she hadn't fled when he'd discovered her first name, even though he didn't know her full identity . . . yet. But she couldn't know that.

The more he learned about her, the more he questioned.

The table was again set for the number of people present, which gave extra space between the guests. With the spread, conversations became clustered and more intimate. He was near the end of the table's left side, while Kate sat close to him on the end opposite of their host. Mrs. Irene Bartrom was directly opposite him, and Miss Clarke was to his left. He ignored Miss Clarke, but it wouldn't have mattered because she spent the entire meal focused on Lord Perry, who was on her other side.

The only outward sign that Kate was still affected by his discovery was the amount of wine she consumed. She picked at her food. The conversation was pleasant as Kate talked with Mrs. Bartrom and him about theater and the arts. Despite her façade being in place, he enjoyed the conversation.

A servant appeared and filled her wine glass for the second time. Her cheeks had started to turn a lovely shade of rose, the effects of the spirits manifesting in a physical form. She was beautiful. Her hair appeared a little darker in the reduced light of the evening. And her eyes had taken on the brown hue that circled her pupils, with the green and blue fading to give her a sultry radiance.

When they stood, she swayed, and he swooped in to take her arm and steady her. She seemed only to be slightly off-balance, but he'd wanted a reason to touch her from the moment he'd left her at the door to her chamber.

As the smaller group filed into the drawing room, he noticed that they'd broken off into pairs, Lord Perry and Miss Clarke had gone directly to the opposite side of the room and settled on a settee to talk in private. The Bartroms and their hosts were discussing books and made straight for the library to look at some volumes.

He had the bonny Kate all to himself.

"Would ye like to stroll around the terrace?" He knew she couldn't refuse because he'd noticed her fascination with being out of doors.

"Aye. I would like that." And although she smiled, the gesture held some reserve.

As they strolled out into the evening air, a weight lifted from his chest. She wasn't going to avoid him completely.

"Ye look bonny tonight."

"Thank ye," she said.

"Are ye angry with me?"

"Nae, how could I be? Ye only did what ye're adept at. Yer job."

Perhaps she thought she was only part of his investigation to him. Was she? She had been, but now, he wanted to know her secrets and how they might affect his mission, but he also saw her as a person. And as the woman who craved the cool waters of the creek on her feet.

One who lied, he had to remind himself. How could he forget what she was? His attraction to her didn't change that she was engaged in some sort of criminal behavior. Could he want her and still be objective? He had to be.

But he also craved to know if she tasted as sweet as the wine they'd consumed with dinner.

"It feels like rain in the air." He attempted to change the topic, but the words fell flat.

"Yes. It does." She didn't offer anymore.

He fought to come up with something else trivial to say, but he couldn't do it. Instead, he offered her the truth. "Ye may have noticed, I'm no' like the others here."

"How is that?"

His remark had finally earned him her genuine smile and a look of interest.

"I'm a common man, a hard man. I don't have it in me to flatter, and I don't waste words."

"I have already guessed this about ye." Her grin lifted higher.

"Then I will speak plainly with ye, and I wish for ye to do the same with me."

"Is there something ye wish to say?" She peeked at him from beneath her long dark lashes.

"Aye."

"I willnae hold yer words against ye. It's actions that should be trusted," Kate replied.

He found her remark rather insightful.

"I think ye should keep yer door locked when ye are in yer room."

She laughed. "That's yer concern?"

"Yes. Yer safety is one of my concerns."

"I typically do keep my doors locked."

"And last night?" He raised an eyebrow.

"'Tis broken."

"Perhaps I should mention it to the Stonehavens."

"Please dinnae. I dinnae wish to be an ungrateful guest," Kate begged.

"I'm certain they would understand."

"May I speak boldly as well?" she asked.

"I would expect nae less."

"If the door were fixed, wouldn't that prevent a curious constable from spying on me?" Amusement returned to her tone, and her grin turned mischievous.

He relaxed, but at the same time, his heartbeat accelerated.

"Did ye find what ye were looking for when ye entered my room?" He wondered how much of his reports she'd managed to read. She'd not been gone long last night, so he knew she couldn't have made it through the majority of the stack.

"I willnae admit to such an intrusion."

He laughed.

He guided her across the terrace to the spot near an entrance to the ballroom where the shadows were deepest, where he knew no one would see, not that anyone present would notice their absence. Even though the others were occupied, he thought it necessary to take her somewhere where he could have her all to himself.

"If I had done such a thing, what would have given me away?"

"Inattention to a small detail, which I will not divulge so that I can catch ye next time, and the lingering scent of oranges, spice, and gardenias."

"Perhaps the culprit should stop wearing perfume," she laughed.

"Nae. The scent is intoxicating. Perhaps it's why a constable would forgive such a breach of trust." He drew her wrist to his nose and inhaled. "This would make a man do things he doesnae understand."

In the scant light, he was still able to make out the dilation of her pupils and feel the quickening in the pulse that beat below his finger as he traced the lines beneath the delicate skin. He'd not wanted a woman in a long time, preferring his duties to the pursuit of pleasure, but everything about Kate called to the part of him he'd neglected for years.

He wanted *her*.

And he desired to throw her off balance. But most of all, he wished to know that she was experiencing the same thirst he was drowning in.

They'd reached the end of the long terrace and were in the farthest shadows. Even if the other guests glanced out the windows, no one would find them here. Turning to face her, he took her other hand and threaded his fingers through hers. He backed her to the side of the house and lifted his hands with hers, placing them on both sides of her head.

She was pinned between him and the wall, and she didn't try to flee. On the contrary, her lips had parted, and the chest rose and fell with the rapid breathing of what he hoped was anticipation.

"I'm going to kiss ye." It was a statement, but he allowed her time to protest.

She didn't. She swallowed, then gave a slight nod before tilting her chin to permit him better access.

Her gaze bored into his, penetrating and needy. He feasted on the sight of Kate wanting him. His body tightened, and his mouth began to water as his heart pounded in his ears.

He closed the distance, placing his lips on hers, and sheer bliss ignited in his core. She slanted up to meet his embrace, and the gasp that escaped her throat was one of pleasure. She liked his mouth on hers, so he deepened the caress, his tongue darting into her opening and tangling with hers. Longing spiked in his core.

He'd never been gripped so tight in passion's embrace. Kate made him feel alive. As she matched his efforts, she brought him to life. For the first time since his parents had left him, he felt wanted, needed, and desired.

She was sweet, better than the finest wine, and he wanted more. Wanted to drink her until he'd had his fill and then continue up to the point where it became impossible. They kissed until he was forced to come up for air—until he feared he would suffocate her if he didn't release her.

When he drew back, the radiance in her eyes floored him. She was a master at deception, but there was no way she could fake the dazed look in her gaze, the flutter of her lids or the way her chest heaved with her quickened breaths.

Kate desired him too, and the knowledge was heady and addictive and powerful. He leaned in and claimed her lips again. This time, his body pressed into hers, and his cock jerked at the touch. It was as if he was a young lad again, unable to control his emotions, his hungers, his body.

A fox shrilling in the distance broke him from the trance. He drew back and swallowed. He needed to walk her to her room and put some distance between them. It wasn't time to take whatever was growing between them to the next phase, but he was now certain that he could not leave this place without knowing what it would be like to lose himself inside of the real Kate.

CHAPTER 8

$\mathcal{K}$ate shut the door and backed to the wall to steady herself before closing her eyes and tracing where Gavin's lips had been on hers. They still tingled, and her body thrummed like the vibrations of a string instrument. Her heart drummed out a rhythm it had never known.

She wasn't sure what the constable knew about her, but he'd discovered her name, and he'd not run for the farthest corner of the world or sold her off to another. He'd made her feel desired. She wanted to push aside the hunger he awoke in her with the simplest touch, but her body wouldn't let her, despite what her brain was telling her.

He had a detailed dossier of information on everyone in her family. She must have escaped the list by being gone for the last six months. It had to have been collected when she wasn't at Camelot because Allison and Joseph Reid were accounted for. If he discovered she was a member of Will's family, how would he feel? He already suspected she held some tie to the group.

Despite the threat, she wanted him. And it wasn't the wine that had loosened her lips and set her heart racing tonight. An immediate attraction had sparked and drawn her to the dark, determined constable the moment she'd met him.

"What are ye dreaming about?" A giggle came from farther in her room.

She jumped and opened her eyes. Isobel sat on her bed.

"Is it the man I heard say goodnight to ye?" A teasing tone rang out from her, and she giggled again.

"Mayhap. But forget about that. What are ye doing here?"

"Flora left, and I need something to do or a way home. I thought I could stay on a little longer and be yer lady's maid for a while."

"I've never had a lady's maid. I dinnae think I need one now," she said.

"Dinnae send me home. I want to stay." Her sister pouted.

Kate inwardly grinned at the girl's enthusiasm.

"Look, I already brought all Flora's new gowns and things in here. She left without them."

"I hope Lord Dunbridge caught up to her, and they made amends."

"Aye. I'm sure they did. He is smitten with her," Isobel sighed.

Kate smiled. "All right. Ye can stay. But if it becomes dangerous and ye need to leave, ye have to promise ye will."

"I promise."

"Did ye shut the window?"

"Aye, 'twas getting cold. I forgot about ye and the windows. I never thought about it, but Flora seems to have a fascination with them too; however, she doesn't leave them ajar all the time."

Kate strolled over and pushed it open. She inhaled a deep breath of the cool night air.

"Get over here and let me take yer hair down. Ye did a marvelous job with it, by the way."

"Thank ye. I think I've become pretty adept at it."

Isobel helped her prepare for bed, then left, promising to return early to assist her in the morning.

Before climbing into bed, Kate grabbed her club and lay it on the mattress. She'd come a long way from the crippling paranoia of her youth, but she still needed the security of it beside her. It was the only way she slept. Her nightly ritual performed, she undressed and climbed beneath the covers.

As she lay there, she considered the way Gavin had kissed her and how her limbs had become weak with want. She thought it might be best if they weren't alone together. She might let him place his mouth on hers once more, and she wasn't sure she would want to stop. Her body ached to feel his again, and that could cause complications she wasn't prepared for.

She would need to keep close to the other guests until she could control her body and discover what he was up to.

❧

The next morning, Kate woke to a click as Isobel closed her door.

"Good morn."

"It's still too early," Kate groaned. It wasn't, but sleep had evaded her most of the night as she thought about Gavin, her reaction to his kiss, and what his purpose here was. She didn't think he did anything without a reason.

Isobel laughed. "I am eager to prepare ye for the day."

Kate grabbed her nightdress and drew it over her shoulders before climbing from the bed. She plodded to the window and looked out at what promised to be another beautiful day. Her attention was captured by a man running beside the far end of the pond. It was Gavin. She studied him as the familiar form gracefully propelled itself forward with the speed of a wolf chasing prey.

"What are ye looking at?"

As the large, dark-haired man came closer, her mouth watered, and the beat in her chest pounded a little bit faster. His legs drove him so fast that she imagined he could outrun a deer.

"Gavin," she answered absently.

"Is he the one who walked ye to yer door last night?"

"Aye."

He wore only breeches and shoes. The tight ropes of muscle on his chest and arms, as they pumped back and forth, moved with his strides, the strength beneath them evident. Her body melted as she leaned in to watch him make his way back to the house.

"Ye fancy him?" Isobel interrupted her thoughts.

"Aye. He kissed me." Even saying it made her feel alive and relive the tingles that had captured her body the moment his lips had touched hers. Her fingertips traced where they'd connected.

"Well, let's get ye ready, so ye can tempt him again." Isobel laughed. "Perhaps ye and Flora will both find good men to marry."

"I shouldn't."

"And why no'?"

"He's a constable from Glasgow, and I found papers in his room about Camelot and everyone living there."

"That is concerning," Isobel admitted.

"Ye were on the list too, Isobel, so stay away from him."

"Was yer name written down?"

"Nae. I think it must have been gathered in the last few months. That's how he kens I'm no' Allie."

She told Isobel everything she knew as her sister dressed her in one of Flora's new morning gowns that looked fancier than most of the clothing Kate owned. The bodice had a pretty embroidered antique frill with rosy-pink accents, and the hem of the cream-colored gown had matching tambour working. She and Flora were close to the same size, and Kate had to admit the quality of material and fit made her feel more like the wealthy merchant woman she was claiming to be.

A little while later, she strolled into the breakfast room and prepared a plate from the sideboard. She claimed a seat near Lady Stonehaven, then shortly after, Irene Bartrom entered and took the chair on her opposite side.

She was heavily entrenched in a discussion with the ladies when she felt eyes on her. Gavin was several places down, next to Lord Perry. They were conversing, but the constable's focus was on her.

A slow warmth began in her belly and radiated outward as she imagined what Gavin might be thinking and remembering the way he'd looked this morning as she'd spied on him. She shouldn't want to touch and explore him up close with his shirt gone, but she had the desire to run her hands along the tight muscles she'd seen working as he ran.

His lips twitched, and she blushed. Had he guessed where her thoughts had gone? Surely not. He only knew that she'd glanced his way.

Could she follow through on her plan to avoid him if all she could think about was being near him again? She swallowed, squared her shoulders, and focused on the ladies beside her, but she couldn't keep her regard from occasionally sneaking glances in his direction.

"I think we could find some more ideas in the library." Irene Bartrom rose.

"That's a marvelous idea," Lady Stonehaven stated.

She stood to follow them and noticed Gavin's steady contemplation watching her as she left the room with the ladies. She smiled at him and his gaze traveled along her movements.

She spent the morning ensconced with the ladies making plans for the rest of the week. When she had the opportunity to slide it in, she mentioned the group possibly taking a tour of Aberdeen the following week. The ladies agreed it was a marvelous idea, and Kate smiled at how easily her plan was falling into place.

Miss Clarke joined them at some point, and she learned the men had gone out for a ride to tour the countryside. She was jealous that they were out in the open, but this room was large enough, and she was having a good time planning out the little plays they would have all the guests act out.

And sequestering herself with the ladies kept her from making irrational decisions involving the man who, although not in the room, was ever present in her thoughts.

The late morning sun glinted from the stones on the great estate as Gavin, Lord Stonehaven, Mr. Bartrom, and Lord Perry rode out of the stables. It was a temperate and beautiful day despite the thickening air that promised rain was on its way. They set a steady pace as they headed out on a tour of the local countryside.

Once he had the opportunity and the others had begun a conversation, Gavin steered his mount toward Lord Stonehaven.

"I've had word that they will arrive tomorrow," Lord Stonehaven said so that only he could hear.

Good. He had work to do. Perhaps the purpose would provide a distraction from the relentless thoughts of the lass he couldn't purge from his mind.

"The one you are concerned with is still ill and will be arriving late."

The news was not what he'd expected, but he could make do. "That may allow me to question their servants without him, although I need to speak with the man's valet."

"He is now scheduled to arrive later in the week. Do you think the guests are safe with them here?"

"Aye. 'Tis only the youngest son who is the problem, and ye have no children about for him to prey on."

Lord Stonehaven pursed his lips.

"I'll be keeping a close watch on him as well." Gavin attempted to reassure the man.

"I instructed my daughter to keep my grandchildren away until I send word."

"Thank ye for agreeing to this. I ken the circumstances have changed yer plans."

"If it means that man will be accountable for his sins, then it will have been worth it."

Gavin agreed.

They spent the afternoon touring the area, then came upon a carriage accident. The passengers had only suffered bumps and bruises, but their group rode into the closest town to get help for the occupants and secure passage for them.

By the time they returned to the Stonehaven estate, it was late, and the air had turned cold and heavy. The rain was now imminent, and although it hadn't begun, his clothes clung to him and were heavy with the moisture that had saturated the evening as they'd made their way back through the heavy fog.

Lord Stonehaven had a meal prepared for them, but the ladies had all gone to bed by the time they were done, so the gentlemen soon followed.

Gavin undressed, and his thoughts once again turned to Kate. He wondered if she was naked under her blankets again. Longing, hot and fierce, claimed his manhood. He had to persuade himself not to take the few short strides down the hall, open the door—which he knew would be unbarred—and join her under the covers.

But although they'd shared a kiss, he couldn't just assume she wanted more.

He did. He wanted to unlock all the secrets she was

hiding, but she had to be willing. He may have to put off that conversation, though.

Tomorrow, the next phase of his investigation would begin. His hope was to learn more of Thomas Fordice, then track down his servants and persuade one of them to give the man up. Surely, they weren't so loyal that they would keep the secrets of a monster. All his hopes relied on getting to them and finding one who would bear witness against him.

Once that was done, he could turn his attention back to Kate.

CHAPTER 9

*R*ain started sometime in the wee hours of the morning. It set a soothing rhythm on the roof, and although it had awoken her, the steady beat soon lulled Kate back into a deep sleep where she dreamed of the constable. Gavin had her arms pinned to the wall as he had when he'd kissed her, but this time there was no fox's alarm to break the spell. This time, he kissed her until her knees were weak, and she wanted to beg him for more.

She woke, twisted in the sheets, flushed and aching at her core. Was she willing to let him take her that far? Would she have the resolve to stop him if he wanted to? She didn't think she could, didn't think she wanted to. She'd never experienced an attraction like this and certainly never let herself act upon it.

She'd been disappointed when he'd not returned by the evening meal last night, despite her promise to herself to avoid him.

Rising, she threw on her nightdress and walked to the window. A deep fog had moved in, and rain still fell, showing no sign that it would slow. In the distance, Gavin took a turn around the pond. For a moment, she wondered if she was still dreaming. The man was everywhere she looked, and when he wasn't there, he occupied her thoughts like the craving for a sweet after a savory meal.

He had almost made it back to the house. Dark hair dripped to his shoulders, and he swiped at the rain on his forehead. He must be pretty dedicated to running to be out in such a mess.

She watched as he came closer. A knock sounded, jolting her from her admiration of the man's physique. The door swung in to admit Isobel.

Taking her time, the lass once again helped Kate dress, paying particular care to sweeping up her hair and letting the right amount of curl fall free in the front.

"Ye are good at this. I hope ye can find a position somewhere soon. I'll ask Miss Clarke if she kens anyone in need."

"That would be nice. I think I would be sad to go to England, but if I made good money, I could send some back to Camelot."

"I'm sure Will would appreciate that."

"This is my favorite color on ye."

"Why's that?"

"The dark-green brings out the emerald in yer eyes. They look quite fetching today."

Her thoughts turned to Gavin, and she wondered if he would like it on her. She shouldn't be thinking to grab his attention. But here she was, being foolish again. His absence had only made her think of him more. She stood and banished the images of his wet body pressed to hers.

When she entered the breakfast room, Gavin was already there. Her heart began to thud loudly, and as she helped herself to a heaping serving of eggs and a honey cake, she wondered what she should do. Turning, she faced the table and discovered his scrutiny on her.

He prevented her from having to make a decision. "Good

morning, Miss Reid. Join me. I'd like to hear about the planning yesterday."

As she eased into the chair beside him, his predatory smile turned victorious.

"We had a grand time organizing. I think 'twill be enjoyed by all."

"Ye look lovely." He leaned in and whispered, somehow turning the simple compliment illicit.

"Thank ye," she returned. "Ye dried off and presented yerself rather quickly."

He moved even closer. Hushed words meant only for her wrapped around her and taunted, "Why, Kate, we're ye spying on me?"

"The way ye would watch and then play tricks on a lass in her bed."

His lips curved up, wicked, unrepentant. "Are yer trying to put ideas in my head, Kate?"

Her body heated. "Nae. I was only pointing out that ye seem to like running because every time I peer out my window, ye are there."

He grinned, seemingly pleased with the knowledge that she'd been watching on him.

"Why do ye run so much?"

"So that I'm fast enough when I need to be." His gaze darkened, and his chest appeared to expand like he was on watch for an enemy to come crashing through the gates and pilfer a village.

Although he left something unsaid, at the same time, he was completely honest. She would let him have his secrets.

"Ye were all gone longer than I thought ye would be yesterday." She attempted to change the subject and lighten the mood.

His gaze turned mischievous again as the shadows vanished from his eyes. "Did ye miss me?"

Her cheeks flushed, then she decided she'd turn the tables

on him. "Aye. I thought ye might wish to walk with me on the terrace again."

"I would like that."

"It seems ye have missed yer chance. It looks like we will be stuck inside today."

"I can think of plenty of places to stroll inside." he paused as his eyes trapped her and turned a deeper shade of blue. "And many locations I would like to explore."

Her breath caught as a wicked grin crooked his full lips. He broke the contact as air swished from behind her. She peeked to the right as Irene took the seat next to her.

"Good morning, Miss Reid." The theater woman glanced past her. "Constable Davidson."

They greeted her in unison.

"I heard there was quite the excitement on your tour yesterday. It sounds as if you gentlemen saved the day," Irene continued.

"We were only helping those in need."

"Well I believe, Charles overdid it. He's sleeping late today."

"He deserves the rest," Gavin said.

She turned her attention to Kate. "I've thought of a couple more we can use. We should be able to hammer out the scripts in the library this morning. Then we can assign the parts."

The conversation flowed, and it wasn't long before they were all rising and heading toward the library. Gavin even joined them and pretended to read a book as the ladies discussed the plays they were going to put on. She wasn't fooled, though. His eyes drifted her way as often as hers sought him out.

Around noon, the butler came in and announced to Lady Stonehaven that her latest guests, Magnus and Stewart Fordice, had arrived. Chills spread down her arms. She thought she had another day, but at least her plan had worked, and Thomas had not joined the men. He would recognize her. As long as he wasn't here, her plan was intact and ready to move forward.

She took a deep breath, then glanced at the man whose attention she'd have to forego to proceed with her reason for being here. Camelot came before her interest in a man. When she glanced at Gavin, she found he was no longer watching her but had his eyes fixed on the door. He was no longer the man who had softened to her but the dark, dangerous constable with a steely determination and purpose.

And that purpose was no longer her was . . . interesting.

"Lovely timing. We were finishing up in here. Show them to the drawing room and we'll join them there."

"Yes, my Lady," the man replied.

"I believe we are done with our planning for the day."

She followed the women's leads, careful not to seem too enthusiastic to meet the new guests. Together, the group strolled into the room where her target stood, staring out the window to the sodden back of the property. Magnus Fordice owned the building that her Camelot family inhabited. Due to her involvement in his youngest son's life, he'd doubled their rent, and then demanded that they leave.

She was here to make certain that didn't happen and seek recompense for those his grown son, Thomas, had harmed.

Luckily, the man and his oldest son, Stewart, had no idea who she was because they hadn't been present when she'd crossed Thomas. She shuddered, thinking about the man. She'd handsomely paid a disgruntled servant of his to give him enough laxative to keep his belly aching and him unable to travel until her plan was complete.

It had also succeeded in keeping Magnus's wife from making an appearance because she was at home nursing their son back to health. Kate couldn't ask for better circumstances to begin her deception.

Introductions were made, but she hung back and began a half-hearted conversation with Miss Clarke. It wouldn't do to be overly anxious. Besides, Gavin kept them busy with questions about their business contacts and relations within Glasgow. It was a shame they were from the same city, and he was so interested in them. She might have to vie for Magnus's attention.

After about a quarter-hour, Stewart excused himself from the conversation and joined Miss Clarke and her. The resemblance to his younger brother was unnerving. He had golden curls, piled slightly higher on top and shorn a little closer on the sides, pale skin, and ruby lips.

Stewart was an attractive man, but his brother had been, too.

"Mr. Fordice, I'm sorry to hear of your brother's illness. I was looking forward to meeting him and hearing about all the work he does with children," Miss Clarke chimed in.

Kate's stomach flipped, and bile rose to her throat. What was Miss Clarke talking about?

"It doesn't appear to be major. I'm optimistic that he will be able to join us soon."

"What type of work does yer brother do?" She hated to ask, but it must be done. She purposely relaxed her shoulders and smiled.

"He works with several orphanages. He's known quite well for finding homes for children who have been abandoned."

She forced a smile as disgust assailed her. She knew too well that finding a stable home for young children was the last thing on that deranged man's mind.

"What do ye do, Mr. Fordice?" Thankfully, Miss Clarke broke back in.

"I help my father with his business dealings. But please, ye may both call me Stewart. Mr. Fordice is my father, and I like to think we'll grow close over our time here."

"That must be rewarding. My brother is a businessman as well."

"Oh, what's his name? Perhaps I've heard of him?"

"Joseph Reid. He works mostly in Inverness, but he's looking to branch out nearby. He acquires buildings in run-down areas and attempts to bring in new businesses and let out space. He's quite busy with it. That's why I'm here alone."

"Sounds like he and I might have things in common."

Lord Perry strolled up to join the conversation. It was probably to stake a claim on Miss Clarke because he'd been monopolizing most of her time the last couple of days. But Kate was glad for the newcomer.

She'd planted her seed. Giving away too much at one time would make this all look like her idea. The sale of the property had to appear to come from the Fordices.

"Mr. Fordice, how were yer travels? The rain must have made the passage a little more difficult," Lord Perry asked.

"We were safe within the confines of the carriage."

A chill racked her.

"Are ye feeling well, Miss Reid?" Stewart asked.

"I am. Sorry, the thought of being trapped in a carriage for so long is distressing," she confessed.

Stewart leaned closer, seeming to want to comfort her, so she played the part of being a helpless lass, wrapping herself in her arms, but at the same time, leaning in to mimic the man's posture.

"Ye don't like travel?" he questioned.

"Oh, I do, but not in such a small space. When I was young, I played hide-and-seek with some children and became stuck in the larder of an abandoned home. It took our parents hours to find me."

"How horrendous," Miss Clarke gasped.

She felt Gavin before seeing him. She swallowed suddenly, too aware of his presence and the distraction.

"Aye. I've never outlived the fear of being trapped in small spaces." She blinked at Stewart because this was partially true, but they didn't need the real story for her to seem vulnerable.

There was no need to try to sway Gavin. She didn't want to be vulnerable in his eyes, but he watched her as if he were questioning her motives, or possibly the interest that Stewart devoted to her.

The older Mr. Fordice broke into the conversation, "Stewart, our rooms are ready, and I believe we should change from our traveling clothes before refreshments are served."

"Yes, Father." He glanced back to them. "Will you excuse me, please? I will put on something more suitable and join you all later."

She watched them go and noticed Gavin did the same. Miss Clarke and Lord Perry had once again resumed a quiet conversation and moved farther away.

"I believe I will take a short rest. I fear the rain has made me tired." She wanted to see which rooms the Fordices had been given.

"Can I walk ye to yer room?"

She considered denying him. They both appeared to have other things on their minds, but when his penetrating gaze met hers, she couldn't resist.

"Aye," she said as she stood.

He took her arm and led her up the stairs. She was thankful Lady Stonehaven shunned the typical English propriety because she was spending too much time alone with this man for it to be considered proper, not that Miss Reid needed to worry about her reputation.

They turned into the hall as Magnus and Stewart entered their rooms on the same side of the walkway as hers, but two and three doors down.

"I wish for ye to stay away from those men," Gavin ordered.

"Why would ye desire something like that?" She blinked, trying to determine if Gavin had already picked apart her plans.

"Because I am here to investigate them, and I dinnae think they are safe."

That did explain his presence and why he was warning her. He knew what sort of men they were.

"Are ye looking out for me, Constable?" she teased.

"Gavin," he insisted.

"Gavin."

"Aye. They are dangerous."

"I have been taking care of myself for some time now. I think I am capable of making my own choices."

His eyes darkened, and he pushed his way into her room, pulling her in and shutting the door.

"Please," he pleaded.

She sighed and glanced away, then attempted to walk past him.

Gavin caught her hand and drew her around. His fingers rose to caress her cheek. "I have a job to do here, and I want to ken ye will be safe."

She leaned into his touch and shut her eyes. When she opened them, his interest had turned hungry with need. "I cannae promise ye this. I am no' yers to command."

His gaze turned stormy as if she had issued a challenge. His arm coiled around her and drew her flush to his hard frame. The smell of fresh wood and smoky bergamot filled her nostrils, and she found herself falling into his embrace. His mouth landed on hers with a hunger that sated a part of her that hadn't even realized it was parched.

And she was wrong. If she didn't have to do this one thing for her family, she'd do anything he asked. She'd do whatever he required as long as he fulfilled this yearning inside her.

But she did owe Will, and Camelot, her life. She would not let them down.

His tongue demanded hers return the embrace, and she did. This was as she had remembered it from before, a kiss that knocked the wits from her, that tormented her senses and stole her breath. She was lost, and she wanted to remain there as every fiber in her being melted into the man who held her as if he'd never leave, as if she were important, as if who she truly was didn't matter.

She sighed and barely caught herself. He was using one of her tactics - distraction. He was damn good at it, and she was so close to forgetting everything except how she felt in his arms, but some small part of her remembered she had a duty.

She heaved her head back and stared up into eyes that were dilated and lost and desiring her as much as she wanted him. Her breath fast, her heart thrumming even faster, she shook her head and dragged herself from his grasp.

His hands fell to his side and his brow furrowed. Waiting for an explanation, he watched her as if she'd dunked his head in a bucket of icy water.

"What is yer interest in the Fordices?" she asked, backing another step so that he couldn't divert her again.

He ran his hands through his hair, his head wavering from side to side. "It is not a pretty business, and they'll harm anyone who threatens them. The less ye ken, the better."

"I think ye should leave." She peered toward the door as she wrapped her arms around her torso.

"Please dinnae get involved," he pleaded, but he didn't know how tied up in this mess she already was.

She couldn't change the course she'd set. "I willnae do anything to incite their wrath." She blinked, then glanced away. "Please go."

When she again met his eyes, he nodded, but sparks flew from his gaze, and his jaw had tightened. He knew she was lying.

He stormed from her room.

Exhausted and remorseful that she couldn't confide in

him, she stumbled over to the bed and retrieved her club from where she'd stashed it beneath the mattress. Placing it on top of the covers, she lay down and shut her eyes.

~

Gavin stalked down the hall toward his chamber. He'd thought they were past the deception, but Kate had kissed him and then lied yet again. His body had gone from pure elation to rage almost instantaneously.

His mind drifted back to a time when he was innocent and couldn't spot lies. The memories took him to a place where the people he had trusted most had destroyed his world and told him the first lie, which set his life on its current course.

It had been a beautiful, early fall day, and his parents had taken him and his younger brother to a tavern to have bowls of soup and bread. They'd even stopped at a bakery and purchased the pair of them a treat. He should have known something was wrong then because it was a luxury his family never indulged in. They hadn't been able to afford it.

He'd been nearly twelve summers, but over the last few months, his body had changed, and he appeared much older than most of the boys his age. He'd also developed a monstrous appetite that kept him constantly craving food and outgrowing his clothing.

They'd all climbed into a wagon and headed out into the country. As Gavin popped a bite of pastry in his mouth, his father had broken the news. "We are taking ye lads to a school for boys. Ye will live at the school, starting this afternoon."

Gavin had stopped chewing mid-bite. His stomach had felt overfull as if it might burst.

"I dinnae wanna go." His nine-year-old brother had begun sobbing straight away.

Gavin's mother soothed, "'Twill be all right. They are going to teach ye all the things we cannae."

His brother had continued to protest, but all Gavin could do was stare out the window until a large home came into view. Boys of all ages had been outside chopping wood, caring for chickens, and dashing around. As they'd hopped down, two men came out to meet them. One had introduced himself as the headmaster and the other a teacher, but something about them hadn't set right with Gavin.

He couldn't place what it was, but he'd been on edge immediately.

"We will miss ye," his mother had said as she drew him in for a hug, her eyes wet with unshed tears.

"Why can't we stay at home?" his brother had asked as his father had peeled him from their mother's arms.

Gavin hadn't wanted to go to the school, either. He was a good student and could teach himself at home or help on the nearby farm for money. This hadn't felt right.

The headmaster had strolled over to his father and given him a wide grin as he nodded his head and said, "They'll do nicely." A bundle that had jingled like coins dropped into his father's hands, then he and his mother had climbed back into the wagon.

"We'll be back to visit soon," his father had called as they rode away.

But that wasn't true. The place wasn't a school at all, and they were never coming back. Neither was his innocent little brother.

He blinked and thought of Kate, who lied even easier than his parents had. He wanted to despise her; he should. Lies were forbidden in his world, and he wasn't sure how he'd let the lass draw him in.

Was she the kind of woman who would leave innocent children at such an evil place? He didn't think so, but he'd also not thought his own mother capable of such an atrocity.

Whatever she was up to, it had to do with their new guests. Taking a seat at his desk, he held up his files.

Could it be that somehow the lovely deceiver down the hall was embroiled in both his cases? Flora MacGregor was in William Douglas's crew, and Kate apparently had a strong relationship with the woman, to the point that Kate had set down an English earl to defend the lass.

Kate had not known the Fordices, or at least they'd not known who she was, so he couldn't see a connection, but she was refusing to stand down from whatever plot was in the unfortunately bonny, little head of hers.

Despite her continued untruths, he was having a hard time believing she was as vicious a criminal as the two men that he'd made it his mission to bring to justice. He would have to watch her as closely as he did the Fordice men. If only to protect her from herself.

After reviewing all his notes again, he made his way back to the drawing room to partake in the fare that was to be offered.

Magnus was seated on the left side of the room, in discussion with the Bartroms, while Stewart was near the middle, surrounded by Lord Perry and Miss Clarke. Since Gavin had already spoken with the father, he sauntered toward Stewart. Perhaps he'd be able to work the younger Fordice brother, Thomas, into the conversation.

"Mr. Fordice, how were yer travels?" Gavin took the seat across from him.

As he did, Miss Clarke turned toward Lord Perry and said something he couldn't hear. They seemed to be looking for the excuse to only speak to one another again.

"Splendid until the rain set in," Stewart's strident voice intoned.

"I was told ye are from Glasgow. I am as well." He smiled, hoping he came off as genial.

"Ah yes, I heard ye were a constable in the city's new force. How do ye like the work?"

The golden-haired man leaned back into the sofa, spreading his arms along the back and relaxing, sprawled out as if he were in his own home.

"It's been rewarding."

"I'm sure it is," Stewart said.

"Tell me more about what ye and yer father do."

"We buy buildings and let out space to tenants. It's been quite a profitable endeavor, but I'll tell you, sometimes we get a bad sort. Now that I have your connection, I might reach out when we need assistance." He seemed eager to talk about the business and himself.

Gavin nodded.

Stewart continued, "Do you ever do any work on your own?"

"Nae. I'm exclusive with the force, but if there is ever trouble, ye can reach out to me directly."

"Marvelous. Thomas and I can usually handle unruly tenants on our own, but it doesn't hurt to have friends."

"Nae. It never does. Is Thomas yer brother?"

"Aye. He helps occasionally, but he has his own pursuits. I do most of the work."

He was about to formulate a reply when he was cut off as the butler came in to announce that the refreshments was prepared.

"Excuse me," Stewart said. "I must see what they've placed out. I'm quite famished." The man rose and darted for the sideboard that had been brought into the room.

Gavin had lost his appetite earlier and chose to wait in the chair. However, the Bartroms took the seat that Stewart had vacated, and he didn't return. He conversed with the pair for quite some time, occasionally letting his gaze drift around the room.

Kate had not reappeared. Her absence was ever present in

his mind. Perhaps it was for the best because he knew for certain he didn't want her around the Fordices, especially if she intended to get near them.

After some time, the guests left the room to prepare for dinner. He did the same.

Once prepared, he considered going to Kate's room to escort her down, or at least make certain she wasn't ill. But if he walked in that room, he might want to kiss her again, and that was a bad idea. His mind and body were in a battle. His head won this time, and he descended the stairs.

Kate strolled in as dinner was being announced. Guests filed into the dining room. He managed to gain a place between Stewart and Charles Bartrom, who sat at the end opposite their host. Mrs. Bartrom was positioned across from him and next to Kate— who was situated directly opposite Stewart.

He'd succeeded in keeping Kate away from them but also keeping himself within the company of the targets of his investigation.

The meal was pleasant until Stewart leaned over to him and said, "Tell me more about that delightful Miss Reid."

Stewart's scrutiny left him and landed on the lass across from him. Gavin had been observing him and knew the man kept stealing glances her way. Thankfully, she was engrossed in conversation with Mrs. Bartrom and paying the man no heed.

"I'm afraid I dinnae ken much." He hedged, but in actuality, he didn't know many facts about where she'd come from, only gleaned glimpses of who she was now.

"Is she involved with anyone? Surely, she has mentioned."

Gavin's fist clenched. He wanted to claim her as his own, but that wasn't true. They'd shared some intimate moments but made no gestures regarding a courting relationship. And he couldn't do so with a woman who would lie so easily.

"She has not." His throat ached as he forced out the words.

Stewart's smile turned predatory. This man didn't appear to have the same proclivities as his brother, but Gavin didn't like what he saw. It might be a challenge to keep Stewart away from her.

"What are yer opinions of the new canal?" Gavin changed the subject, and Stewart went into a litany of how it was good for business and how he was taking advantage of the project. Talking about himself, the man's interest in Kate faded to the background.

When dinner was complete, the men retired to the game room for cards, drinks, and smoking. He purposely kept the Fordices drinking and talking late into the evening but gained no information. That was what he'd expected, though. It was going to take tracking down one of their servants to pull the pieces of his inquiry together.

By the time the group rose from the revelry and moved back to the drawing room, Kate had already gone to her chamber. He'd succeeded in keeping her away from the men, but it had also meant he'd not seen her.

CHAPTER 10

*K*ate sat up and stretched, then donned her nightgown. She was refreshed. Between her long nap yesterday and a good night's sleep, she was ready to get the day started and work on her plan.

She walked to the window, not out of habit, but to discover if she would catch a glimpse of a shirtless Gavin running about the pond. She was in luck, but he was still headed out in the other direction. She was given a nice view of the broad expanse of his back. She'd bet if she were closer, she'd be able to see muscles ripple as his arms moved in time with his powerful legs.

Although a light drizzle clung to the air, the day promised a clearing as hues of red and orange occasionally broke through the lingering clouds. Gavin became a small dot on the landscape as he neared the crest of his loop.

A whoosh of air in the room alerted her to the door swinging in. The lock might not work, but the hinges were well oiled and made no sound.

Isobel greeted, "Good morning."

"That it is."

She thought of her tasks ahead and how she would work

what she needed into conversation with the Fordice men or if it was too soon or suspicious to plant more seeds. She decided she needed to wait until at least the afternoon before proceeding.

Stewart was either going to be especially easy or difficult to sway. He'd been watching her last night, and she'd done her best to make it appear as if she didn't notice. She needed Magnus to sign the papers, but if she upset Stewart, they might both turn their backs on her *deal*. She wished she'd found a way to keep Magnus's oldest son away as she had with Thomas, but the older man might have changed his plans had she attempted such a thing. Besides, it had been hard enough to plan Thomas's delay.

She had no room for second-guessing anything right now. It was time to move along with the scheme.

"Make me as bonny as possible today. I have things I have to convince men to do."

"Oh, that will be easy." Isobel laughed.

"We can only hope."

A little while later, she strolled into the breakfast room, prepared a plate, and sat next to Lady Stonehaven. The Fordices came in shortly after. She was pleased that Magnus took the free seat next to her before Stewart could make it to the table.

"Good morning, Mr. Fordice. Did ye sleep well?" Kate asked the older man.

Magnus's hair was somewhere between a golden blond and ash gray. He kept it longer and slightly parted to the side to cover the hint of a receding hairline. At one time, he'd probably been as handsome as his sons, but he'd put on weight that was hidden on his face with his neatly trimmed full beard.

"I did. It was easy with such nice accommodations." He glanced past her to include Lady Stonehaven in the conversation.

"I'm pleased you chose to join us." Their hostess gave a bright smile.

They talked about Scotland and the weather and the food. As they did, Gavin came into the room and was forced to take a seat several places down on the opposite end of the table. He glowered at her, and she ignored him.

"I hear your brother also deals in properties."

Perhaps she wasn't going to have to wait until this afternoon to insert more suggestions. Magnus was ahead of her.

"Oh, aye. He enjoys investing in poorer neighborhoods and turning them into thriving areas."

"That's noble of him."

"In a way, but I think he does it as much for the challenge as the rewards."

Magnus nodded like he could appreciate her "brother's" sentiment.

"What areas do ye invest in?" she asked.

She already knew the answer, but she had to play her part. He only bought in highly sought-after areas. Magnus owned the building Camelot was in because it had been packaged with another property in Edinburgh's high-class district. After the previous owner's death, his family had had to sell to cover debts, and they would only sell the two together.

The piece of land where Camelot sat was not one Mr. Fordice was interested in maintaining or had even wanted. That was why any upkeep on the place had been performed by Bran, who had become quite efficient at restoring and refinishing places.

"I just look for the right opportunities." He laughed.

Lady Stonehaven broke in with a question, but it was great timing. She'd accomplished what she needed. Giving too much information at first would make her offer suspicious when it came. This transaction had to appear to come from Magnus.

They conversed a few more minutes, but then everyone stood and made their way into the drawing room to continue the conversation. The afternoon would revolve around music and right now was a casual conversation time.

She was now engrossed in a conversation with Lord Stonehaven and Lord Perry. Gavin had claimed the Fordices' attention, but his stony resolve still drifted her way occasionally to study her movements. She was also stealing glances in their direction.

The butler marched into the room and over to the group of men, a silver tray in his hand. He offered a letter to Magnus. The older Fordice man took it and excused himself from Gavin and his son, preferring to move to the corner to read it in private.

A frown formed on his face before he walked back to the group and said something she couldn't hear to Stewart. The men said a few words to Gavin, then walked from the room.

Kate made an excuse and followed. The pair walked down the hall and into the library. She passed the room and went into the next. The study had a door that led into the library and she might be able to overhear their conversation if she were lucky.

Easing the study entrance open, she sneaked in and pulled it behind her. She hurried to the connecting door and placed her ear to it, putting a hand to her other so that she could concentrate on the conversation.

Magnus's voice breached through the wood. "It says that the tenants on the second floor have been damaging the property and that the ones on the main floor have started a brothel."

There was a muffled reply from Stewart, but she couldn't make it out. This was the missive she'd had delivered. It had come from Magnus's solicitor's office with his seal, but it had been one of the man's assistants who she'd convinced to prepare the letter. She'd had it made up early and trusted one of her brothers, Callum, from Camelot to send it on the prescribed date. Callum would be reappearing in her plan later if everything else went the way it should.

Magnus spoke again. "That property has been nothing but trouble. The sooner we are rid of it, the better."

Yes, she cheered internally. Everything was proceeding nicely.

A strong hand latched onto her arm. She gasped and turned, bumping into the door. Gavin's penetrating gaze pinned her with fire.

"What was that?" Stewart shrilled.

"It sounded like something in the adjoining room." Magnus's voice got louder as if he were coming closer.

Gavin drew her to the side, glanced around, and then headed toward the nearest door. Everything in the room blurred as he darted straight into what was a small closet. He gently pulled her in and sealed the exit closed before she could protest.

The world collapsed on her as if she were a tiny boat encapsulated by an angry sea. She shivered as a prickle of sweat erupted on the back of her neck.

"Nae," the strangled word left her lips as fear set in. She shook her head. It was dark, and she could barely make out anything as breathing became nearly impossible.

She could make an excuse for being in the room; she just couldn't stay in here. Her legs threatened to give beneath her as a wave of dizziness struck.

She scrambled for the knob, but somehow Gavin's hand grabbed hers and latched onto it.

"I can't." Panic lit her voice.

He didn't respond but put a finger to her lips in a gentle request to stay silent. He might mean well, but he didn't know what he was asking.

A little louder, she choked out, "I can't."

She was about to scream out when Gavin silently turned

her in his arms so that her back was flush with his chest. He drew her close and put his hand over her mouth to stop her protests. With his support, she was no longer worried that she might fall over, but now, being restrained by his efforts reinforced and magnified the terror that she knew was unreasonable but couldn't keep at bay.

Beads of perspiration developed on her temples, and despite her nose being clear of Gavin's grasp, she couldn't fill her lungs.

She struggled, but his arm tightened around her, and he pushed her into the wall to stop her feet from kicking out. She thought she would drown—as if the world was going to swallow her up, and she'd be trapped here forever.

She was entombed in one place, but really, she was falling through a void of anxiety and tumbling into the past. She tried once more to break free, but her limbs didn't want to cooperate, and her feeble attempts did nothing.

She was thankful when blackness closed in around her.

What the hell was wrong with the lass? She'd shown nothing but controlled composure under every circumstance he'd seen her in. The voices of the Fordices now came from just outside the closet door. Somehow despite her mouth moving behind his hand, he was able to keep her quiet.

She didn't know who she was dealing with. What might they have done to her had they discovered her spying?

Something slick met his fingers and palm—tears. He'd never hurt a lass, and while his grip had been firm, it had also been gentle. Whatever had happened to Kate was not a typical response he would expect from someone in her position.

Her struggles ceased, and her body went limp. He

released her mouth as her head lulled back against his chest. Fear beat in his own, and he tried to figure out what was wrong. Voices still came from the room, or he would burst out with her. He put his ear to her mouth to check her breathing. Relief swallowed him as a solid in and out of breath met his efforts.

The men stayed in the room for far too long, discussing some property where they had issues with the tenants. He willed them to go away.

If he made a sound now, Magnus and Stewart would discover them, so he held her, hoping she'd revive as soon as the men left. The only thing that kept him calm was that he could still feel the steady inhalation of air entering, then leaving her body.

After several more minutes, the men's talking became lower, and he waited a few moments longer to be certain they were gone before he peeked out the door. Cradling her in his arms, he slowly urged the small closet door open into an empty room.

The sun shone through the window, and he let his eyes adjust to the increased lighting. He glanced at her. Kate looked peaceful, but her cheeks had lost her usual rosy color, and salt from tears lingered on her soft skin.

His chest ached. He'd been trying to protect her. What had gone wrong?

Scooping her up, he bolted for the exit and glanced down the hall in both directions. No one was about, so he fled the room and headed straight for the stairs, then her bedchamber.

As soon as they were in the room, he tore toward her bed and lay her down gently, then retrieved her dressing chair and placed it under the doorknob to bar anyone who might walk in on them. Once he let his racing heart stop, and he felt comfortable, he ambled back to the thick mattress and eased down to sit on the bed beside where she rested.

"Kate," he whispered as his fingers pushed a strand of hair from her forehead.

She didn't respond. He took her head in his hand. He cradled it and ran his thumb along her cheek. Leaning down, he placed a kiss on her temple, then another.

"Wake up, Kate. I need to ken yer all right." If her breathing hadn't returned to normal, he'd still be worried, but the color was returning to her cheeks.

Her lashes fluttered, but remained shuttered.

"Kate. Kate," he insisted, saying her name louder.

Her lids opened to slits and she blinked a few times before fully taking him in. Confusion met his regard, and then clarity shone in the depths of her eyes as she remembered what had occurred.

She scooted back on the bed and inhaled sharply, gasping for air. She sat up as her hands clenched onto the blankets.

"It's all right."

She nodded, but it took her breath a little more time to slow. Her gaze traveled past him.

Skirting around where he was seated, she bolted for the window. It was open, and she stuck her head out as far as she could. He let her be, knowing she was the only one who could stop whatever was going on in her head.

He patiently waited for her to get her fill and then turn back around. When she finally did, she swallowed, then moved toward him. Easing down onto the mattress's edge, she placed both her hands in her lap before meeting his eyes.

"I dinnae do well in small, enclosed places."

"I was trying to protect ye. I didnae ken."

He tried to think what he could have done differently, but the only other thing would have been to push her against the wall or desk and thoroughly kiss her, make it look as if they had been in the room carrying on as lovers do. There had not been time to get out of the study before they were discovered.

"I ken that, but I cannae stop the panic. It's a part of me."

"Why?"

Her arms crossed her chest, and she hugged herself. She sat there, unable to give him an answer as her chin trembled.

"I promise ye can tell me. I willnae judge ye."

She took a couple more breaths, then the resignation in her gaze turned to determination.

"I never knew my father. When I was a child, my mother and I traveled to . . ." She cut off, her eyes glazing with panic. He guessed she'd almost given away some bit of information she hadn't wanted to.

"My mother was looking for a passage to Canada or America. We moved for more than a day. I dinnae even ken how long it was. She didnae have money for two fares, and I was small and talked a lot, so she bound my mouth and hands, and put me in a trunk so that the hack driver wouldnae charge her for me."

He didn't know what to say. How could a parent do something so cruel? His mind was reeling that she'd been through such an ordeal.

She shook her head, and a tear fell down her cheek. "Ye can leave now."

His brow furrowed as she looked away.

"Why would I leave?"

"I told ye the truth. That's what ye wanted and now ye can go." She squared her shoulders as if she expected him to sprint out the door and never look back, as if he would blame her for what she'd been through.

"I'm sorry. I didnae ken, but now I do. I'm happy ye told me." His thumbs made little circles on the soft skin of her hands. She'd not pulled free from his grasp.

He licked his lips and said, "I understand the past can cause demons. I have some of my own. What yer mother did was wrong, and I'll never subject ye to such a small space again."

She gave a thin smile.

He reached forward and pried her hands from her sides, drawing them in and holding them as he scooted closer. "I'm no' going anywhere."

Relief flashed in her eyes before confusion replaced it. Her eyes crinkled with surprise. "Ye're no' leaving?"

"Nae. But next time I have to save ye from yerself, be prepared to risk yer reputation."

Her head tilted as a blank expression came over her face.

"The only other thing I could have done was made it look like we'd gone to that room for an assignation."

She blushed an appealing shade of rose, and he was tempted to lean in and kiss her now, but they were sitting on a bed, locked in her room, and if he did put his lips on hers, they might become lovers after all. And he couldn't take advantage of her after she'd just gone through an ordeal.

It was enough that every muscle in his body was tight with the sensation that traveled through his body from where they were joined.

"How are ye feeling now?"

"Much better, thank ye."

"Are ye going to tell me why ye were spying?" he questioned.

"No," she stated matter-of-factly.

At least she'd not lied about it.

"Ye dinnae make a good spy."

"I agree. I dinnae have the nerves for it. I'm a planner and not spontaneous."

"I think I need to warn ye again to stay away from them." He didn't have to say who. She didn't question.

"I am capable of looking after myself."

"I'm sure ye are, but it never hurts to have someone else watching out for ye."

Her gaze shifted to study the floor. Did the lass have no one she'd ever depended upon?

His thoughts turned to her known associates, William Douglas and Flora MacGregor. Perhaps she didn't—although after meeting Flora, he wasn't sure his opinion of her was all accurate. That reminded him that Kate wasn't who she said she was, and he found himself enthralled by a lass who was incapable of telling him the truth about who she really was.

He needed to go because he was starting to question his standards. He wanted her, but somehow, he was forgetting that lies were lies—black and white. Lines etched in stone he shouldn't cross or forgive.

"I'm glad ye're recovered. I have matters to address."

"Thank ye," she said.

But he wasn't sure what she was thanking him for, saving her downstairs, carrying her up to her room, listening to her story, or leaving. He didn't ask and blocked the thoughts out because he wasn't certain he wanted to know.

He released her hands, stood, and bolted for the door before he was tempted to stay and wrap her back in his arms. He had work to do, and the faster he could accomplish his goal, the sooner he could take the men into custody. His mission seemed especially essential now that he knew for certain that Kate had a secret agenda involving the men.

Gavin traveled down the back of the hall and took the steps to the main floor, where he exited near the rear of the house. He strode straight for the stables. The rain had stopped, and the sun shone bright, although the grass was still sodden with moisture. He arrived at the building and walked in to search the stalls.

Luckily, the stablemaster quickly directed him toward the coachman for the Fordice men, Eddie, because he'd just come in from giving the horses some exercise. Gavin stopped at the entrance to the stall where the man stood.

"Hi Eddie, I'm Gavin Davidson. Are ye here with Magnus Fordice?"

Eddie nodded.

"Are ye from Glasgow?" He wanted to establish where the man was from before relaying his position with the Glasgow police.

"Aye. Lived there all me life."

"Beautiful city. I've been there most of mine." He stuck out his hand, and the man took it.

"Pleased to meet ye. What brings ye out this way?"

"I'm a constable with the city's force," he said.

The man's brow creased.

"I'm looking into a matter that may have affected the Fordice family." He wanted to word this in a way that wouldn't shut the man down straight away because he expected resistance to his questions. Especially if the man was loyal to his employers. He needed answers, and intimidating people who might have the knowledge he sought could drive them away.

"What can I help ye with?"

"I've heard the youngest Fordice, Thomas, may have recently been assailed by a violent family that accused him of some awful crimes. Did ye hear anything about that or the circumstances surrounding it?" he prodded.

Gavin wasn't going to reveal that the family members had pursued Thomas after learning the man had possibly harmed a child that had been entrusted to his care. The child, in this case, remained missing.

"Oh, nae. I wish I could help ye, but I only began working for the family a few months back. I've no' even met Mr. Fordice's youngest son yet."

"Do ye ken what happened to the man before ye?" Gavin queried.

"Nae. I've never been told and haven't asked. They're a secretive lot."

"Thanks for yer time. If ye hear anything on the incident or see anything suspicious, will ye please reach out to me?"

"Oh, aye. I will."

"And please dinnae let Mr. Fordice ken I was asking. I dinnae want him to worry that there may still be a threat out there."

Gavin wasn't going to tell Eddie that the threat was coming from him and that it was more like justice. From his quick assessment, he'd liked Eddie and believed the man would reach out if he saw something untoward.

"Absolutely. I willnae trouble them."

Gavin thanked the man, then turned and left the stables.

Plodding back across the expansive field toward the estate, Gavin noted that he needed to track down the last coachman who worked for Magnus Fordice. Perhaps if the man were let go, he'd be willing to share misdeeds by his old employer and his family. He went straight to his room to pen a letter to a colleague on the Glasgow force, then handed it to the butler to have it sent out that day.

The rest of the afternoon was spent listening to music by various guests, then a meal and retiring with the men to play cards again while the ladies stayed in the drawing room to converse.

By the time he emerged from the game room, Kate had already gone to bed.

CHAPTER 11

$\mathcal{T}$he new day promised to be a beautiful one. As Kate broke her fast and talked to the Bartroms, rays of light lit the breakfast room with dancing prisms and lent an air of magic to the morning. Gavin kept stealing glances at her, and although she was embarrassed by yesterday's events, something in her recognized that he knew one truth about her and hadn't disregarded her.

There was so much more that she kept hidden. No matter, she decided she liked his dark, brooding regard focused on her. The intensity of his scrutiny made her feel alive.

Only one other person on earth knew more about her than Gavin currently did. The closeness she felt toward him was both exhilarating and terrifying. With Camelot's leader, she'd only told him her secrets because she'd been young and desperate for a place to stay. She'd told Will secrets out of obligation and necessity. She wasn't quite sure yet why she'd given Gavin the truth of what her mother had done.

The group finished their meal. Then, after a leisurely stroll through the gallery with Lord Stonehaven explaining the portraits hanging on the walls and expounding on family stories and legends about each ancestor, the guests exited the back of the house. Since the incident yesterday, she'd not had a moment alone with Gavin or Magnus Fordice, but that worked well on both accounts.

She'd also managed to stay close to their hosts and the Bartroms in an attempt to keep Stewart at bay. He'd discovered her in the hall as she'd left her room to go to dinner last evening and took her hand, called her Allison, and leaned too close in a suggestive manner that had made her skin crawl. She could do without ever being near him again. She didn't know if he was as sick as his brother, but she wasn't going to take any chances.

Gavin was correct about Stewart, and she would avoid him as much as she could without alienating his father. She might even insist that Isobel kept her company when she was not with a room full of guests.

The sun was now high enough in the sky to shower light on this side of the house. The lawn was a vibrant shade of green and had dried from the rain of days past and the early morning dew.

The guests strolled to a row of tall, meticulously trimmed bushes that formed a wall that extended as far as the eye could see. The dark-green of the yew bushes was formidable and contrasted sharply with the other landscape's open plane. They towered above her head, indicating they'd been planted a long time ago.

Lord Stonehaven stopped at what appeared to be an entrance. His silvery voice rang out, "This, my dear friends is more than a mere maze. It's a labyrinth that is built to guide you to your purpose."

He paused, then glanced at each of them.

Lord Stonehaven cleared his throat and began again, "It has been said that a labyrinth represents a journey. A path that helps us find our way to our center and leads us back out into the world again with a new perspective. I hope that you are able to find your purpose as you wander through this place of meditation."

Lord Stonehaven's introduction was given with a flourish that left her with gooseflesh. She imagined a magical world where one could find answers to questions that they had never thought to ask. She'd never been in a maze and was suddenly captivated by the idea.

"It's more intriguing if you enter on your own and seek to follow the path where destiny guides you."

"How long does it take to complete?" Irene Bartrom asked.

"This particular labyrinth is larger than most. For a novice with this layout, anywhere from an hour to three, so be prepared if you wish to enter that your sojourn may be long."

Worry clouded the older woman's eyes as her hesitant voice questioned, "And what happens if ye cannae find yer way out?"

"If that happens, call out, and I'll have my man, Fredric, come in to retrieve ye. He'll be stationed out here."

Stewart was the first to bow out. She supposed because he'd told her when he'd captured her attention the evening before that one of his legs was paining him due to a recent incident where he'd saved a lass on a runaway horse. Parts of his tale were quite boastful, and she imagined that not all of it was accurate. Both Bartroms followed his dissent, then Magnus.

Kate was fascinated with the maze, and she wanted to avoid Stewart anyway, so why not take a chance on seeing if she could locate the center and cleanly make her way back out? She might never have the opportunity to try again.

Their host guided them through a pattern of alternating entrances, giving a few minutes between each guest as they disappeared into the thick brush. Lord Perry went first, followed by Lady Stonehaven, who possibly knew her way to the center and back again with ease, then Miss Clarke, and then Kate.

As she stepped in, the first thing she noticed was the deep shadows cast by the tall hedges. She paused for a moment, second-guessing whether she could do this. The path was wide enough for two people to pass each other but still tight.

She pushed away the tension in her stomach. Anytime she felt uncomfortable, all she had to do was glance up to the sky and see the wide expanse of blue greeting her with its reassurance that she wasn't trapped. Taking a deep breath, she moved farther in and examined the first path to the right.

Running her fingers along the branches' soft leaves, she imagined how much work it would involve to prune and maintain the maze. She turned left, then right again, and continued to meander around twists and turns. It wasn't long before the path to the exit was forgotten to her.

The random nature of the increasingly twisty shrubberies seemed turbulent and unbalanced. She came to a dead end. Turning from the impasse, she glanced up to the clear blue sky and took a reassuring breath, then returned her attention to the path before forging back in the direction she'd come from.

How had she found herself in this turbulent, chaotic place?

Only six months ago, she'd been carrying out one of her typical scams. Her deceptions were typically aimed at a well-off gentleman who wouldn't suffer from her interference in his life but would also give her the funds to survive for a bit longer. Will had taught her only to target those that she couldn't irrevocably harm from her actions.

That seemingly normal man had been Thomas Fordice. She'd been dining at a hotel in Glasgow when she'd seen the elegantly dressed man give a large amount of coin to an unsavory looking fellow who seemed eager to take the offering and flee. Thomas Fordice must be well off if he had money to spare for such a man down on his luck. She almost felt guilty about targeting a person who might have such a good heart.

A little while later, when she'd seen the same ragged man tear through the lobby with two children in tow, she'd thought nothing of it. He was probably treating his son and daughter to a view of the small pond of fish that had been set as a display in the lobby. She hoped the concierge wouldn't hold their lack of proper clothing against them. The children looked frightened to be dragged through such a sophisticated setting.

As the well-to-do man she'd been eyeing left his table, she followed him through the short lobby and watched as he strode confidently toward the stairs. The children and their father were no longer in sight.

She stopped at the desk.

"Excuse me," she said to the clerk.

"The gentleman who just left." Kate made certain that the clerk could see the man's back before he stepped out of view on the steps. "He purchased my lunch for me because I couldn't find my coin. Do you ken his name and which room I can find him in? I was able to find it and would like to repay his generosity."

No one ever questioned the request she'd made many times.

"Oh, aye, madam. That's Thomas Fordice. He's one of our best clients and always stays in room 303."

"Thank ye. I shall reimburse him straight away." She'd smiled in a way that implied gratitude, then turned to follow Thomas.

A vision of the now intruded. Lady Stonehaven popped from behind a bush. "Hello there, dear." She was flushed and excited. Her rosy cheeks made Kate smile.

"Are ye done?"

"Oh, aye. I've done this several times, but I can't believe

that Miss Clarke and Lord Perry beat me to the center. That niece of mine has an amazing memory."

"This is fun." Kate smiled despite the memories that had tainted her journey thus far.

"Keep going. You are headed in the correct direction." She winked at Kate and continued without another word.

"That's good to ken." Kate laughed, and Lady Stonehaven disappeared around the corner.

A cold breeze blew through the maze, and she shivered. As Kate navigated another corner of the endless ever-changing puzzle of hedges, she was reminded of winding and turning about the stairs on her way up to Thomas's room on that fateful day.

Gathering her breath, Kate had knocked lightly on the door to room 303. No answer came. Perhaps this would be easier than normal if Thomas had already left his room. Her brother Bran had given her a basic tutorial on picking locks, and she'd become quite good at it.

Her usual response would be to tell the guest there was an issue with their bill, and they were wanted at the front desk to ensure no one was taking advantage of their accounts. She was normally able to charm her mark long enough to stuff a small piece of material in the door slot so that it didn't close properly when the man left. This usually gave her enough time to whisk in and out quickly.

She typically gave herself five minutes at most. She knew all the hiding places that careful men chose, so it was easy to take everything of value and be gone down a separate set of steps before the guest returned. Upon leaving, she would remove the cloth and bolt for the exit. She was usually long gone long before anyone ever realized she'd been in the room.

Trying the handle, she discovered the lock had not been engaged. She snuck in and pulled the door silently behind her, thankful she'd not had to spend the time retrieving the long thin object to pick the lock which rested in her handbag.

This was one of the nicer hotels in town, so she entered a sitting area and got her bearings before heading to the bedchamber, which had been shuttered. She eased open the thick, wooden barrier. Shock pelted her at the sight that greeted her.

The gentleman from below was shirtless and had his trousers about his feet. He wore a maniacal grin that twisted into an expression promising ill intentions. The children she'd seen were both in the room with their hands and mouths bound.

Her stomach lurched as the food she'd eaten threatened to climb up her throat. She must have moved or made some noise because Thomas had turned her way and his evil smile faltered, and his gaze became panicked.

"Who are you?" the man had croaked as he'd reached down to pull up his clothing. Losing his balance, Thomas had toppled over and hit his head on the nightstand.

She didn't think, just reacted. "Come with me. I'll see to it that ye're safe." She'd held out a hand to the frightened children and motioned for them to follow her.

Luckily, they hadn't hesitated. Thomas had recovered and was again on his feet but still attempting to right his clothing. Kate had bolted through the door with the children. Bounding down the back steps, they'd reached the bottom and exited the back of the building before she was able to catch a breath.

"Come," she had instructed again, and the boy and girl didn't argue as she led them to the hack she'd rented and had prepared for her fast getaway.

As they were pulling away from the street, the man had sprinted from the hotel, pants righted and shoes on as he attempted to catch her. He ran a short way after them, but she focused her attention on the children and removing their bindings before she had turned back and realized Thomas Fordice couldn't catch them.

She'd taken the boy and girl back to Aberdeen, to safety, to Camelot. But what she'd not known until later was that Thomas had someone follow her, discovering who she was and where she'd taken the children.

It was bad luck that his father had owned their building, and then doubled their rent when she and Will refused to return the children. Now the Fordices had decided that wasn't enough, and her family was going to be forced out onto the streets. Will had been looking for a new flat to rent but was having trouble finding anything in Aberdeen that had room for all of them.

It was all her fault, but she would save those kids again in a heartbeat.

She stepped out into an open area, and relief rushed through her. This was the center of the labyrinth. A lone bench rested in the midpoint. She sat on it and fought the sting in her eyes.

Her purpose was to protect Camelot and all who lived in it. Her family shouldn't pay for her part in incurring the wrath of a sick and sadistic man. And she was on the right path to ensure that Allison and Joseph Reid received justice for what Thomas had been about to subject them to. If only she could help all the children that Thomas had harmed.

Gavin stepped into the maze and inhaled the scent of evergreens, earth, and fresh air. He moved forward, then headed toward the path he'd seen Kate take. Shortly, his way became blocked, and he was met with clearances that led in two directions. He aimed left, thinking it might guide him toward the center.

He followed, coming to another obscured aisle. The

bushes that blocked the way seemed to have been forgotten and needed a trim compared to the rest of the neatly pruned rows. He reached out and fingered the wild, extending branches. The prolonged overgrowth reminded him of where this journey had begun and where the child had been found. A vision of the lad's small, bruised, and broken body invaded his head and infuriated him. Bile rose in his throat.

It had taken him months to track down the boy's family, only to discover he'd been left at an orphanage because they'd been evicted from their farm. The parents had hoped to give him a better life by leaving him in a place that would provide food and shelter for him long enough to earn the coin to find lodgings and provide a normal home.

They would never get that chance. Gavin wondered for the first time if perhaps his parents had told the truth and had intended to come back for him and his brother. He'd never thought to seek them out and question them. Even now, he wasn't certain he could ever face them again.

Gavin had visited the location where the mother and father had left the boy. He'd been disgusted by the conditions at the home. The director had spoken with him but claimed the boy had run away.

"Why didn't ye report it?" Gavin had asked.

"Kids always run away. They dinnae want to live with my rules. I have no responsibility for the ones that leave on their own."

After questioning all the staff who had given him no clues about what could have happened to the lad, he'd asked the stableman. The older man, who'd lost most of his teeth and had lines around his eyes, had leaned in and confidentially told him that he'd taken the director with children on several occasions to meet a man at the Glasgow Majestic Hotel.

"The kids never come back with him." The elderly man had shaken his head.

"Do ye ken who he meets with?"

"Nae. I always wait outside, but it never sits right with me. I can't say anything, or I'll be out of position."

"Aye. Thank ye for yer time."

The next couple of weeks were spent moving in and out of the hotel, covertly keeping an eye on all the guests. After maintaining a detailed journey of people coming and going, he started questioning the staff. It was another week before he tracked down a maid that confided in him that the only regular guest that caused shivers to run down her spine was Thomas Fordice. She'd once heard the cries of a child coming from his room.

"And that man has nae children," the lass had stated, shaking her head, and giving him a disgusted look.

Gavin turned and found his path obscured with another hedge. Rotating back toward the way he came, he moved forward, then took the opposite direction. He let the rambling rows lead him, and his mind, as it drifted, and he remembered why he was here at the Stonehaven estate.

When he'd discovered the Fordices' plan to attend this house party, he'd reached out to Lord Stonehaven and told the man of his suspicions. No one else in attendance was aware of why he was here. But this was his best opportunity to question the Fordice staff without opposition and get the answers he needed. If he couldn't do it here, he would sprint back to Glasgow to seek out the servants who had stayed at their home while the family was here.

It had been quite a disappointment to discover Thomas and his valet had been detained by some illness. Thomas's valet was most likely the one with any proof of wrongdoing, but he might also be the hardest servant to convince to turn king's evidence on his employer.

He'd heard whisperings of the other Fordice men covering up for Thomas, so they were as complicit and dangerous as the predator in his mind. Gavin had to keep moving before another innocent child was hurt, but so far, he'd not found one person who had enough insight or evidence into the man's proclivities to detain him.

He needed a witness.

When he turned another corner, the bushes opened into a comfortable clearing. Kate sat on a bench in an area that must be the middle of the labyrinth. Her glazed eyes caught on his, then cleared as she smiled.

She wore a bonnet today. It framed her face, and she looked bonny in it, but he longed to see the sun-kissed tresses of her hair in that swept up way he'd become accustomed to. In actuality, he'd like to remove the pins that held her locks in place and discover what the silky strands looked like falling down her shoulders.

His mind and body were still not in unison on the subject of Kate. She was a skilled deceiver, and although he wanted to believe there were only straight or crooked lines one could follow, something was hiding in her deceptions. It was almost as if an altruistic aura about her made it impossible to glance away. And the acknowledgment had him questioning the way he viewed the world.

He stepped forward and sat on the bench next to her. The solid stone structure was large enough for at least two more people, but he sat close, craving the intimacy of something pure after reliving the last few months in pursuit of evil. Their legs brushed against each other, and he relished the comfort of her nearness.

"Greetings," he said.

"'Tis a lovely spot here." She sighed and glanced up.

He followed her movements and watched a moment as puffy clouds drifted by on a sea of blue.

Her voice was wobbly when she queried, "Did ye believe what Lord Stonehaven said?"

"About what?"

"Finding our purpose."

"I've known mine a long time. It didn't take a labyrinth for me to find it," he confessed.

She glanced up at him, her eyes appearing green, set off by the hedges and grass. Her lips pursed slightly. She looked lost and confused. "What if I still haven't found mine?"

"Then perhaps thinking about it has set ye on the right course."

She scrutinized her hands as she wrung them in her lap.

"When did you find yers?" Her curious gaze once again met his, and the honesty in her questioning struck him. Here, out in the open, she was again that lass that he'd seen wading into the stream.

"I found my reason for being on the day my family left me." A twinge of anger ran through him, but also a dawning realization that he was proud of what he'd become despite—or perhaps because of—what his parents had done to him.

"That's odd."

"Why?"

"That's the day I lost mine." The vulnerable smallness of her voice reached a place in him that wished to believe she wasn't a criminal in league with the likes of William Douglas, that she was just the lass that he longed to get to know.

He didn't like to see her melancholy, and he wanted an excuse to touch her.

Standing, he reached a hand out to her. "Come, let's find our way out together."

"I'd like that."

She thrust her palm in his, and he drew her from the seat, then held her hand as he turned toward the possible exits. The smell of spices, oranges, and gardenias once again called to him.

As they strolled through the tangled, twisting path, he asked her questions that he thought would give him a good sense of who she really was but wouldn't be of such a personal nature that she'd feel the need to lie. He'd concluded that her lies were a means to an end, but more so, a shield she held up so that no one could get near.

He yearned to be the one to break down those barriers.

"If ye were able to learn a new skill, what would it be?"

"I would like to teach others. There is a special light that comes into one's eyes when they learn something new." She laughed, and the sound reached in and wrapped its way around his chest.

He guided them around another turn.

"What about ye?" she asked.

"I would like to ken how to grow my crops."

"An admirable goal. Do ye like working with yer hands as well as with that sharp mind of yers?"

"Aye. But mostly, I like being able to provide for others."

As they took the next corner, he resisted the urge to pull her close and place his lips on hers. He did hold her hand a bit tighter. To stop himself, he thought of another question. "What's the first thing ye think of when ye wake in the morning?"

"That I need air."

At first, he was taken aback by her quick reply, but then he remembered what she'd been through as a child, and he understood. Her trusting eyes glanced up at him as they rounded a corner as if she were waiting for judgment.

When none came, she continued, "I always run to the window to take a deep breath, just to know I'm still alive and that I can."

He smiled down at her and nodded.

"And what is yer first thought upon waking?" she prodded.

He stopped and met her eyes straight on. "That today, I'll be fast enough." Visions intruded of waking in a field near a burning building in the landscape. He pushed the past away to concentrate on the lady by his side.

She leaned in, and her eyes peered up at him through the

longest, darkest lashes. "I've seen ye run. I think ye've mastered that one." Perhaps admiration lit her gaze, but whatever it was, he felt as if a wall between them had begun to crumble.

As they continued, he recognized the overgrown bush he'd passed earlier. He knew they were almost to the exit, but suddenly not wanting their time to come to an end, he continued with his questioning, "What do ye look for in a friend?"

When she didn't answer, he stopped. Curious to know what she valued in another, he wouldn't allow her to disregard his query.

Her gaze darted away, and he thought it was fear that had sparked in her eyes. She didn't blink; she didn't lie. She told the truth when she said, "I don't."

"Ye don't look for friends?"

He saw the lump she tried to swallow and the regret in her eyes. She pulled at his hand, wanting him to keep moving and forget this question. But he wanted to know why she hid herself away.

"I dinnae need complications." She lied, but the untruth was told more to herself than to him.

"Everyone needs friends."

She withdrew as the progress they'd made slipped. He wasn't going to lose that ground—wasn't going to let Kate put that wall back up. He wrapped his arm around her waist. The feel of her body next to his sent waves of hunger cascading over him like a sea starved for the shore. She melted into him, and her head tilted back.

Her lips parted as she realized his intent. When his mouth crashed down on hers, her defenses seemed to disintegrate as passion grabbed them both. She relaxed as he drew her nearer, pulling her up on her toes as the hand holding hers released it and clasped onto her tightly rounded rear. Need clawed at him as his fingers curved to the soft contours.

He moaned into her mouth as his eyes rolled back in pleasure. He wanted to drive harder, to push against her so that there was no barrier left, but he was afraid the bushes would poke into her back and ruin the moment.

His tongue swirled with hers as pure longing and lust consumed him. Her innocent movements matched each stroke as her arms clung to his side, giving him her complete trust. He was intoxicated by the need that pumped in his veins and made him feel as if she were the only woman for him.

This was Kate, the woman in the water, the woman of his dreams. In this one embrace, he could envision them together on his land, her dipping her toes in the stream as he planted his first row of crops.

The kiss broke, but only long enough for them to catch air. His mouth was on hers again, thirsty for the pleasure he knew he would find in her arms. His body was tense and painful with the need to push whatever had grown between them to the next logical step. It no longer mattered what his mind said.

His body had won, and it demanded his reward.

It demanded Kate.

If they were in her room, he would lean her back on her mattress and slowly claim her body with his, but he couldn't give in to that temptation here. If she were to allow it, he would not take her on the ground where anyone could come upon them. He could retreat with her back to the center of the maze, slowly undress her and draw her down on his lap so that he could delve into the sweet spot between her legs. Surely, all the others were gone by now, but they were only feet from the exit.

Just as he thought it, voices filtered into his ears. He cursed the luck of his timing. Pulling free, he gazed down at her lips, a ripe, swollen red from his attention. Her bonnet was askew, and he wanted nothing more than to rip it free from her head and release the glorious curls hidden beneath.

He still held her rear and kept her captive next to his engorged manhood. "I warned ye no' to make me want ye."

Kate's chest rose and fell in a rhythm that matched his pulse. "Ye should never caution a lady who enjoys a challenge."

"Then sparring with ye is turning into my delight, Kate." He dipped his head and nibbled on her ear. "'Tis both of our pleasures I have in mind."

She sighed and tilted her head. He withdrew, knowing if they didn't stop, he'd be throwing her over his shoulder and running back to that bench. With the distance between them, blood once again began to flow to his head.

He led her around the next turn, then the straight path to the exit. Perhaps he had found a new purpose in the labyrinth; if not that, at least a pastime he wanted to indulge in.

The tangling turns of the living puzzle had changed him.

As they stepped back into the light of the day, he had become certain of two things. Her deceptions were used to protect herself. And despite whatever tie she had to the man he'd been hunting for years, he wanted to know her in a way he'd never wanted any woman before.

Her charm had pulled him in, and they might both end up hurt before this party was over.

*a*s Kate sat down in the drawing room for tea with muffins with jam and a warm cup of tea, her gaze drifted to the large, open window with a view of the gardens and pond. The labyrinth wasn't visible from her position, but in her mind, she could still imagine herself in the tall greenery and remember Gavin's dilated gaze after their kiss.

Movement from the other end of the room caught her eye as the butler walked in with a tray and strode to the man she'd just been thinking about. Gavin took the missive, thanked the man, then dashed from the room.

Magnus Fordice entered and claimed the seat beside her.

"It has turned to a lovely day."

"I agree. I'm looking forward to the walk in the gardens. Will ye be participating in the talk?" she asked.

Lady Stonehaven had arranged for their gardener to walk the grounds with them and explain where all the flowers and plants had come from, along with how they were tended.

"I'm afraid I will miss it. Stewart and I have some business we need to see to in Aberdeen, so we will be visiting the city."

Her limbs went numb, and she nearly dropped her teacup. This was the worst news possible.

She required that Mr. Fordice remain here to finish her plans. Did he have some connection in Aberdeen she hadn't counted on? Although they were still almost a week away, she felt forced to bring up her brother again now. She hadn't thought her time so limited, but if she pushed, he might see through her urgency.

"I hope ye enjoy the city. I plan on going next week when my brother arrives."

"I should like to meet yer brother."

"I'm sure he'd be pleased with that as well. Perhaps ye can. I'll be visiting with him on Tuesday when our whole party goes to Aberdeen. I fear he'll only be there for a couple of days."

Magnus only nodded his head, making no commitments to go back to Aberdeen. She needed him there next week. The muffin began to feel like a stone in her belly.

Stewart appeared and joined their little group. They spoke for a while until the butler popped into the room and told the Fordice men that their carriage was prepared. The men excused themselves, then headed out the door, dashing her hopes of moving along her plan.

Gavin stewed in the study as he turned over the information from his colleague in Glasgow. Dread filled his mind, gripping his head in a tight vise and making it ache. They'd been too late.

The Fordice's previous coach driver had been found . . . dead.

It was only by chance that an old farmer had been roaming a secluded spot on his land not far from Glasgow, near the town of Bishopbriggs. He and his dog had come across a recently moved pile of dirt. The dog began digging in the mound. It uncovered a shallowly dug pit that had been filled with an oversized, wooden box and the dirt that had been thrown back on top to cover the hastily built coffin.

At first, he was surprised that they'd taken the time to find the crate, but the next words in the letter had turned his gut sick with disgust.

Marks on the body and the condition of the top of the sarcophagus indicated the man had still been living when he'd been nailed inside. That led Gavin to believe that the tomb had been used to inflict as much anguish and suffering as possible. He'd either died from the absence of air or, worse yet, lasted for days and perished from lack of nourishment. There were no wounds on the body that indicated a struggle. It was as if the man had willingly given into his captor's demands to lie there as he was sealed inside.

It had taken the watchmen in Bishopbriggs several days to find the man's family and have him positively identified. His wife had immediately reached out to the Glasgow police since Gavin had already been to the home, trying to locate the man. When she'd not found Gavin, she'd reported the news to his friend, who had sent word straight away.

Gavin's newest letter to his contact asking him to intensify the search for the man probably hadn't even reached Glasgow yet.

Gavin shook his head. His mission here was now even more critical. He was certain that Magnus and Stewart were behind it. Thomas didn't seem the type to soil his hands with the hard work of burying a body. Today, he would increase his efforts to reach out to the Fordice's servants. He had to come up with something because he didn't think this was the first time the men had sought their own justice, and he didn't think it would be the last.

He penned a new missive to his contact and asked that he look into coffin makers in the area to discover if the wooden torture device could be somehow traced back to the purchaser. He also requested that the man head out to Bishopbriggs and question anyone who might have witnessed strangers in the area acting suspiciously.

Pocketing the letter, he stood and took a deep breath. He'd been relaxed and happy this afternoon when he'd emerged from the maze with Kate, but she was a distraction and involved his next case. This was the one that needed his attention.

If someone else were harmed, it would be on him.

He charged back toward the room of guests. Magnus and Stewart had left, and Kate sat alone on the sofa. He wanted to go to her, draw her near and tell her how infatuated he was with her, but work came first. Giving her a tight smile, he turned and strode from the room to track down Stewart's valet.

When he discovered the men and all their help had left for a visit to Aberdeen, he shut himself in his room to study his notes. He had to be missing something. He was swept away and didn't leave his desk until late in the evening, searching for some sustenance from the kitchen.

Everyone else was peacefully sleeping, but he knew that he wouldn't be tonight.

He'd gone to bed the night of the fire, and he'd woken up to complete devastation. Now, when he was engrossed in a case, sleep wouldn't come. The ever present fear gripped him, and he couldn't push it away.

He was not going to be fast enough to save the next person.

CHAPTER 13

$\mathcal{K}$ate stretched and rose. She threw on her gown and headed for the window.

She had a new routine now. Instead of breathing in the air, the first thing she did was scan the landscape for Gavin. Either he'd wasn't running today, or he'd been out early. Either way, she came away from the view deflated.

Isobel had burst into her room early and informed her she'd be heading to Camelot to retrieve some more of her belongings. Miss Clarke had agreed to take her to London and set her up with one of her friends as a lady's maid. It was a great opportunity for Isobel. She would return from Aberdeen Sunday evening.

Kate was thankful that Isobel had been quick with preparing her for the day. She'd dressed her in one of Flora's new gowns. It was a deep blue that reminded her of Gavin's eyes. She wondered if he'd like it on her because last week when he'd laid a gown out on her chair, it had been a lighter shade of blue. She ran her palms down the material on this one. It had to be the finest she'd ever touched.

She'd feel invincible, except that he'd ignored her yesterday afternoon. When he'd poked his head into the drawing room after the Fordices had left, Gavin had given her an obligatory smile and exited the room, not to be seen again.

She was trying not to let the lack of his attention bother her, but she couldn't stop herself.

Had she revealed too much yesterday?

She thought back. Their kisses had been magical, and she'd thought he was coming to accept her, but he'd retreated. This was the first time in years she'd risked getting close to someone, and the pain was already wishing to cradle her in its arms and brush her temples with its spiking tentacles.

Had he rejected her before she'd had the chance to retreat?

She had descended the stairs and entered the breakfast room to discover she was the first to arrive. After preparing a plate, she took a seat at the table and ate slowly. She was on her second bit of eggs when Charles and Irene strode in, holding hands. They were an adorable couple.

"Do ye ken what Lady Stonehaven has planned for the day?" Kate asked.

"No. I'm afraid I didn't think to ask last night. I was exhausted from all the walking. I do believe I will stay in and catch up on the news from London today. A post has arrived," Lord Stonehaven said.

The talk veered to theater as it had many other days. Kate enjoyed the conversation.

Gavin strolled into the room, filled a plate, then sat across from her and conversed with Lord Perry as he ate. She kept her gaze on Mrs. Bartrom, afraid if she looked his way, it would be to find that he was no longer interested in her.

After the meal, she strolled into the drawing room with the guests when Gavin approached.

"Miss Reid, will ye walk with me? 'Tis a bonny day."

"I'd like that." She smiled.

Gavin guided her out onto the terrace. "I have a surprise for ye. Follow me."

Her brow tightened.

"Dinnae tell Isobel I'm outside," she whispered conspiratorially. "I barely escaped her trapping my head in another bonnet today. I practically had to beg." Kate laughed at the girl's enthusiasm to follow the English protocols she had been studying. She was thankful Isobel had taken off the next couple of days and wouldn't catch her.

"I'll no' tell her, but I won't be responsible for her wrath because of yer defiance." He smiled.

They strolled straight through the gardens. "Ye missed the talk yesterday."

"I was detained on business matters."

"Have ye completed yer tasks?" she asked.

"Nae. But they will have to wait."

"Until then, I am worthy of yer affections." She wasn't sure if she was swiping at him or pleased that he thought of her when his mind wasn't on work. She hadn't realized how acutely she'd experienced his absence and believed it a measure upon her that he'd stayed away. It was silly to be envious of his work.

His lips thinned.

"I'm sorry. My words were uncalled for. I found my mind drifting during the talk and imagined ye gardening," Kate cajoled. "Although crops are different, I think ye would have appreciated the information."

And she had been second-guessing everything she'd said to him in the maze. She had been too honest, and that left her raw and unnerved.

"Perhaps ye can teach me," he said.

She laughed. "Ye wouldnae want for that. I am unable to keep the simplest of plants alive."

They came to the end of the rows of flowers and stood at

the edge of the pond where there was a short pier she'd not spied before.

"How quaint," she said as he guided her out onto the planked wooden surface. A small boat, tied to a beam on the end, caught her attention.

When they reached it, he released her arm, took hold of the pier, and stepped down into the rocking vessel. He turned back toward her and held out his palm up to assist her. She took it as her fingers trembled, not out of fear but surprise.

He remembered. She'd never been on any kind of boat. It had always been a dream, something she'd never thought to have the opportunity to do.

Gavin untied the rope and used a paddle to push off from the mooring. Then, he dipped the oars into the placid waters and propelled them forward. As he rowed, a butterfly landed on his shoulder.

"Ye have unexpected company." She pointed and smiled at the delicate creature who had chosen such a hard, determined, and dark man as a perch. But she knew then that she would choose him too.

He glanced down and smiled at the wee thing before continuing his efforts.

The colorful creature flew away. The fragile butterfly was like her, only landing somewhere long enough to drink in the view but not get comfortable. She'd never stayed anywhere longer than a few months. Gavin was a good man, and he deserved better than her type of crazy. She wished that she could be someone different, a person who stayed, but fear won out every time.

He stopped rowing and looked all around. "We are here."

Her gaze traveled around, and her eyes watered. The world was open to her on all sides. This was the most precious gift anyone had ever given her. While she wanted to lean back and revel in it, all she could think of was that she and Gavin were alone, and that if they weren't exposed to the view of others, she would let him have her body.

With this gesture, he'd already crawled into her heart.

"What do ye think?"

When she said, "It's beautiful," she wasn't referring to the scenery or the carefully crafted view. She was referring to him and his soul.

"Come here." He set down the oars, crooked a finger at her, and smiled.

She took the hand he offered as he drew her near. Guiding her around, he inched back on the seat so that she fit into the space between his legs. His arms wrapped her in warmth as he whispered in her ear, "It's no' the canal, but I hope 'tis still enjoyable."

"It's more than I could have dreamed."

Relaxing onto him, she sighed and forgot about the world, letting the moment seep into the marrow of her bones. She felt safe in his embrace as a gentle breeze blew across her face, the sun casting a soft glow on them and the beauty of the open space. The boat gently rocked and lulled her into a place of tranquility.

She looked out across the expanse and took in how truly large the pond was and just how far he was running.

Glancing over her shoulder, she asked, "Why do ye no' think yer fast enough?"

∾

Gavin swallowed. As many times as he'd relived the events of that fateful night, he'd only recounted them once—the next day when he'd told the authorities what had happened. He thought to deny her, but Kate's hand landed on his thigh. He guessed she was possibly unaware that she'd made the comforting gesture.

She'd opened up to him about her mother. Perhaps he

owed her a little bit of his trust. "My parents deserted my brother and me to a home for the unwanted when we were but children."

Her hand tightened on his thigh. "I'm so sorry. I ken what it's like to be left behind."

He continued, "They did horrible things in that place. We'd been there almost a year. One night, I was jolted awake in the field near the house. I saw two boys I was friends with run off into the woods."

"That's odd."

"When I turned toward the house, flames were devouring the structure. I didn't ken where my brother was. So I ran, but I didn't get there in time. I attempted all the exits, but the fire blazed hot. I could not get near." His arm twitched at the remembered burn. "There was no one else about to help. I watched the place burn, knowing my brother and all those boys were trapped inside.

"When morning came, one of the town's watchmen escorted me to his home, and his wife nursed me back to health. I had a burn and a gash on my head and suffered from dizziness and headaches for days. Since I had nowhere to go and they had no children, they took me in. They became my parents, and I learned everything I know from them.

"I'm convinced that I survived that night to save others and to find justice for those who didn't make it out."

"Is that why ye became a constable?"

"Aye."

She wiggled in his grasp, turning to face him, now sitting sideways in front of him. Kate's gaze was clouded with moisture. He wanted to look away because of the shame, but at the same time, the compassion in her hazel gaze drew him in.

"Is that where yer scar came from?" She traced the outline on his temple with the tip of a finger. The sensation of her caress sent shivers through his body.

He nodded.

Her palm cradled his jaw as her thumb caressed his cheek. The touch had to be the gentlest he'd ever felt. He tilted his head into it.

"I am sure when the time comes, you will be fast enough." She couldn't know what those words meant to him, and that she had the faith in himself he lacked.

He dipped his head and claimed her mouth. With those words, she had shown that she understood the madness that consumed him. She had attempted to wash away the fear he'd not shared with anyone.

His lips on hers were soft but firm. It was more than the embrace of passion; this was comfort and familiarity. With the touch, he told her he appreciated her—but at the same time, the gesture spoke of a trust he'd placed in her.

When he withdrew, he said, "Thank ye."

They sat there a while longer as he cradled her in his arms, content in the magic of the moment.

He could imagine them doing this on his land, the parcel he'd saved for and bought. No one else had wanted it because it was where the orphanage had been. But he had seen the opportunity to replace it with something good. Over the last few years, he'd been able to expand the holding to include a parcel that had a pond like this one, and also a stream that ran through the property on the other side.

The sun began to grow high in the sky. When the fiery ball went behind a cloud, he glanced down to notice a blush on her cheeks from the rays. "I believe ye should have let Isobel talk ye into that bonnet."

"Why?"

"Ye are starting to color. We need to head for shade."

He didn't want to go back and think about anything beyond Kate lazing in his arms, but he didn't want her to burn either.

He reluctantly rowed them to the dock.

CHAPTER 14

*K*ate held Gavin's arm as they strolled toward the house. The beauty of the morning's clear sky was fading as gray clouds gathered in the sky. The rain was imminent, but at least they'd had this time outside. Gavin had given her a memory that would last long after she was gone from this place.

The thought of finishing her task and leaving became sad. Not only would she truly miss this man, but she was also growing close to the Bartroms.

By the time she and Gavin made their way back inside, the guests were already starting with afternoon tea. They helped themselves, then split apart to mingle with the other guests. She couldn't stop her gaze from drifting toward the man frequently. Several times, she caught him glancing in her direction as well.

Before long, the pocket doors to the music room were opened, and Miss Clarke played the pianoforte again. Lady Stonehaven sang for the gathered party, then encouraged Kate to do the same. She enjoyed singing but typically only did so when alone.

The afternoon went quickly, and before long, she was

once again in her chamber, dressing herself since Isobel had taken today and tomorrow to go to Camelot. Isobel's influence was still present because she had put out the items that she wished for Kate to wear tonight, along with detailed instructions.

Isobel had also left a decanter of wine in the room. Kate poured a glass before starting the process of changing.

Once she'd donned the dress, complete with a matching necklace that she'd promised Isobel she would wear, Kate glanced in the mirror. She was always changing her looks, but this time it felt wrong. For one, the bauble around her neck was probably worth more than she'd ever made in her "business." After letting her guard down with Gavin this morning, she felt odd once again erecting her shield, one that had never before included overpriced jewels.

And that was trouble. She shouldn't care so much, but she knew Gavin saw past her deceptions, and she found herself being more honest with him at each meeting. It had to end before she got hurt.

But was whatever happened between them worth the loss she would have to endure when he discovered the truth?

She finished the wine and left the room to slowly wind her way down the stairs for the late meal. When she stepped into the drawing room, everyone but Gavin turned her way. He wasn't there.

"Miss Reid, it's such a pleasure to see you again." Archie Clarke, the Stonehavens' nephew, reappeared, and he was suddenly at her side, offering her another glass of wine. She took it, and they began a casual conversation about his recent exploits.

Dinner was announced, and she followed him in as he told her of his trek to track down a villain for Flora's earl. He'd been part of the plan to free her from Drostan's clutches. Kate delighted in hearing the story, but she never let on to Mr. Clarke that Flora was anything more than an acquaintance.

Flora had seen to it that Kate had been educated while sacrificing her own cultivation for the benefit of all their adoptive family. She was looking forward to Isobel's return so she could get the whole story of what had happened after Lord Dunbridge and Flora left.

Kate was so interested in how her sister's return to safety had played out that she didn't notice Gavin had come in and sat several spots away on the opposite side of the table. When she did glance his way, his gaze, dark and angry, pinned her. He gripped his eating utensils as if he were ready to stab a person instead of the slab of beef on his plate. She couldn't think of what she could have done to upset him.

With the meal, she had another glass of wine, but it never seemed to run out. She eventually noticed a servant, who would fill her cup as soon as she'd almost emptied it.

When they rose to head back into the drawing room, a flush reached her cheeks, and her legs felt as if they'd lost their substance. Mr. Clarke took her arm to steady her. He smiled down at her.

"Thank ye," she said.

They stepped into the other room, and suddenly Gavin was at her side. His gaze pinned Mr. Clarke, then dropped to where he held her.

"Good evening, Mr. Clarke. Nice to see ye have returned." But the tone in Gavin's voice said he was anything but happy that the man was back.

"I'm sure my aunt has missed my presence." Mr. Clarke laughed.

"Miss Reid, I'm pleased to ken our activities today didnae tire ye." He addressed her, but his focus remained steadily on the man at her side.

Why on earth would he think her exhausted from leaning against him in a boat? He'd done all the work to get them there and back. Her breath caught. He was jealous, and she'd had too much wine to stay alert as to what was going on.

A long stare passed between the men before Mr. Clarke grinned and released her arm and backed away.

"Excuse me. I must greet my cousin." Mr. Clarke stepped to the side and made his way to Miss Clarke.

"Walk with me?" Gavin's gravelly voice asked as he held out a hand. He procured another wine glass from the sideboard and handed it to her before taking one for himself.

Gavin guided her out of the room, then to the left, before hooking another left and heading toward the back end of the house.

"Did ye have a nice conversation with the Stonehavens' nephew?"

"Aye. For a member of the English ton, he's quite easy to talk to."

Gavin scowled and turned into the ballroom, then led her about halfway down to a spot where a window admitted a little bit of the late evening light. The afternoon rain had lightened, but it was still cloudy and darker than typical for this time in the evening.

He motioned for her to take a seat, and he pulled the nearest one so close that they could have almost been sitting on a sofa.

"And what did he say that was so interesting?"

She took a sip of her wine before answering. "He was telling me about a villain he tracked down to help Flora."

"Was she in danger?" he queried.

"Och, yes. That Drostan can be an awful fellow." She shook her head.

It appeared as if Gavin's nostrils flared, but it was so hard to see in this light. "Tell me about this Drostan." Gavin's voice became guttural and gruff. Had he heard of the King of the Docks?

"What do ye wish to ken?"

"What does he do?"

"He owns ships. He and Will dinnae like each other."

Gavin grasped her free hand and held it. The touch was possessive but also seemed laced with something she couldn't place. His grip was tight, but he leaned away from her. Perhaps she'd had too much to drink. He seemed angry again.

What had she done to incur his irritation? Perhaps the anger was directed at one of the men they were discussing. She took another gulp of the wine.

~

G avin was shocked at the information Kate divulged, and she didn't seem to understand the significance. Even though she admitted to an acquaintance with William, perhaps she wasn't one of his people.

If he'd known how honest Kate could be when plied with spirits, he would have done it before now. Although guilt stabbed at him, her honest answers could save lives.

How could she not know the connection between William and Drostan?

"What is Drostan's surname?"

She tilted her head. "I think 'tis Webster."

The last name proved it. There was no coincidence. William Douglas was keeping more secrets than the people close to him realized. What had happened between William and Drostan?

Kate glanced at the cup in her hand, then frowned. She seemed to realize how it was affecting her finally. "This is why drinking is against Will's rules."

Rage, raw and hot, hit him square in the chest. She was one of William's associates if she abided by his directions. What part of his world did she inhabit? And why hadn't she shown up in his bloody research?

She must have seen her mistake in his eyes. She pulled her hand free from his, set the cup on the floor, then stood. "I think I would like to leave."

He couldn't let her go now. She might be his best link to the man he'd been tracking for years. And although it appeared that she would attempt to protect the arse, Gavin would get the truth from her. Now would be a good time since she'd suddenly developed the inability to lie.

She turned and rushed down the center of the room, headed back toward the other guests and safety from his questioning. He bolted forward and caught her wrist. She stopped but kept her head down, eyes averted.

"Dinnae go," he commanded as he would in his official capacity, the words coming out as a demand even if he meant it as a plea.

Silence lingered.

After a moment, her sad eyes glanced over her shoulder at him. "I have an obligation to protect people, and I seem to be incapable of doing that in yer company."

"Stay," he said, easing his temper and the authority in his voice.

He'd spent so long getting close to her, and now that he was making progress, he'd let his anger with William Douglas cloud his interaction with Kate. Now she was withdrawing, and it was his fault.

"Let go." The distance in her voice sounded strained, as if she were having a hard time gathering the reserve to push him away. She pulled her arm as his grip lessened.

"Please don't leave," he pleaded as he released her. "I'm sorry. My anger is not with ye."

She twisted toward him, her gaze wary and mistrusting. He'd done that, and now he was furious with himself for causing the carefree spark she typically had to evaporate from her eyes.

"Ye are forgiven, but I do think I must retire."

She retreated toward the back of the room. He followed.

"May I escort ye to yer chamber?"

"Very well," she said, but she didn't offer her arm.

They took the back stairs, and he changed the subject, hoping to bring back the ease they typically shared. He didn't like the chasm that had forged a cavern of mistrust between them.

"I enjoyed our time together today."

He truly meant it, but he was worried that she would think he'd been trying to manipulate her after he mentioned it. He hadn't. Since pulling her into that closet, he'd been haunted by the look on her face. He'd wanted something to erase her pain for a little while.

"I did as well," she acknowledged.

"I think we made it back from our excursion just before the rain."

"It was a beautiful outing. Thank ye again." Her words were still wooden and on guard.

"Yer company and hearing ye sing this afternoon was more than enough of a reward." He wanted to take her hand and wipe away his angry accusations. He craved the closeness they'd begun to develop. And his words were true. He'd sat in the corner and listened to each note of her lovely voice as the music had engulfed him.

She smiled but didn't respond. They crested the steps.

"I didnae notice ye running this morning," she said.

He was thankful for the opening.

"I couldn't sleep, and so I went out early," he confessed.

They'd reached her chamber. He twisted the knob and pushed in the door. She stepped inside, and he boldly followed. He'd never muscled his way into any lass' room, but he was hoping she'd forgive his rash behavior, and he craved her touch.

She didn't object to his company, but she did wrap her arms around her waist as if comforting herself. The gesture made her look vulnerable. He preferred the confident woman who didn't seem to be afraid of anything.

"Do ye want me to open the window for ye?"

She glanced over as if she'd forgotten it. "Aye. Please. The Stonehaven servant who took the tray I had must have closed it because of the rain."

He flung open the shutters, then returned to her side.

"Thank ye." She smiled up at him with rose-kissed cheeks. Her hair framed her face as if it were a masterpiece painted by an artist. He'd never been so intensely attracted to anyone.

"Ye look lovely tonight."

"Thank ye." Her eyelashes fluttered, and her lips parted. She released her crossed arms, and her fingers touched the necklace. "This isn't mine."

He stepped close. "Good, because I wasn't referring to anything ye were wearing. What I'm seeing are bonny hazel eyes, hair the color of golden wheat, and cheeks that are flushed with either desire or from our trip out onto the lake."

Kate's eyes dilated and fixed on his.

"I see a lass who lets herself go and holds her face up to the wind and one who cares more deeply for others than she is willing to admit."

He leaned in and touched his cheek to hers as he inhaled deeply. "What I smell is a scent so intoxicating that my body tightens and yearns for yer touch anytime ye're near."

His head dipped, and he whispered in her ear, "Everything about the real Kate enthralls me."

Her hands clasped onto his waist as she exhaled a sigh. He kissed her ear, then nibbled at the bottom as her fingers tightened on him.

Trailing kisses down her neck, he lost himself in her sweet response as she arched into his attentions. Her breasts pushed against his chest, and a shot of urgency ricocheted to his core. He nibbled and sucked until she was boneless in his arms.

Then he pulled free, seeking her mouth as his desire burned uncontrolled. He closed his lips around hers as he cradled her head. As their tongues danced together, his fingers spread into her hair and began removing the pins that confined the tresses to her scalp.

When he withdrew, her lips were red and swollen, and the thought that he'd made her look thoroughly kissed like that drove him mad with desire. She panted as her chest rose and fell. He continued to eye her as he tugged the rest of the placeholders from her hair and removed the red beads that had been threaded through her glorious mane.

Her hair cascaded around her shoulders. He delved into the silken strands, massaging her scalp. She craned her neck into his movements.

She was beautiful.

Guiding her toward the dressing table, he set the hair clips and beads down. She shivered as his fingers trailed across her shoulders, then draped her hair to one side as he worked to unfasten the clasp at the back of her neck. He removed the necklace and set it down.

She swallowed as her mesmerized gaze watched him in the looking glass. She took in every move he made . . . inquisitive, intelligent, and uncensored. His heart beat loudly in his chest.

Only Kate stood before him now. Not some woman she was pretending to be. There was no way to fake the hunger and curiosity blazing in her eyes, and it stole his breath that she was looking at him with the same need that coursed through him.

Somehow logic broke free from the cage in which he'd locked the unwanted lucidity. As much as he craved this, he wanted Kate to give herself to him without the aid of spirits. Yes, this was her—this was the woman he yearned for, but it had taken wine for her to expose herself to him tonight.

He wanted her to come to him on her own.

"I want ye. But no' like this, not now."

Confusion set into her hazel gaze. She straightened her shoulders, tilted her chin in the air, and turned. She'd put her walls back up.

He caught her hand and spun her back around. "If we take whatever this is to the next step, we both need to be aware of what we're getting into." It commanded every bit of strength he had to hold out, but her total and unencumbered surrender would be worth it.

She nodded, then smiled as she swayed a little.

"Do I need to get yer maid for ye?"

"Ye ken she's more than that? She's like a sister," she admitted.

He had realized the lass had worked for Flora, but this was new to him. Instead of being angry, he was pleased that she couldn't stop incriminating herself when she had too much to drink. And, she was undeniably charming.

She continued, "Nae. She's no' here tonight, and I'm no' use to having a maid anyway. I prefer to undress myself." She hiccupped, and he laughed.

That's because I have no' undressed ye yet.

The thought had his cock jerking to attention. Hell, he had to get out of here before he changed his mind.

"Good night, Kate." He took her cheeks in his hands and placed his lips on hers for a sweet, lingering kiss.

She smiled when he withdrew. "Sleep well."

And with that, he made his way back to his room. Sleep easily came as he drifted off thinking of the lass down the hall and what he might do with her on the morrow.

CHAPTER 15

*D*espite the lingering drizzle, Kate rose to the sound of birds chirping. She donned her gown and moved her club to lean against the wall between the night table and the bed. The hefty weight in her hands was reassuring, but so was the thought that Gavin might already be up and running around the pond.

She strode over to the window and was rewarded with a nice glimpse of his back as he dashed to the far side of the body of water. His routine was comforting. After everything that had escaped from her lips last night, he was still here.

He hadn't left.

Gavin now knew she was well acquainted with Will and Camelot. Damn that delicious wine and her worry over her plan. The combination had caused her to make some vital errors, but she wouldn't do it again.

They'd almost become intimate last night. But she couldn't blame that on the spirits. Even this morning, she craved to feel his lips on her mouth, his skin next to hers. She wanted that intimacy with him. She was shocked because she'd never felt the urge to be that close to anyone. If he came to her room tonight, she would let him teach her what it was to know a man. She was, after all, close to twenty-one years of age. It was time she experienced being with someone.

She dressed herself, then went down to break her fast. Shortly after she sat, Gavin walked in and took the seat next to her. The conversation was light, about the weather, what was going on in the papers, and the activities planned for today. It was nice and comfortable, and they fell into a rhythm like old friends. Even when there was silence between them, it was a relaxed calm of just being in each other's presence.

Other guests poured into the room, and soon the space was filled with a buzz of constant voices. After the meal, she was whisked away with the ladies to finish preparing for the afternoon's entertainment. She'd never been to one of these house parties before, but she had to admit she fancied the project they were working on, gathering costumes, and preparing for people to play parts in their little skits. The act was similar to preparing for one of her jobs, but this was for smaller parts, and the stakes weren't as stressful.

She truly enjoyed this.

As she and Mrs. Bartrom finished pulling the last of the costumes together, Lady Stonehaven appeared in the small parlor they had used to prepare. It was a room next to the study where Gavin had pulled her into the closet. The chamber was decorated in a more feminine style and served as a study for Lady Stonehaven when she had correspondence to prepare.

"Magnus and Stewart have returned," Lady Stonehaven announced.

Relief flooded her. She would be able to proceed with the plan today. The tension she'd held in eased slightly.

"Wonderful news," Irene proclaimed. "Miss Reid, did you select a part for them?"

"Aye. I have one, but 'twill take us a few minutes to prepare costumes, and I think we need to get the Fordice men their sections to practice. We should be able to start after tea."

The rest of the early afternoon was spent with the guests memorizing their lines, then a light refreshment before everyone returned to their rooms to dress for their parts.

When the music room's pocket doors slid open, the first actors stepped into the space that had been designated as their stage. The rest of the guests were seated to view the performances. First up were Miss Clarke and Lord Perry, who played the part of Romeo and Juliet. It had been the perfect part for them since they seemed to be forming a strong bond. It appeared a marriage was imminent, due to Lady Stonehaven's efforts.

As Miss Clarke said Juliet's last line, "O happy dagger! This is thy sheath; there rust, and let me die." She plunged the fake knife into her gut, and applause rang out from the rest of the guests.

Next up was Gavin, who portrayed Macbeth. According to Irene, most people in the theater community were superstitious and only called it "the Scottish play."

Kate was spellbound by Gavin's appearance. He always looked imposing, but he wore a tunic that cut across his chest and accentuated his muscles. The tights he wore clung to his legs and showed the power beneath. Irene had even fashioned a crown for him from an old trencher she'd found in the kitchen. Charles had somehow hollowed it out and left the perfect size ring. Although it didn't appear that he was thrilled with acting, his dark gaze and serious nature lent a strain of credibility to the monologue where the Scottish king was opining on the death of his wife.

"Bravo," she cheered when he finished, as the assembled guests clapped.

Lord Stonehaven played Hamlet's father's ghost as Mr. Clarke played the namesake of the play. They worked well together and gave a flawless performance.

Magnus and Stewart acted out Caesar's death, and then Kate had a monologue from *The Eumenides,* where she played the part of Athena. Lastly, Lady Stonehaven had a monologue from *Cleopatra.*

After the presentations were done, Irene stood in front of the group. "Thank you to all. We were pleased with your participation. I also have to say a special thanks to Miss Reid, who did a wonderful job pulling this together."

She blushed. It was the first time she'd ever done something she was proud of. It was silly to feel such joy at something that in the scheme of life was trivial.

Irene and Lady Stonehaven were at her side, discussing how the parts had gone and how well everyone had done. She'd never participated in something that seemed to bring smiles to so many faces. The experience had her giddy with glee.

As they talked, she peeked over at Gavin. He was speaking with the Fordice men, even though she occasionally caught him throwing glances in her direction. Eventually, guests began to retreat to their rooms to prepare for dinner.

Lady Stonehaven was making her excuses when Gavin appeared at Kate's side. "May I escort ye to yer chamber?"

"I would like that. Thank ye."

Stewart's gaze had continually drifted her way, his expression one of determination. She didn't want him to find her alone anywhere.

"I enjoyed the activity this afternoon," he said as they started toward the reception hall and the main stairs. His words were genuine, but there was something stiff and measured about the conversation.

"It was a delight to organize," she admitted.

His blue eyes met hers, and she imagined he was looking at her with approval instead of the mistrust which sometimes darkened his gaze.

"Ye make a good king."

"Why do ye say that?" he asked.

"It's that shadowy, serious nature of yers. Like ye have too many burdens to bear."

His lips pursed as he mulled over her words.

As they ascended the steps, his solemn gaze dropped over his shoulder as if watching to see if they were being followed.

"Is something bothering ye?"

His brows knit together, and he debated his answer before admitting, "I dinnae like the way Stewart Fordice watches ye."

She couldn't admit that she was put off by his attention as well, but she needed to stay close to Magnus, so she wouldn't be able to avoid his son.

"Ye need to stay away from both of them."

For the afternoon's event, she'd worn a white, flowing gown that exposed her shoulders. She'd also had a shield and spear for the part, but she had left them downstairs. She wished she could hold them up now until she could think of a response. She'd even consider telling Gavin what she was up to, but he had some ill will toward her brother, and she wouldn't share any information about Camelot with Gavin. She wanted to trust him, but her family was too important.

As they crested the top of the steps, she attempted to lighten his somber disposition. She stopped, and her gaze roamed over him for the first time in private. She placed a hand on his chest and said, "Ye may be dressed as a king, but ye cannae order me about," she laughed.

He didn't find humor in her reply because his steady, watchful eyes darkened and dilated. His body tensed, and the muscles beneath her fingertips jumped. Suddenly, she was hot, so she backed up, and he took her arm to continue down the hall.

They'd made it about five steps when his husky voice scorched her with intensity. "I warned ye."

"About what?" She peeked up at him.

"No' to make me want ye."

They'd reached her chamber, but instead of pushing in the door, he spun her around so that her back was against the cool wall. His focus blazed on hers as desire spread in her core, and then his gaze dipped to her chest. His penetrating stare spoke of illicit desires, and she wanted to know them. Instead of being frightened by his intensity, she yearned to discover what he would be like as a lover.

His strong hand moved from her arm to rest at her waist. The heat seared through to her flesh. The thrill pumping through her veins was anticipation. She licked her lips as his head began to dip, and his fingers melded to her curves.

The door swung in beside them. A sigh, like the pressure escaping from a dam, released from somewhere in his chest.

Isobel's smiling face popped out from within her chamber. "Oh my. I thought I'd heard something out here."

"I believe it is time to prepare myself for the evening meal." She didn't recognize her raspy voice, and despite her words, the last thing she wanted to do at the moment was concede her time alone with him to a dining room full of people. Hell, where had her senses gone?

He nodded. "I will see ye there."

Gavin turned and strode toward his room.

She turned to Isobel. "I didnae ken ye were back."

"I told ye 'twould be a short trip."

"Ye missed it. Gavin took me out on a boat yesterday." An odd lightness invaded her senses. *Is this what giddiness feels like?*

"I think he fancies ye." Isobel craned her neck into the hall, and they both watched as he disappeared into his room.

She sighed. "I like him, but 'tis no' a good idea to get involved with him," she admitted as she stepped into the room and drew the door shut.

Still, she wanted to. Just once to feel close to someone again. No, her mind fought her. She couldn't want that because he was going to leave. Why was she setting herself up this way? But she knew she was going to give in anyway.

"I have to give ye all the news." Isobel broke into her contemplation.

"Well, what did ye learn?"

"That Flora is safe, and the business with Drostan is done," Isobel blurted out.

"Thank heavens. I dinnae ken what it is with Will and Drostan that they must terrorize each other." Kate had never met Drostan Webster, but she had heard the tales of the two men's rivalry.

"Anyway, Drostan went back out to sea, so all is well now."

"Good. Will doesnae need the troubles," Kate said.

"Sit," Isobel instructed. "We need to start preparing ye for the meal."

"And Flora's earl?" Kate asked as she sank into the seat.

"He's apparently still in Aberdeen. I think she might marry him. So, everyone is well and safe."

But her sister was wrong. None of the Camelot Crew was safe. "I have to tell ye something."

"What's that?" Isobel asked through a pin she had pinched between her lips, as she pulled one of Kate's stray curls back in place.

"I'm here to save Camelot."

"What do ye mean?"

Now that the Fordices were back, she'd been able to breathe again. Worry had claimed her yesterday and had driven her to drink too much wine. Now, relief settled in, and she thought she could discuss her plan.

"The Fordices. They are the ones that own the building." She glanced up at her sister.

Isobel gasped. "Stewart. Is he the one that . . ." the girl couldn't finish.

"Nae. 'Twas his younger brother. If Thomas were here, he'd recognize me in a heartbeat."

"But he's supposed to be coming." Isobel's eyes widened.

Her sister pinned the last of some shimmery beads that looked like pearls in her hair.

Kate ignored the worry in Isobel's voice. By her calculations, she had several more days before she would need to worry about Thomas showing up. She had a swift departure planned. "I'll be gone before he arrives.

"Stand, let's get ye in a proper gown." Isobel fastened the dress she'd chosen for Kate.

She had to admit, it was a beautiful shade of sapphire, and the cut was quite flattering, showing just enough of her shoulders but entirely too much of her chest. She almost looked as if she belonged here.

"I'm going to get the Fordices to sign the deed over to Joseph."

"And how are ye going to do that? He's but nine years."

"Callum and Cole are going to help after I get the Fordices to Aberdeen." They were twins that had arrived at Camelot the same time she had. They would help her with anything that meant keeping the family safe.

"I dinnae like the sound of this."

"Nae need to worry. I have everything in place." She swallowed the anxiety that clung to her throat.

"Kate, ye should talk to Will."

But she couldn't do that. She knew Will wouldn't let her risk it. Then he would have to uproot everyone and possibly stay in the streets until they found another place they could afford. She couldn't let that happen. They had a babe they were taking care of as well—living and roaming from alley to back alley was no place to keep the children healthy.

Isobel's doubt put a damper on her mood.

"Ye look lovely. Oh, one more thing." Isobel reached down

and came back up with another necklace that also comple-mented the ensemble. It looked dreadfully expensive.

"Where'd ye get that?"

"Lord Dunbridge got it for Flora. She won't mind if ye borrow it."

Kate shook her head but agreed to wear it because it furthered the ruse that her brother was wealthy. She needed Magnus to believe it.

By the time she arrived, most of the guests were already present in the dining room.

~

G avin strode down the hall to his room.

Kate was playing a dangerous game. Not only with the men capable of killing her, but with him. He'd warned her. Until Gavin could make progress with the Fordice servants, he had a new purpose. She'd toyed with him long enough, and it was time to take whatever she was willing to give. Judging by her reactions, that was whatever he wanted.

His whole body was tight with anticipation and hunger. He didn't have many weaknesses, but Kate was one of them. The desire to know her fully, who she really was, and what she felt like wrapped in his arms was all-encompassing.

Dressing quickly, he made his way back to the drawing room and struck up a conversation with Charles Bartrom. He'd grown quite fond of the theater owner and his wife. He could see why the Stonehavens had invited them here from London. They were good company and even better people.

When Kate stepped through the door, everyone turned her way. She knew it too, the little siren. She was aware of her effect on people and used it to her advantage. He'd admit he was as captivated as everyone else, but he wouldn't let her enchantment rule him.

He was in complete control.

When she'd stepped out in her little play this afternoon, she'd kept them all raptured by her portrayal of the goddess Athena. She was even more alluring in the deep-blue gown she wore tonight.

Fury ignited in his chest as she peeked his way, then ignored him in favor of walking up to the man who was most likely a killer. Did she think her acting skills were going to save her from the man, or even from him now that she'd tempted him too far?

"She's a lovely creature." Charles Bartrom broke into his thoughts.

"I was staring," he acknowledged.

Charles laughed. "You are not the only one." He nodded toward Stewart and Mr. Clarke.

At least Mr. Clarke had the sense to glance his way and wink, acknowledging that he recognized Gavin had staked a claim on the temptress. Stewart, on the other hand, openly drooled. Perhaps if he couldn't keep Kate from playing with the affections of other men, he would have to warn Stewart of his interest in her.

That wouldn't jeopardize his mission.

His fists tightened as he realized his interest in the lass might scare the man off. His hands were tied with that, but tonight, he would find pleasure in Kate's arms and then let her know what the Fordices were capable of. Perhaps afterward, she would have the sense to keep her distance from them, but it would be too late for her to do the same with him.

"I am not a matchmaker, but my wife thinks the two of you would suit nicely."

"Does she?" Gavin's eyebrows shifted up.

"I know what you're going to say, though."

"What's that?"

"That you do not have time or the want of a wife."

Gavin nearly choked on the air in his throat. He

swallowed.

"Ye would be correct." He'd never thought of taking a wife. Everything in his life had led him toward a goal of seeing that victims were given justice. Outside of that single purpose, he'd never made room for thoughts of what his own life should be.

"What it's hard for a bachelor to see is that life's burdens can be eased with the right woman by one's side."

Gavin's gut began to twist. This was not a conversation he wanted to have. He was about to tell Charles his feelings on the matter when the arrival of Lady Stonehaven saved him.

"What did you think of the entertainment this afternoon, Constable?"

"I enjoyed it. Thank ye for yer efforts and continuing to host me at your home."

"Mrs. Bartrom and Miss Reid did most of the work," Lady Stonehaven said as she glanced around the room.

He wasn't positive that Lord Stonehaven had told his wife why he was here, but they seemed to have a comfortable companionship, so he guessed the man might have given her an idea. He noticed that she greeted Magnus and Stewart politely but attempted to stay away from them.

He wished Kate would do the same. His attention traveled her way, as it did every time she was in the room. She'd said something to Magnus that had him laughing as the man soaked in her radiance. Gavin inhaled and reigned in his temper. She was playing with fire by earning the notice of the Fordice men.

Maybe he'd been wrong and Kate didn't fully understand her effect on the men around her.

He'd cautioned her not to make him want her, but she hadn't stopped tempting him, and every time they touched, she'd melted into him as if she welcomed his affections. Now, he desired her fiercely. His mind had caught up with his body, and she'd tempted him too far.

It might lead to something dark and tragic for her when he discovered the true nature of her association with William Douglas. He hoped she wasn't involved in the man's endeavors, and he didn't have to lock her away.

But the men she insisted on getting close to were not the only danger.

Tonight, their yearning for each other would take them down a path from which there was no return.

CHAPTER 16

*K*ate stepped into the drawing room and their gazes met. Appreciation was in Gavin's regard as it roamed across her body and absorbed either her or the deep-blue gown she wore. He stood tall, wearing his dress jacket and kilt again this evening. She liked how it looked on him and was thankful that the ban on them had ended some time ago.

His shoulders were held back as he remained on alert and watchful, but Charles occupied him. The imposing figure he cut still emanated danger, and she was drawn to it like a beacon, but she knew that she would drown when she gave into him.

She was surprised the desire in his study hadn't frightened her. He was a turbulent, crashing ocean that would consume her, but she didn't care. She was ready to let him pull her under and surround her in his darkness because she'd not let herself feel for so long.

Instead of strolling up to the man who watched her as though he were going to swallow her whole, she tore herself away from his stare. Despite knowing Gavin wouldn't approve, she sidled up to Magnus. She might plan on letting

Gavin lead her down a path of destruction, but she still had a job to do here.

And that came first. Time had become an enemy.

She smiled and took the seat next to the elder Fordice. "I'm glad ye are back. I was afraid ye had left us."

She lounged back on the settee, mimicking his posture to put him at ease.

"Nae. We're having too good of a time. We had some business to see to."

"In Aberdeen?" She leaned closer.

"Aye."

"My brother will be there later in the week to close on some properties. I wish ye could meet him." She blinked innocently.

"I would like that." His reply was genuine and sent a shiver of hope that she could still see this through to the end.

"He had planned to join us after his visit, but he sent word that he'd been called back to Inverness."

Guests began filing into the dining room, and she moved to follow Mr. Clarke, who had been speaking with his aunt. Magnus entered behind. She mulled over what to do. What if Magnus decided the trip back to the city was too much for him? She couldn't let that happen.

It was time to plant another seed, one that would promise an introduction to a prominent family . . . the Sutherland clan. She'd never met any of them, but Magnus wouldn't know that until after her deception was done.

"That is a shame," Magnus said as he pulled her chair out for her.

"Thank ye," she said as she eased into it, and he pushed her closer to the table, before taking the seat next to her.

She continued, "Oh, it is. We were going to visit the Sutherlands after I met up with him, but alas, seeing our dear friends will have to wait."

"You have a connection with the family?"

"Joseph and their son are quite friendly. We go to see them often."

Magnus's gaze lit.

"If ye would like, my brother or I could make an introduction. I'm sure they would be honored to meet a man of yer status." She wanted to wretch but knew flattery, and promises she couldn't keep, would be her way to woo Magnus into the deal.

"Lady Stonehaven has planned for all of us to go to Aberdeen this week as a group. Will ye be joining us?"

"Aye. Yes. She mentioned it. Stewart and I plan on going."

"That would be splendid. I'll write to Joseph to see if he'll be able to spare time. Perhaps we can have a meal together."

They continued to eat and talk through the meal until Mr. Clarke drew her into a conversation, and Magnus turned toward his son and Charles, who carried on a lively debate about relations between England and Scotland.

After dinner, Kate approached Lady Stonehaven and Miss Clarke.

"Will we still be traveling Aberdeen on Tuesday? I've learned my brother will be there for a couple of days on business."

"I am sorely disappointed he won't be able to join us here, but yes, our excursion is still on. I'll remind everyone tonight, and we'll see who wishes to join us. It's short notice, but I think it would be grand, and we could leave by mid-morning on Tuesday. That gives us a little over a day to prepare."

Kate conversed with Miss Clarke as Lady Stonehaven circulated the room, then made it back to their side. "I believe we are on, and all persons have agreed to the outing."

"I'm thrilled not to be going alone. I think we'll all enjoy it." Relief set in, and she let out a genuine smile. She'd managed to get Magnus back to Aberdeen, and it appeared to come from Lady Stonehaven.

Lady Stonehaven excused herself as the guests began to disperse into different directions. Instead of heading into the game room with the rest of the men, Gavin sought her out.

"Would ye do me the honor of taking a turn out on the terrace with me, Miss Reid?" His husky voice washed over her, sending shivers of awareness spiraling through her veins.

"I would be glad for the air, Constable."

"Please excuse us, Miss Clarke," Gavin said as he extended an arm, and she threaded her hand through it. He guided her out the large, windowed doors into the fresh night air.

The sky was clear, and stars had begun to cut through the twilight. As they sparkled in the distance, she soaked in the spacious views and the alluring scent of the man beside her. He seemed intent, striding with purpose toward the long end of the terrace. She followed, content to be by his side and out in the open. She took in a deep breath to inhale him as he guided her toward the dark end of the promenade.

Was he going to kiss her again? Eagerness coursed through her.

"Ye ken I am here for reasons other than pleasure?" His taut voice dampened her expectations.

Fear spiked.

Had he discovered who she was? His hurried pace and determination made her aware that he might not be pulling her away for intimacy, but to interrogate her.

"I thought as much." She swallowed the lump in her throat as a tightness invaded her neck and shoulders.

Why else would a constable be unexpectedly present at a gathering such as this? She'd known from the start that his presence here hadn't been planned. Her research had been meticulous.

"Then ye need to ken that Magnus and Stewart Fordice are capable of murder." He stopped at the back door of the house.

Ice stabbed her and strode through her limbs. Her steps faltered, and she glanced up at him, not bothering to hide the worry that crept in. Fingers tightening on his arm, she held on as the implications washed over her.

She'd thought the men entitled arses, but not killers.

She would take precautions and never be alone with the men, other than leading them to the solicitor who would have them sign the building over to Joseph. Then she would disappear and never have to face them again.

Gavin drew open the house exit and held an arm out for her to enter. Her brow creased, but she didn't argue as she stepped inside.

"Thank ye for the warning."

"I dinnae wish to see ye harmed." He grasped her hand and led her up the back stairs. "'Tis time ye ken I'm here investigating them for unspeakable crimes."

"I will be on guard."

If she could abandon the plan now, she would because these men were not like the ones she typically dealt with, but her family needed her, and she owed them. She wished she could tell Gavin the whole truth, but his animosity against Will would likely see her brother in prison.

They passed by her door. He led her on until they reached his chamber. Pulling out the key, he slid it in the lock and turned it, then pushed open the solid wood plank. He drew her in behind him before shutting and relocking the exit.

He twirled her around and backed her to the solid timber. "I dinnae think ye comprehend the danger."

And she suddenly wasn't certain if the threat Gavin was still speaking of was the Fordice men or him.

"I am a grown woman." Perhaps her throaty reply was an unfortunate choice of words that seemed like a childish reply, but she did know what kind of peril she was dealing with, and it didn't matter. She had to follow through.

"I know." The coarse growl that came from his throat had

her rethinking how he took in her response. His gaze traveled down to her chest, then back to her eyes. The awareness that met her was blistering and filled with a hunger she'd missed before.

She had been the prey this whole time, and now she was cornered. Even during his warning and reprimand, his sole intent was on her. She'd been so focused on the news he'd given her that she'd followed him blindly. Excitement spread out into her limbs, causing her body to thrum with anticipation.

His fingers threaded into hers, then brought her hands up to pin them above her shoulders. Her mouth watered as his intention for sneaking her to his room became clear. He thought he was in command, but this was what she'd hoped for.

She licked her lips, and they parted as she prepared for him to kiss her. His scrutiny remained fixed on her. In his gaze was a struggle for control, as if a war raged inside him. He wanted this but was trying to hold back. They both knew there was no future between them, which was what made this perfect for her.

She would be gone in a couple of days' time, and he could go about with his business.

"Kiss me," her breathy voice pleaded.

"Oh, Kate, I want so much more than a kiss."

Tingles of anticipation thrilled the back of her neck and spread out in all directions.

"Then take what ye want." She'd never been this bold. She'd never desired the touch of a man, but she wanted Gavin.

He inhaled sharply as his lips turned up into a satisfied grin.

When his mouth collided with hers, it was with a thirst that took her breath away. As his tongue filled her entrance and tangled with hers, she was swept away on the tide of his dark desires. She let it pull her under and surrendered herself to the force of his need, which only fed her own.

As the embrace continued, she tilted her head to give him better purchase. Her fingers tightened in his as she wished to put them on his chest and finally feel the strength beneath the muscles, but he kept her pinned. Her knees became unsteady, and his effort to hold her still might have been the only thing keeping her upright.

He drew back, and the glazed concentration in his eyes was evident even in the unlit room. Enough light filtered in from the late summer sky to show his chest heaving in and out as if he'd lost his breath. Her core became wet and slick with the knowledge that her kiss had made him breathless.

But suddenly, she was aware of the stakes of this game. She was not in control, and he would be the one to leave. She was headed straight into the arms of a man who was going to wreck her.

He blinked, sensing her hesitation.

But she couldn't, and didn't want to, stop him. She was going to let him drive as fast as he could, and no matter the danger, she was in for the ride, even if the collision would destroy her. Kate's lips fell open, and she nodded for him to keep going.

He noticed her capitulation because his mouth curved in a victorious grin. Her inhalations were ragged and out of time.

Gavin's head dipped as he placed caresses on her shoulder, then followed the slope to her neck. Chills, and sensations of coming undone, skated down her spine. When his teeth skimmed the sensitive flesh, then nipped, she gasped and arched into him.

A satisfied rumble escaped from his chest. In one swift move, he drew her from the door and twisted her around in his arms so that her back was flush with his front. One hand kept her pinned at the waist to his hard frame, a bulge pressing into her back, as he continued to lavish attention on her neck.

She felt as if she were falling into sensation. She was barely aware of his free hand pulling at the ribbons on the back of her gown.

There was something heady about giving up her control and letting him lead. She was so accustomed to always being the one who planned for every eventuality. Here, she didn't know where they were headed, but she did know it was going to be explosive.

And despite the pain it might bring, she knew she wanted it.

∼

G avin hadn't expected her to be so responsive to his touch. Really, he'd not known what to anticipate. He'd only known that he could hold out no longer. If she'd said no, he would have backed away, probably muttered a few curses, then an apology, and licked his wounds.

But Kate had come alive. She was so eager to put her hands on him that he'd become rock hard the moment they'd locked eyes upon entering his chamber.

He'd seen a flash of unease in her gaze, but she'd wiped it away and then urged him on.

Her gown already loosened, he worked at the laces on her stays, pulling them free. Reaching down, he gathered the garments over her head and tossed them on the floor. He liked the blue on her but decidedly liked it more where it presently lay.

She didn't protest. She turned in his arms to face him and began tearing at his jacket and shirt.

"My eager little Kate," he breathed as he helped her with the fastenings.

When he drew them both off, her hands traced the lines

of his chest. Need exploded in his groin at her tender exploration.

She licked her lips and seemed to be mesmerized by his bare flesh. Watching her reaction drove him mad with lust. He needed to get back in control because urgency beat at him and drove him out of his senses.

He put her at arm's length and scanned what remained on her. A short chemise that didn't leave much between them. The length of it was the reason he'd been able to see the outline of her lower legs through her gossamer gown. Now, the spot between the end of the material and the top of her stockings left a tease of flesh exposed to him. He licked his lips, wanting to taste all of her.

He took the hem of the garment and peeled it over her head. She was left exposed but for her slippers and stockings. Every part of him tensed, and he ached with the need to plunge into the spot between her legs and claim her.

He kicked off his boots and unfasted his belt before tearing the rest of his clothing from his body. As he did, she moved toward his bed, and he was given a lovely view of the globes of her ass. He couldn't wait to have her perfectly rounded rear in his hands.

She sat and removed her shoes and stockings, and he finished undressing before she was done. He was nude, but he didn't move because there was something fulfilling and erotic about watching her slow, measured movements as she rolled down the stockings to expose her dainty ankles and feet as if she were savoring the act of teasing him.

When her attention turned his way, her gaze raked his body in a slow, intense study that told him she appreciated the care he took in maintaining his form. He stepped closer and noticed she'd grabbed onto the covers and gripped them.

Extinguishing the distance between them, he leaned down and claimed her mouth with his once more. The honeyed taste of her nearly had him mad with desire. She returned the embrace as her hands rose and clung to his thighs. The hunger to drive into her surged, and his penis began to throb with need.

He pulled himself away from her lips, barely able to contain his breath. Instead of guiding her back on the bed, he wanted to prolong this encounter, so he knelt on the floor before her and spread her legs so that he could fit his chest between them. He began by placing small kisses on her thigh and trailing his hand along the other.

Then he could wait no longer to touch the center of her. He drew back to look, as his thumb found the bud between her legs. She whimpered at the touch, so he did it again and her breath hitched. She was watching every move he made as if curiosity was winning out over the sensations.

Sliding his fingers in a delightful rhythm across her slick passage, he thrilled as she threw her head back and surrendered to his ministrations. That was what he wanted. He wanted more than anything else for her to lose control and reveal the true Kate. Forget being someone else and become the woman he wanted to tame.

He inserted one finger into her passage, then moved forward to taste her. He licked and sucked at the nub at her core as he pumped the finger in and out of her. She whimpered, and he was able to peek upward as she arched her tense body. He intensified the movements. She cried out as her fingers threaded through his hair and clenched around the strands.

Several strangled gasps escaped into the air as her release hit her fast and hard. Then, mewling sounds escaped from her throat as the clenching around his finger continued.

Her head thrown back and the trembling of her legs staggered him off balance, and he knew he needed to be inside her as the convulsions of her climax still rocked her body. He stood and guided her on the bed.

Positioning himself between her legs, he drove into her.

The pressure was exquisite, and he nearly lost himself in the one stroke. A pant escaped from her lips as her fingers tightened on his sides. She held onto him as if he were the only thing keeping her afloat.

As he gazed down at her, he was captivated by the dazed look in her eyes, her mouth open as gasps continued to come from her throat.

Kate was the most beautiful creature he'd ever seen.

He plunged deeper as urgency beat at him, each stroke milking him and tightening the pleasure that pleaded to break free. He lost himself in the sensations as he thrust in and out of her warm sheath. He'd never felt such ecstasy.

When his release came, it was harder and more intense than anything he'd ever experienced. Rapture reached into every inch of his being as he spilled the evidence of his desire within her channel. Still, he moved until the contractions stopped and sanity began to return.

This was the first time he'd ever lost control and let himself feel completion inside a woman. He stayed there inside her as her sated gaze met his. He was instantly aware that this one time with her wasn't enough. He wanted to have her again and again, possibly in merely a few minutes.

He'd never known bliss like this. He kissed her with a fierce satisfaction that he hoped told her that this was only the beginning of them enjoying each other. She had to know that he intended on drowning in this feeling until both of them were so satisfied that they couldn't move.

After taking her mouth in his, he finally withdrew and rested at her side. He drew her in so that she fit between the crook of his shoulder, her soft skin flush with his. He was suddenly exhausted and needed to shut his eyes a few moments before they began again.

"Did I do it right?"

He thought it an odd question after what they'd both just experienced.

"Aye. Ye were perfect."

He nestled into her and breathed in the familiar scent of spiced oranges and gardenias. His eyes shut, and he drifted off with the woman who had been vexing him still in his arms.

CHAPTER 17

*K*ate opened her eyes, a grogginess washing over her as she tried to make sense of where she was. She had drifted off, only to wake again in Gavin's reassuring arms.

She felt cherished and respected. His scent covered her, and she inhaled to take it all in. His fingers were curled around her arm with the gentle weight of possession.

She felt wanted.

Then, she felt sick. She couldn't breathe. Despite his large room and the comfort of his flesh next to hers, she knew that when he discovered the truth, he'd reject her like a piece of refuse.

Her own mother hadn't wanted to keep her.

She wasn't worthy of his affections, and he'd find out. Her lungs began to close in on themselves, and she glanced over to find his window was shut. She had to get out of here so she could breathe again. She needed the cool night air.

Sliding from his embrace, she was careful not to wake him. He sighed and rolled over. She scooted off the bed, drew on her chemise, and then gathered up the rest of her belongings. She took one more glance at the man who had made her feel ultimate pleasure, the one who was going to discard her, and she fought the prick of pain in her eyes.

Easing open the door, she glanced into the hall and looked both ways. No one was about. She slipped out and shut the door quietly, rushing for her room.

When the door swung open, she dashed in, shut it, and pushed her back against the solid wood as she caught her breath. Dropping her gown and slippers to the floor, she sprinted across the space to the already open window and the rejuvenating, cool night air.

How was she supposed to feel?

Her lungs were having difficulty filling.

Should she have stayed in his room? Would he be angry that she'd left? She shook her head. No, she'd done the right thing. If she hadn't left, he would have woken up and realized he'd made a mistake with her still there.

"Where have ye been?"

She startled at the sound. Isobel sat on her bed, thumbing through a book, which she placed on the nightstand and rose.

Kate was so disoriented that she had no idea what time it was, or how long she'd been in Gavin's room.

"Are ye crying?" Isobel stepped forward.

Was she? What was wrong? She was sweating and her breath was tight. Fear had taken root in her chest, but she couldn't say why.

"Nae. I'm fine." She waved Isobel's concern away with a shake of her head.

"Did ye come from the constable's room?"

All Kate could do was nod.

"Sit down. I'll undo yer hair and get ye in bed."

She obeyed and moved to the dressing table, thankful to have some kind of direction.

"He's no' going to leave ye," Isobel consoled.

Her eyes widened as she shook her head. How had Isobel

known? Taking another deep breath, she put on a neutral face and hid all her emotions. That was what she was good at. She was in control.

Closing her eyes, she opened them again and said, "I willnae let him. I'll go first."

"Och, Kate. Ye have to let someone in. He cares for ye." Isobel smiled.

But Isobel was wrong.

Gavin had wanted her, but that was over. He'd be done now. Perhaps it was a good thing because now he wouldn't care if she was involved with the Fordices. She could finish her plan and vanish. Once she did, this time perhaps she would go somewhere far away, possibly France. If she couldn't speak the language, she wouldn't have to get close to anyone.

"Thanks for being here." She had to admit it, though, that it had been nice to have a friend nearby. She would be sad to lose Isobel's company.

"I'm quite enjoying my time." Isobel smiled.

"Did ye ken we are going back to Aberdeen this week? Ye could have postponed yer trip."

"I did, but liked seeing everyone. I'll miss them when I leave for England, so the extra time was well spent."

"That's great, Isobel." She jumped up and hugged her. The gesture did a lot to soothe her as well. "Ye deserve happiness."

"So do ye, Kate."

She gave a quick smile and skirted around Isobel for the bed.

"Now, get some sleep. It's late, and we have a busy day of packing and traveling tomorrow," Isobel said as she walked toward the exit.

"Aye. I will."

She climbed into bed, and as she lay there, she attempted to think about what she had to accomplish over the next couple of days. Her mind kept returning to the man down the hall and what they'd done together. She didn't regret their actions, only the consequences.

She now felt vulnerable, and she'd not let that happen for years. It was the reason she moved about so much.

It was a good thing they would be in Aberdeen soon. Perhaps Gavin would decide not to go; then she could swing by to retrieve her things and be on her way somewhere else. As long as she didn't get any closer, perhaps she could avoid what might come.

She tossed and turned all night, barely resting at all.

The next morning, she rose late as Isobel pushed in her door, followed by a couple of servants holding a big basin of wash water. After sponging off, she felt refreshed and ready to start the day.

When she finally walked into the breakfast room, only one guest remained . . . Gavin. His eyes didn't leave her as she prepared a plate. She purposely sat on the opposite side of the table instead of walking around to be right next to him, which she'd done on previous occasions. In this position, across from him with the solid surface of the table between them, they could talk, but she could still keep her distance.

"Good morning," she said after slipping into the seat and glancing over to meet his steady gaze.

"Good morning, Kate." His voice was rough, and he'd used her given name in public.

He didn't attempt to hide his displeasure with her, and the vibrations in his tone sent shivers skating down her spine. Her eyes widened. She glanced back over her shoulder to see they were the only ones in the room.

When she glanced back at him, there was no remorse in his direct stare. "Did ye sleep well?" His query was clipped and angry.

She opted for the truth. "Nae. I barely slept at all."

"Perhaps ye should have stayed." He folded his arms on the solid wood and loomed closer.

Hell, was the man going to let everyone know what happened between them? He didn't seem the type to boast about a conquest, but perhaps she'd misjudged him. Glancing over her shoulder again, she saw they were still without an audience. Her seating choice seemed unfortunate because her back was to the room, and he had to speak louder to reach her across the table.

"I couldnae breathe, and I didnae wish to wake ye," she whispered, this time electing to use a partial fact.

His regard softened as his brows crinkled. "The window?"

She nodded and averted her gaze, certain her cheeks had colored with embarrassment. The waves of anger wafting from him appeared to dissipate.

"Are ye prepared for the journey?" he asked as she stuffed a forkful of eggs into her mouth.

She chewed, then swallowed. "Aye. Is that where everyone else is?"

He nodded. "Since ye are taking yer carriage and I dinnae have one, I'd like to accompany ye." Now his voice was all authority, the constable again, as if she didn't have the choice of refusing him.

How was she to avoid him when he insisted on such closeness? Not having a logical reason to refuse his request and not sure if his comment was a demand or a question, she said, "I would like that."

And truly, she meant it, but at the same time, she knew the proximity would be torture.

"What time would ye like to leave?"

"Whenever ye are ready. The Bartroms are preparing to leave now, and I believe Mr. Clarke is going with them. The Stonehavens have a full carriage with Miss Clarke, and Lord Perry and the Fordices are coming later."

She'd been aware the Bartroms had wanted to depart early but hadn't counted on all the others leaving at different times.

She took another bite and then washed it down with a sip of water.

She placed the cup on the table and noticed the tremble in her own hands. How was she to survive a carriage ride with Gavin? How was she to make it the next few days without growing closer to him? She was always the one to rush out the door. Her ability to retreat had kept her sane.

Everything was different now. She didn't want to leave Gavin's side, and that scared her more than the thought of the Fordices discovering her plan.

~

Gavin stared across the expanse that Kate had put between them. She looked lovely. Her cheeks were flushed in a way they hadn't been when she'd entered the room. He wanted to close the distance between them, take her in his arms, and quell the unrest that had settled into his bones after her departure.

She was purposely avoiding him. Had he hurt her in his haste? If so, she'd given no indication last night. Was that why she'd come down so late as well?

The tension that had racked Gavin's body since he woke up to find Kate gone this morning still had not abated. After he'd risen and thrown back the covers, he'd noticed small splotches of dried blood on the mattress. Why had she not said something?

He'd stifled the urge to burst into her room and demand to know why she'd left, instead opting to go for a longer than typical run. It had done nothing to suppress the confusion circulating in his head. Afterward, he'd bathed himself, then headed down to the breakfast room to wait for her.

Everyone had come and gone by the time she strolled into the room. He wanted her more right now than he had last night as he'd guided her across the terrace to sneak her to his room.

How had this happened?

It was her fault for being so responsive . . . then for leaving.

Now, this thing between them had become even more enticing as she tried to pull back. He was going to chase her, and he knew she wouldn't be able to outrun or outmaneuver him. He didn't know how long this would last, but he was going to enjoy it for the duration.

After she deposited her fork on the table, he stood and strode over to where she sat. "I'll escort ye up to finish preparing."

She stood and took the arm he offered.

"Ye smell lovely."

Her scent conjured images of her beneath him as he claimed her, apparently being the only man who ever had. He shouldn't let that color his interactions with her, but something about the trust she'd placed in him made him feel a primal burst of emotion that he couldn't name.

"Thank ye."

They headed out of the room, and he guided her through the reception hall and to the main steps. After they crested the top, he could take the silence no longer.

"Are ye all right?"

She smiled and nodded at him, but then she blinked twice. Dread invaded his chest. What had gone so wrong with her when he'd thought their time together had been perfect? The only thing that would have made it better was waking to find her still in his arms.

He pushed her door open. She walked in, and he followed to see if her lady's maid was present. She wasn't, so he shut the door, then drew Kate into his arms. He had to know if her interest in him had dimmed.

When his lips met hers, she tilted her head into the

embrace as her fingers curled onto his ribs. The kiss started sweet and innocent but quickly morphed into an intense burst of desire. As he pulled back, he studied her dazed gaze and parted lips, which seemed to be still begging for more. Relief flooded in.

Kate did still want him.

Blinking, she shook her head slightly as if to brush off the effects. She seemed frightened not of him, but of her reaction to his touch. He, too, was having a hard time understanding what was happening between them, but at least that was something he could strive to remedy.

He released her and put distance between them so that he could think clearly.

"About last night . . ." he started, but then the door slid open, and Kate's *maid* strolled in. He'd figured out that the lass was on his list as well, Isobel Ferguson, one of William's crew.

Gavin still hadn't discovered Kate's place among them, but he was willing to take his time with her to pry all her secrets loose. He was having too much fun with her to rush it. Knowing she would be part of his next mission no longer angered him—it thrilled him that he'd need to keep her close still once the Fordice issue was resolved.

"Oh, forgive me. Am I interrupting anything?" Miss Ferguson stepped forward with a knowing grin she didn't try to contain.

"Nae," Kate answered too quickly as her cheeks turned a pale rose.

"Miss Ferguson," he greeted.

She smiled at him, then appearing a bit flustered, turned back to Kate. "Someone is coming up to get yer trunk. Do ye want to make certain ye have everything ye need before we close it up?"

"Can ye give us a few moments, Constable?" Kate said with a straight back and tilted chin.

He didn't like that she'd reverted to calling him by his title. He wanted to plant his lips back on hers and kiss her until the only name she could think to call him was Gavin.

"Aye. My belongings have already been delivered to yer coach, so let me ken when yer ready, and I'll escort ye down." He didn't want her to have a chance encounter with the Fordice men without him around.

He strolled from the room as the women finished their packing.

A short while later, a light knock sounded at his door. He stepped out, locked the room, then held out his arm for Kate. She took it. Miss Ferguson followed as he led them down the stairs, then out the front door where the carriage had been retrieved for their convenience.

He helped Kate enter, then Miss Ferguson, who thankfully claimed the seat facing the rear of the carriage. That left him the option to take the spot next to Kate. The boxed-in area was on the smaller side, and Kate was already opening the window and breathing in the outside air.

When he eased into the space next to her, his leg was flush with hers, and a thrill shot through him that they would be this close for the several hour journey into Aberdeen.

As the buggy jolted to a start, Kate jumped and tried to balance herself. Her hand landed on his leg, and before she realized what she'd done, he took it in his and held on. He imagined that the maid knew they'd spent time together last night, and this wouldn't come as a shock to her. Miss Ferguson saw his gesture and smiled.

"Miss Ferguson, are ye from Aberdeen?" An opportunity presented itself. Why not take advantage of the time?

"Oh, aye. Lived there all my life." Miss Ferguson was happy to share.

He grinned on the inside, careful not to show his satisfaction. "Tell me a little bit about yer family and life there. I've never been."

Miss Ferguson opened her mouth to answer, but Kate interrupted, "Constable, I'm sure Isobel would like to rest. She's had a long morning of packing and preparing for the trip."

"I thought we were on more familiar terms, Kate. I prefer when ye call me Gavin." He pinned her with the irrational irritation that had been brewing since her swift departure from his bed.

He turned back to Miss Ferugson, who looked amused. "Miss Ferguson, did ye ken that Miss Reid's name is no' Allison?" He tilted his head forward, and his eyebrows rose. "I'm fairly certain she's no' really even a Reid."

The lass paled, and her jaw went slack.

"Ye dinnae have to answer any questions." Kate's frantic reply seemed breathy, and her voice quaked.

He waved his free hand as if to dismiss her words. Perhaps she was worried now that he was once again probing for answers.

"Gavin, please leave her be," Kate pleaded, a rising tide of panic reflected in her gaze. Her inhalations became a little more erratic.

"Well, we need to talk about something. I know, Kate, tell me more about yerself."

The carriage bounced through a rut in the road, and her fingers tightened in his as she flinched. Her palm had heated in his hand, and her face had turned ashen.

Kate's breathing seemed inconsistent and her eyes wild. She normally kept her cool with him, so what was happening?

His gaze traveled the expanse of the coach, looking for an external reason for her stress. The only other thing in the cramped space was Miss Ferguson.

It was the confines of the carriage. Her reaction also explained why he'd seen her by the side of the road on that first day. Had his curiosity and insistence worsened her reaction? He suddenly felt the need to shelter her.

"It's going to be all right, Kate. Come here." He twisted sideways and pulled her into the space between his chest and arm. She clung to him with both hands as she fought to control her breathing.

"Lean back. There's plenty of room in here, and we can get out anytime ye need." He spared a glance to Miss Ferguson, who had drawn out a collapsible fan and waved it in the air to circulate it. He gave Miss Ferguson a small smile of encouragement.

"No rush, relax," he said as he stroked Kate's cheek. She was shivering, and her eyes had frosted over, but she relaxed into his arms.

"Close yer eyes, and I'll tell ye about my home." He fingered a stray lock that fell down the side of her temple, then pushed it back out of her face.

She nodded and shut her lids but still kept her grip on his arm.

"Ye ken the home I told ye about that burned?"

She nodded again, and the talons wrapped around his forearm eased as her breath began to steady.

"I saved up and bought the land it was on. No one wanted it." He paused, talking in shorts bursts and in a slow, measured tone to convey that they were in no hurry.

"There's a stream that runs to the west. The water can be about waist-deep and cool and refreshing. The brook makes a soothing trickling sound, and sometimes I sit by it and watch the water flow by."

He paused and ran his thumb across her cheek, then continued, "I could see ye stepping into that water and glancing up to bask in the sun."

A smile broke across her lips, and her breathing evened out.

"There's a wide, open field nearby where I'm going to try

to grow barley." His fingers had moved to her arm, where they traced soothing circles.

Glancing over, he found Miss Ferguson watching them with a grin. The lass gave a short nod and turned her attention out the window as if giving them privacy.

Returning to Kate, he said, "There are mountains and when the sun sets, it's one of the prettiest sights ye'll ever see. The clouds turn pink and orange."

"It sounds lovely." Her voice was soft, and all traces of panic had vanished.

"Would ye visit me so that I could show it to ye?" He could imagine sharing his world with her and the pleasure on her face as she took in the open views and the fresh air. A tightness tugged at his chest as he waited for her answer.

"I would enjoy that."

"Ye would like it," he assured her.

"Why did ye choose a place with such bad memories?" she asked.

"Because it reminds me of where I came from and what I can accomplish. I also feel closer to my brother there."

"I didnae have any blood siblings. I'm sorry ye lost yers." Her eyes fluttered open, and she glanced up at him.

"He's still in my heart."

She'd volunteered new information, and he thought to question her on her mother, but he'd only now gotten her calm again, and he liked the soft weight of her in his arms.

"Tell me more about yer land." She closed her lids as peace washed over her face.

And as he gave her every detail about his home, her body became limp. After a while, she eased off into a peaceful sleep. He watched her for a long time, wondering what she would think of his land if he took her home. Maybe when all this was over, he could convince her to stay a few nights. He certainly would not be averse to having her warm his bed for an extended period.

He caught himself smiling at the thought, and then he remembered they weren't alone. Glancing over, he was surprised to notice that Miss Ferguson looked pleased that her friend had fallen asleep in his arms.

"I've never seen anyone calm her like that," she whispered.

He was afraid to wake Kate, so he asked softly, "Does it happen often?"

"Nae, but the couple times I've seen it, no one can ease her fears, and she usually runs off after it happens."

"How long have ye kenned her?"

"Long enough to ken that she never lets herself get close to anyone." Miss Ferguson bit down on her lip, probably in an attempt to keep her thoughts to herself.

That was an interesting little nugget, considering Kate seemed to have so many friends.

"That's all I'm going to tell ye. She's warned me no' to talk to ye."

"So, ye dinnae plan on telling me why she's pretending to be a child that lives with ye and William Douglas?" He attempted to hide the ever-present anger and resentment that emerged when he thought of the man he'd been chasing for years.

"Nae, but I will tell ye she risked a lot to save those kids. She didnae have to do it."

His brows knit together, and he broke from the maid's gaze as he glanced down at the woman in his arms. This was a new lead as well. He'd have to look into Allison and Joseph Reid's backgrounds.

"Who did she save them from?"

As far as he could see, they were still living with the worthless William Douglas, but that didn't mean they'd always been there. His information only went back several months; perhaps that was where his blind spot was with Kate as well. He'd not gone back far enough.

"I'm no' telling ye anything else. Ye can get the answers

from Kate." Miss Ferguson turned her head and glanced out the window, a clear signal she was done with his interrogation.

He turned his attention back to the sleeping lass in his arms. More questions now plagued him.

Time passed as he studied Kate. By the time they hit another bump that woke her, his shoulder had been tingling for a good half hour. He'd not wanted to move. Holding her hadn't made up for waking without her this morning, but it came close.

Her eyes blinked open, then glanced up to where he watched over her. A lazy, sleep-kissed smile spread across her lips. If they were alone, he might have set her in his lap and filled her until they were both panting, but they weren't. The thought made him ache with need.

She sat up and stretched without taking her eyes from his. "How long was I asleep?"

"Most of the trip," he whispered as he held his finger up to his lips and nodded his head in the direction of the dozing Miss Ferguson.

"Did ye harass Isobel while I was asleep?" She leaned in to whisper.

He couldn't resist. He took her cheeks in his hands and thoroughly kissed her. When he released her, she looked thoroughly dazed and compliant. He was looking forward to the evening when he'd seek her out and they'd have a repeat of last night.

"Why did ye no' tell me ye'd never been with a man?"

"Does it matter?" She turned red and averted her gaze.

He took her chin and tilted it up to meet his gaze. "Aye. I feel as if I've taken something I shouldnae have."

"There is no need for regret. I'm pleased with my choice."

Pride swelled in his chest. "Then ye have a desire to come to my bed again tonight?"

She paused. There was an instant of hesitation before she

took a few breaths and then met his regard straight on. "Aye, I would like that."

Yes, he screamed in his head as his whole body tensed again.

"Thank ye," she said.

"No need to thank me. Anytime ye want, I am ready."

"Nae." She laughed, and the sound wrapped its way around him and drew him in. "For talking me out of the fear." Her gaze darted away for a brief moment before returning. Her cheeks had reddened again.

He smiled. "You're welcome. How are ye feeling now?"

"I think I should be good for the remainder of the journey."

He was glad he'd been able to put her at ease.

"Yer home sounds lovely."

"It is." He could imagine them resting on a blanket near the stream, and then him consuming everything she would give as the golden rays of the sun lit her face beneath him. He'd never envisioned someone being in his space, but he would share it with her.

"I think we're close now," Kate said as she pointed at the window.

Just then, Miss Ferguson stirred, and for the rest of the ride, the maid pointed out landmarks and explained them.

The carriage pulled to a stop outside the Aberdeen Imperial Inn. Gavin helped the ladies down, and they strolled in to speak with the man at the desk.

When Kate's back was turned, and she was speaking with Miss Ferguson, he leaned in toward the man. "Could ye please be certain my room is near the lasses'?"

"Aye. That's easy enough." The clerk nodded his head discreetly.

"Also, two men are coming in later today. Fordice is the name. Please make certain they are on a different floor."

"I can do that as well."

"Thank ye." Gavin slid several coins as a tip toward the man.

"Here ye go, room 204 for ye sir, and 205 for the ladies." He bowed his head. "Just up the stairs. Yer belongings will be brought up shortly."

"Thank ye," Kate said as she clasped onto the key.

As they navigated the steps up, Gavin decided that while he'd initially been hesitant to take this trip, he was pleased that it would keep Kate away from the Fordices and that he would have more time with her.

It might also prove that he had better access to question the Fordice valets. He didn't hold out hope they would be helpful, but he still had to try speaking with them. He escorted the ladies to their room, then washed up and headed back down to meet Kate.

CHAPTER 18

*A*s Kate washed using the basin that the hotel had sent up, her thoughts strayed to Gavin. He'd been so kind today, and somehow talked her through her attack. She'd never had one dissipate so quickly, but she'd felt so cherished in his arms, and he'd known exactly what to say to break through.

Isobel insisted on repining parts of Kate's hair, so she sat at the dressing table and let her poke pins about her head. "The constable fancies ye."

She smiled, then reality broke in. "Men's affections are fleeting."

"I think ye like him too," Isobel teased.

And that was the problem. Kate had come to care for him, but the hard, dark man of the law had shown with his actions that he had a good heart. She enjoyed his company, even when he was interrogating her.

Letting herself care always led to heartache. She was already in too deep and had agreed to spending another night with him.

"I wish I didnae," she confessed as she met Isobel's study.

"He's not like Fiona."

She'd not let herself think of her childhood friend in years. Fiona's father was a cobbler, and they lived several blocks away, but the girls had formed a fast friendship after meeting at a local park once she'd come to live with Will's family.

They'd been so close until Fiona's parents discovered she was one of the children of Camelot and the King of the Streets's crew. They had forbidden her to see Kate, and the girl cut her off right away. They had let her visit one more time but came with her and told Kate she was rubbish and that she was never to seek out Fiona again.

Fiona had left and never turned back. The reminder had her gut twisting in knots.

"It doesnae matter, Isobel. When he finds out where I come from, he'll be done with me."

"I think ye're wrong, and I think when ye go to leave, he's no' going to let ye."

Kate stood and turned to face her sister, who she knew meant well. "I'm a criminal. The world is black and white to him. If I left and he hunted me down, it would be to put me in prison."

"Ye didnae see the way he was looking at ye while ye slept in his arms. Do ye ken that man didn't move for hours because he didnae want to disturb ye?"

She didn't want to hear anything else that made her care for him. She hadn't succeeded in putting distance between them today. Instead, it had been the opposite. "I cannae talk about this right now. I have other things to worry about."

She strolled over to the door.

"Kate," Isobel's voice called. "Ye deserve to be cared for. Let him in."

She shook her head, then walked out into the hall, shutting the exit behind her.

A few moments later, she pulled in her chair at the table with Irene and Charles as she looked at the plush surroundings.

She'd spent time in many hotel dining rooms, but never this one. When she was in Aberdeen, she typically stayed at Camelot, so she was certain the staff here wouldn't recognize her. Also, Camelot was about a twenty-minute walk, so the likelihood of running into her family unaware was slim. Although she knew Peggy worked in the nearby bakery. As much as she'd like to see her, it was best to stay away from any of them until her deal was done and Gavin was no longer a threat to Will.

She'd decided that once this was all over tomorrow, she was going to ask Gavin straight out why he was after Will and try to talk him out of whatever he'd found Will guilty of. She knew Will had done some awful things in the name of keeping them safe, but she didn't understand how any of it would involve the law from Glasgow. Her brother never left Aberdeen.

The Bartroms enjoyed a dish called whim wham, small bowls of sponge cake with crème and raspberries. She'd seen it before but never indulged in the delicate-looking treat, which had been topped off with slivers of almonds. She ordered two additional servings, one for her and one for Gavin.

"So glad you made it safely," Irene Bartrom beamed.

"We had an uneventful journey. How was yours?"

"We made excellent time."

"I thought Mr. Clarke was with ye."

"Aye, he was, but he took off on some errand as soon as we arrived. He was eager to get here. That's why we didn't wait this morning," Charles said.

Gavin strolled in. His chest was held back, and he glanced around as if inspecting every corner of the room, always on the alert for some sort of danger. A thrill shot through her. She knew Isobel had been wrong, but she had been too.

He wouldn't be able to care for her, but it was too late for her; she had already gotten too close.

He drew out the remaining seat, and her heart began to beat faster at his nearness.

She smiled at him. "I took the liberty and ordered ye a treat. I hope ye dinnae mind."

"Good afternoon, Constable Davidson," Charles greeted.

Gavin nodded. "I trust ye are all settled in yer rooms."

"We are." Irene beamed. "This is such a lovely hotel. And what a marvelous suggestion to come into the city, Miss Reid. I dinnae believe we would have done it without your urging."

She felt Gavin's gaze physically as he turned toward her and pinned her with mistrust. She had been hoping the ladies would claim that the idea was theirs, but now Gavin probably surmised she had a reason for dragging them on this journey.

Once the tea and biscuits were set in front of them, and Gavin began eating, his scrutiny softened, but the damage was done. As they dined, the four of them had a pleasant conversation, and when she wasn't watching for Magnus and Stewart to arrive, her mind was drifting to being wrapped in Gavin's arms again.

"There is a shop we must visit. The clerk was talking about a place called the Aberdeen Atlas Emporium. It's a short walk from here, and then we can visit the bakery that's next door to it." Irene glowed with anticipation.

Charles laughed. "Yes, apparently they make the best queen's cakes in all of Scotland. It sounds like something I must not pass up."

That meant going into the bakery where her sister Peggy worked, but she was fairly certain the lass wouldn't give her away. She'd been aware this might happen.

"We'll have to pick up some extra for Mr. Clarke. He said he had something to see to once we arrived, and he took off. Said he might not be back tonight."

"It seems he's learned the area well," Gavin suggested as he mulled over something in his head.

She wondered what he could be thinking. "This was delicious. I'm looking forward to the late meal when we return. I believe they will have music as we dine."

"Oh, that will be lovely." Irene smiled.

"Shall we head out? I don't think the Stonehavens will mind us getting started without them."

The group rose from the table and headed toward the front hotel exit. Gavin extended his arm, and she took it. The gesture was becoming too familiar, too comfortable, but also too tempting to decline. She was now craving the feel of him next to her. Her bid to put distance between them seemed to be over, and she'd failed miserably.

A short while later, the four of them were strolling the shop-lined street with the damp afternoon clinging to them. Although the rain hadn't yet started, the humidity in the air had made the curls in her hair springy, and the chill had her walking a little closer to the warmth of Gavin's body.

They came upon the well-kept storefront of a warehouse that seemed to stock almost anything a modern home could want. The open windows gave a nice view of some of the wares it had to offer. This was the place the hotel clerk had insisted they visit, the Aberdeen Atlas Emporium.

They'd made it several steps ahead of Charles and Irene, who had paused to look in the windows of another establishment. Gavin pushed in the door, and a bell that had been attached to it rang and announced their arrival.

People dallied about different areas of the filled space, and as Kate took them in, a familiar face came into view. A momentary flash of panic seared her insides.

Kate's steps faltered as her attention focused on one of her brothers from Camelot. He'd seen her too because his brow crinkled when he glanced up from the bonny lass he'd been speaking with.

What the hell was Bran doing here?

She straightened in an attempt to hide her discomfort and shock. But her composure had come too late. Gavin's arm tensed. His whole body suddenly seemed to be standing on edge, and she knew that in her surprise, she'd given herself away.

Upon exiting the hotel for their walk, she'd thought the worst that could happen was that they'd run into Peggy in the bakery. She'd chosen this area of town because her family wouldn't be near. Now she was thinking she'd chosen poorly, although there hadn't been many options fitting for the social station of the Stonehavens.

She'd have to make the best of the situation.

Bran cautiously stepped toward them as if he already sensed something wasn't right. He practically exuded unease at her appearance, and caution pulsed from him in almost visible waves as her brother measured up the threat that was Gavin Davidson.

She gave a slight shake of her head as she shifted her gaze between Gavin and Bran, hoping that Bran would catch the warning in her eyes.

Bran was the golden boy of Camelot. He had a way of winning others over with his quick smile and wit, but what Bran was best at was stealing. She'd eaten many a night only because of his efforts to provide for those at Camelot.

It had been Bran, Will, and Flora that had formed Camelot all those years ago and begun bringing lost kids home to save. She was one of those unfortunate souls, and she owed Bran for what they'd done to try to make her a whole person again.

Bran eyed Gavin as if he'd already determined he was dangerous. Bran was correct. They watched each other openly as if they were two giants in an epic standoff that would determine the fate of the world.

Gavin had stilled, and his imposing figure studied his

surroundings. He hadn't missed her subtle attempt at subterfuge, but he didn't openly acknowledge it either.

She wanted to throw her arms around Bran and hug him. It had been ages since she'd seen him, and it tore at her heart that instead of embracing him and telling him how she'd missed him, she pretended not to know him. Even if Gavin knew something was amiss, she had to play out her deception for Charles and Irene, who had entered behind them.

"Welcome to the Emporium. Can I help ye find anything?" Bran tried to act casual, but tension was etched on his face.

"We were told by the clerk at our hotel that this was the place to be and a must-see stop on our visit to the city." Kate put on her best smile.

Gavin's scrutiny glided cautiously between her and Bran. His deep-blue eyes had darkened with displeasure.

"Aye." Bran attempted to laugh, but it came out as a choked chortle because, at that moment, he apparently noticed the pin on Gavin's shirt that indicated he was on the Glasgow Police Force.

"The Emporium has the finest wares in all of the city," Bran continued as if he worked in the place.

When had he had a legitimate line of work other than day labor on the docks? Perhaps she'd been away from Aberdeen for too long. She had to applaud Bran for turning into a well-adjusted store clerk.

He truly looked the part.

"Ye seem familiar. What's yer name?" Gavin's deep and foreboding voice bounded through the store.

"Breandan MacKay at yer service." Bran gave a slight smile as he used his full name instead of the shortened version that all his friends and family used. Perhaps it was an attempt to hide his identity.

She tried to think back to Gavin's list. Had the shortened version of Bran's name been on it? One look at Gavin told her it didn't matter; the mistrust in the depths of his limitless eyes was on full display. He knew exactly who Bran was.

"And who am I assisting today?" Bran's voice had deepened as he made a point of trying to act normal.

Kate chimed in, "I'm Allison Reid, and this is Constable Davidson, here from Glasgow."

Bran's eyes flared, and she wanted to punch him for being so obvious. She should have known using Allie's name would shock him. His face reddened, and she knew if he thought he could, he would curse her for bringing one of their family into her scheme. She'd wished she'd not had to as well but taking on the moniker of the Reid family had been necessary.

Gavin said nothing, and it was obvious that Bran was having difficulty with how he should respond.

Kate saved him. "I think we will browse on our own. Thank ye."

"I'm here if ye need anything." Bran put inflection on the last word. A signal to Kate that if she were in trouble, he would be there to help her despite his anger.

Kate led Gavin toward the linens. To put off his interrogation, she began a conversation about the material with the other lass working in the shop. Gavin's regard never wavered from an intense study of his surroundings, and of Bran, as he spoke with the Bartroms, who were asking questions about some item Irene couldn't find on the shelf.

Kate had begun to grow hot, so she drew Gavin toward the exit. "I'd like to get one of those queen's cakes now. Mrs. Bartrom, we are going to step right outside. Take yer time."

It appeared the Bartroms were making a purchase.

As they breached the doorway, the breeze caught her hair and blew a spiral of curls into her face. It tickled, so she pushed it back.

She wanted to rush headlong into the bakery and have a reason not to address any questions from Gavin, but Peggy was probably in there. "Can we stroll for a few minutes? I need some air before we enter."

She pointed through the window of the bakery. The space for customers was smaller, and it appeared to be crowded with families making late afternoon purchases to supplement their evening meals. "I think 'tis best to do it before the rain sets in proper," she continued.

"Aye," he said. His voice was rough, but she could tell he had calmed quite a bit since his initial reaction to Bran.

"What do ye think of Aberdeen?"

"All the buildings are gray, but 'tis a clean city."

"The docks are just down that way, past our hotel. You can also look out to the ocean."

"Is that where ye said Drostan stays?"

He seemed overly curious about Will's rival. She held no allegiance to the man, and so had no reason to guard what she knew of Drostan.

"Aye. He seems to be an angry man. He's known as the King of the Docks."

"That's interesting."

"People say he can be quite ruthless," she continued, telling Gavin everything she had ever heard. It seemed to pacify him, and she was pleased to have a safe subject to discuss.

Just a couple of minutes later, they had reached the end of the block. "We should probably turn around. The Bartroms should be done by now."

They did and began strolling back toward the bakery. Both of them seemed to be lighter, and as they moved forward, their companions exited the Emporium and strolled into the next shop.

Once they reached the storefront, she stayed out of view of the windows and kept her back to the shop as she pretended to study the ones across the street.

She used her weakness to her advantage. "I'd rather stay

in the air. I dinnae need to purchase anything, but if ye would like, ye may go in."

It was sad she wouldn't be able to see Peggy, but she couldn't afford setting Gavin on edge again, and the girl might not be able to contain her excitement upon seeing Kate. She made a pact that she would come back and visit Camelot before she left for an extended trip. Although she never stayed for long, it was a place of comfort and acceptance for her.

"Nae. I'll pass as well." He continued to ask questions about the ship captain, and she gave honest answers until the Bartroms reemerged with bundles and praises for the smell of the pastries.

The group spent a little while touring the rest of the area, then headed back to the hotel to prepare for the late day meal. Upon entering the lobby, they discovered Magnus and Stewart had appeared. Relief flooded her that her plan was still on track. She warmly greeted the father and son, who informed her they were headed to a local tavern for a drink and to discuss business. The duo planned to return for the meal.

The letter she'd had sent to the hotel for Magnus was in his hand.

Tension eased from her body as he smiled at her as if he'd already read the contents and was deeply intrigued.

Gavin escorted her to her room. "I have some things to attend to, and I'll see ye at the meal."

"Aye," she said.

He turned and strode down the hall. Was he already putting distance between them? He'd not taken her mouth with his, not made sure she was inside her room as he typically did, and not insisted that she stay away from the Fordices.

Gavin seemed preoccupied, but shouldn't she view that as a good thing? If he were focused on other matters, she wouldn't have to worry about how to avoid him when the time came. She needed him far away when the events she'd planned came to fruition.

~

G avin dashed down the hotel hall and back toward the lobby. He regretted the way he'd deposited Kate at her door and fled. He thought he might have seen hurt or confusion in her eyes. Still, now was his opportunity to seek out the Fordice valets and question them without Magnus or Stewart knowing of his investigation.

This was the opportunity he'd been waiting for more than a week for, and he couldn't let his desire to hold Kate interfere.

Upon sharing his credentials, the clerk gladly gave him the Fordice room information. They were two floors above him and Kate. He hurried up the steps hoping the men he was looking for would be in their employer's rooms unpacking their belongings.

He knocked on the door to Magnus's room first.

A middle-aged, straight-backed man with a sprinkling of gray in his brunette hair answered. "Can I help ye, sir?"

"I'm Constable Gavin Davidson of the Glasgow Police. Are ye Andrew Tuft?"

"Yes, I am, but Constable Davidson, Mr. Fordice is not in. Should I tell him you are looking for him when he returns?"

Gavin skirted past Andrew and walked into the room.

"Nae. I'm here to see ye."

Andrew fumbled with shutting the door, turned toward him, and scratched at his temple.

"What can I do for ye, sir?" The valet asked, his lids rapidly blinking as he gave Gavin his full attention.

"I have a few questions." Gavin strolled over to the closest chair and slid into it, attempting to convey an air of nonchalance. He didn't want to scare the man off or make him think he was in any trouble.

Andrew nodded.

"How long have ye worked for Mr. Fordice?"

"Approximately two years, sir," he replied as he hung the pair of trousers he'd been holding in the wardrobe, then turned back to face him.

"And in that time have ye witnessed any activities that cause ye concern?"

"No, sir," he said quickly, his brows knitting together.

"What about his son's activities?"

The man stilled momentarily but then went right back to his work by pulling another item of clothing from Magnus's bag. He appeared to be using his efforts to put a barrier between them.

"It is not my place to have dealings with his children." The man's voice shook a little, and he turned to put the next item away.

"But ye have heard whispers?" Gavin could sense the valet was holding back, but this had been his concern. Those companions closest to the Fordices would be the ones most likely to keep their secrets.

Andrew stopped fidgeting with the clothing to give Gavin a disapproving stare. "I don't give credence to rumors, Constable. I am a loyal servant. I suggest if ye have any problems with Mr. Fordice, ye take the matter up with him directly."

"One last question. What happened to the valet before ye?"

The man's face paled. "I only ken that he was gone upon my arrival in the household."

"Very well then. if ye decide that yer conscience needs to be cleared, I can always be reached at this address."

Gavin handed him a piece of paper with the street

number of his Glasgow office. Andrew took it but only bowed his head.

"One last thing. I prefer that ye dinnae inform him of my visit."

Andrew nodded.

Gavin pulled open the door, "If he thinks ye have talked to me, ye might find yerself in danger."

The valet's lips thinned, apparently convinced that Gavin's words might be true.

Gavin scooted down the hall to Stewart's room. He had no such luck there, either. The questioning seemed to follow the same pattern. Both men were either too loyal or too scared to speak up.

Discouraged, he headed back to prepare for dinner and write to his colleague in Glasgow to ask him to follow up on the whereabouts of Magnus's last valet. Stewart's had been with him for many years.

Upon arriving back at his room via the steps near the rear of the building, he caught sight of a large frame standing outside Kate's door. The man knocked, and every hair on Gavin's arms stood to attention.

The figure was none other than Bran MacKay. William's second-in-command at the house called Camelot and a thief. When they'd run into him in the shop, he had been surprised to see them, then pretended not to know Kate.

Gavin pulled into the shadows of his doorframe and covertly watched as Kate's door swung open.

She was barely visible as she threw her arms around Bran and the two embraced. Fury exploded in his chest. Gavin was tempted to stride down the hall and punch the arse for touching her, for even knowing her.

After the initial shock, clarity returned, and he wanted to start asking questions, but he stayed back to discover what the two of them would do as rage bubbled and burned in his chest.

They released each other half a second before Gavin would have made the choice to rush down the hall and pull them apart. Kate didn't let the man in her room, but that was little relief as the pair began an animated conversation.

Had he not experienced and known the truth of her innocence, he would have thought them lovers. Still, his stomach roiled with something rotten and gnawed at him to challenge the man for seeking her out.

Snatches of conversation reached his ears, but none of it landed coherently or made sense.

A moment later, Bran was backing away, and Kate closed the door. Relief washed over him that at least she'd not invited him into her room.

The thief stalked down the hall to the exit but turned to glance over his shoulder before descending the stairs. They locked gazes, and Bran seemed tempted to retrace his steps, then challenge him. He must have thought better of it, or Kate had instructed him to stay away because instead of returning, he turned and disappeared.

Gavin had suspected earlier today that they'd known each other, but Kate had purposely distracted him. Bran's presence had told him one thing. He would no longer wait for answers—he was going to push for them again tonight.

Over the past week and a half, Kate had shown no inclination to divulge information about William and his crew, but that needed to change. Perhaps since they'd become closer, she'd feel safe to confide in him.

He found her loyalties perplexing.

Kate was intent on protecting William, yet she held no such reluctance to speak about Drostan. Could it be that no one here knew the connection between the men?

But that wasn't his focus right now. Why was Kate talking to another man at her room? No other man should be at her door, especially not one who was part of his investigation. He recognized the fire that blackened his insides.

He was jealous.

And tonight, he needed to prove to her that he was the only man who should be near her chamber.

He let himself into his room. His anger festered and seared as he prepared to join the others for the meal. Once ready, he sat down at the desk, wrote his correspondence, then headed down to the front desk to have it delivered.

As he descended the steps, Kate came into view, and his body instantly thrummed to life. Her lovely sun-touched curls were once again pinned up, and she wore an emerald-colored evening gown that made the green in her eyes stand out, even from across the room.

As Gavin reached the bottom of the stairs, she turned toward Magnus, who had approached from her other side. They stood there talking and waiting for the others to arrive for the meal. Gavin stepped up behind them and ducked into a shadowed corner as the elder Fordice began speaking.

"Yer brother has written to me," Magnus declared.

"That's nice. I received a letter from him upon my arrival as well," Kate crooned in a voice that sounded enthusiastic.

Gavin had been with her when they'd checked in. There had been no such letter for her. What was she up to? He stayed back as not to interrupt the conversation.

"We will be dining tomorrow at an establishment nearby. I'm looking forward to seeing him."

"He has asked that I join you," Magnus stated.

"Oh, that would be lovely. I'm sure that ye will get along nicely." The excitement in her voice sounded genuine.

Gavin's brow crinkled. He'd have to find out more of this planned lunch with a brother that was nine and didn't truly belong to Kate. He might have to follow them to see who would be there.

"If ye would like to head that way together, I can be ready by two and will wait for you in the lobby," Magnus offered.

"I would like that," she crooned. "It will be nice to have company on the walk."

The Stonehavens appeared and joined them. The conversation turned to small talk about the rain.

Gavin removed himself from the alcove and headed toward the front desk. Once he'd deposited his letter, he turned to look at Kate as she continued to charm everyone in her company.

He chose not to sit near Kate at dinner. He was too tempted to pepper her with questions, and he needed some time to clear his thoughts about everything that had happened during the day.

The stall on his investigation, Bran at Kate's door, and Kate lying about receiving a note from a brother that did send one to Magnus all swam in his head, causing it to ache. He ordered a whisky and relished the burn as it spread down his throat.

Kate's gaze kept drifting his way. Her hazel eyes were colored with concern but also laden with a healthy dose of caution.

Perhaps she sensed his irritation.

He didn't take her arm as the group made their way up the stairs to retire. Miss Clarke and Lord Perry were also on their floor, so he still made no move toward her as they all said goodnight and headed toward their separate rooms.

Once inside his chamber, Gavin paced. He wanted to trust her, but more than anything, he desired for Kate to have faith in him. Worry that her scheming was going to get her hurt overwhelmed him, but mingled with the thought that he'd warned her, and she hadn't listened.

If something happened to her, it would be no one's fault but her own.

After a sufficient amount of time had passed, he dashed down the hall and rapped lightly on her door.

She cracked it open and peeked out. A bonny smile lit her

face when she saw it was him, and he almost chose to forgo everything he needed to discuss with her in favor of drawing her in for an embrace. She pulled the door wide, and he stepped in.

Kate's trunks were open and unpacked, but Miss Ferguson was nowhere in sight. He studied the room. Kate's window was open, and her odd club was already out and on the bed. It was as if she were ready to bash any intruder bold enough to enter her room without permission. He decided he liked that she was a prudent woman who wouldn't hesitate to defend herself.

He thought to put her at ease. "Ye look lovely this evening."

"Thank ye."

"Will ye join me in my room? I had some wine delivered, and I'd like to have a chance to talk since we were no' able to at the meal." He'd thought about questioning her here, but the chance of being interrupted by Miss Ferguson was too great.

They needed complete privacy.

"Of course. I'd love to join ye." She blushed as she already knew talking wasn't the only activity he had in mind.

His hands itched to touch her, to caress her curves, explore her flesh, and memorize every last detail of her, but that would have to wait. He wanted to taste her again, but he knew if he put his lips on hers, he wouldn't be able to stop.

He'd had enough of her games. Tonight, he wanted answers before they found bliss in each other's bodies.

He motioned for her to exit and then led her down the hall to his room. She silently followed.

Once in his room, he turned, shut the door, and locked it.

He moved over to the small table where he'd put the tray and poured them both a glass of wine.

"Did ye enjoy dinner?"

"Aye, I did. What did ye think?"

"The fish had a nice taste," he said, and although he'd savored the first bite, the rest had seemed bland as he'd watched Stewart ogle her over his plate.

She took a sip. "This is delicious. Thank ye."

"Are ye liking Aberdeen so far?" he asked.

"Aye. I always like visiting this city."

"Is it because ye have so many friends here?" He attempted to sound casual.

Her shoulders drew back, and then she took a large gulp of the wine as she thought of a reply. "I have spent a good portion of my life here. I do have many acquaintances."

"And Bran MacKay is one of those men." He raged inside but tried to keep it bottled up, even though he knew his voice sounded coarse and accusatory.

His hand tightened around his glass.

"Yes," she admitted without any remorse for associating with known criminals.

"I dinnae understand why I'm surprised that everyone ye seem to associate with is a malefactor."

"Bran is a good man." She sighed and shook her head.

"How well are ye acquainted?" he asked.

She blew off his question. "Can I open the window?"

"I'll get it for ye."

As she evaded his question, he understood that not only had her deceptions angered him, but her lack of trust wounded him.

"Why did he come to your room this afternoon?"

Her eyes flared, then she shut them, resigned that he'd discovered her secret. "If ye must ken, ye frightened him."

"I find that hard to believe. I thought he was ready to brawl when I saw him leaving."

"He only wanted to be certain I was safe. After ye stared at him with yer accusing eyes at that shop, he thought ye might mean me harm," Kate said.

"That's insane."

"Aye, but he was no' aware of that."

"How do ye ken him?" he rephrased the unanswered query.

"I cannae tell ye that." She stood straighter and set her glass down on the table.

"I insist."

"I wish to leave." She stepped toward the door, and he gently latched onto her wrist.

"Don't."

"Are ye keeping me here against my will?"

"Nae, I would never do that." Gavin shook his head.

She closed her eyes, and his free hand rose to her cheek to caress the tender skin. "Please, I want ye to trust me," he implored.

"I do, but I cannae give ye any information that might harm Will, and I ken that's what yer after."

"Why do ye protect such a villain?"

She shook her head. "Ye dinnae understand Will, and I'll never betray him because I would no' be standing here today, were it no' for him."

A shudder spread through his spine. What had she gone through that William Douglas had been the only man to save her?

The arse had not saved his brother. He had not saved any of the kids in the fire. Gavin had seen William running from the flames that night. He withdrew his hand and drew away from her, but she followed him, placing her hand on his chest.

"I ken what ye think yer are doing is the right thing, but I dinnae think ye ken Will's true nature." Her hazel eyes implored, looking for some sort of understanding he wasn't capable of giving.

Gavin rubbed at the scar on his temple. William was one man he couldn't forgive, and he needed to change the subject before fury took over.

He wanted to question her intentions with Magnus, but he didn't think she would answer. And he would wait to learn what happened tomorrow with this meeting she had somehow scheduled. He'd follow them to see where they were going, and he didn't want to mention that he knew about it because then she might change whatever plan she had concocted.

She had her secrets, and she wasn't ready to share.

Although she wouldn't confide in him, there was still something honest in her eyes as she gazed into his. She seemed to be pleading with him for understanding. He wished he could give it to her.

Clasping her hand to his, he drew it up to smell the place where her pulse beat. The familiar scent of Kate washed over him and called to the male part of him that could overlook his worries long enough to enjoy what she would willingly give.

"I would do the same for ye. I would never betray ye," she confessed, and he saw the truth in her eyes.

"I want to believe that, Kate, but how can I when ye continue to lie?"

"Ye only have to trust me." Her eyes beseeched, and he wanted to squash the doubt that he couldn't shake.

Her free hand rose to his chest in a soothing gesture, as if he were a beast to be tamed. He clasped on and moved her fingers to his side so that he could get closer. Suddenly, his body was in flames again, and everything outside this room melted away.

There was only Gavin and Kate, and he burned for her. Desire shone in her eyes.

Her lips parted, and she tilted her head up. Then he put his lips on hers—urgent, hot, demanding. Although he was still learning her, there was something comfortable and reassuring in the way they moved together as their tongues tangled and she began to come alive in his arms.

Need coursed through him and burned stronger than the most potent whisky. He pulled her flush so that he could feel the length of her body pressed to his.

They disrobed and landed on the bed in a blur of speed. When he entered her, all the tension that he'd felt since waking to find her gone evaporated. He slowed to savor every second, not wanting the completion of being inside her to end, but when it did, the explosion rocked him harder than anything he'd ever experienced.

It would be a long time before he got his fill of Kate.

As they lay together, he ran his fingers up and down her curves, learning her, memorizing every inch. He waited for her to fall asleep. For now, it was enough that she trusted him in this way, but before long, he would demand more. Because he wanted everything from her - her secrets, her desires, and her dreams.

He craved the real Kate, but soon, he'd no longer be able to tolerate the one that lied.

He'd locked the door, and the window was open. Hoping he'd wake if she attempted to leave, he finally closed his eyes.

CHAPTER 19

*K*ate woke to Gavin's fingers dancing across her flesh. As yearning built in every nerve he touched, her first thought was that only a short time had passed since they'd been intimate. But when she glanced over to the open window, it was to discover the sun rising in the sky.

She'd slept through the whole night in his room.

"Good morning." Gavin's lips curved up in a lazy, seductive smile as his eyes pinned her with need. It was heady to be wanted by such a controlled and measured man. Something about being able to undo him called to that part of her that wanted to test his limits.

She let out a sigh and stretched into his touch as he caressed her side, and tingles spread to her core. Instead of waiting for a reply, his mouth claimed hers as his hand dipped to the spot that was already craving him. He tested the wetness there, and then she felt the grin of satisfaction that spread across his mouth as he continued the embrace.

Suddenly, he was on top of her and filling her as she arched into him. As he moved in and out, his eyes never left hers, and a primal possessiveness lit in the depths of his pupils. He moved slow, drawing out every movement and driving her to a peak so fierce she lost awareness of everything except the waves of pleasure that beat at her with ecstasy.

He continued to move as if he was greedy for the response that he elicited from her. And she knew that when he left, she would be grateful for this time with him. Thankful that he'd found such bliss in her, even if it might be fleeting.

When he stiffened and cried out with his pleasure, she couldn't help the smile that reached her lips.

He stayed in her for some time before saying, "I'm glad ye didnae rush out again last night."

"Me too," she purred. And she was surprised that she meant it.

He moved and lay beside her. She turned onto her side to run her fingers up and down his bare flesh. A small patch of uneven skin on his arm caught her attention. "What happened here?"

"The fire. I got it when I tried to go back in to save the others." He shrugged it off.

"That must have been painful. Is that how ye got this too?" She trailed the line of the small, whitened scar that zagged across his temple.

"Aye." His eyes darkened, and he looked as if he were about to say something that she wouldn't like, then thought better of it and held his tongue. She hated that he couldn't trust her, but it was her fault for being who she was.

He scooted off the bed, and she felt his absence immediately. She sat up and clutched the covers over her breasts.

"We should get ye back to yer room so that ye can head down and break yer fast." Was he purposely putting distance between them?

"Are ye going to dine with us as well?"

"Nae. I have some business to see to this morning. I'll be back sometime this afternoon."

She wanted to ask but decided not to pry because she didn't want him questioning her movements today. "Then we shall meet back here later." She rose, and a blush heated her skin as he watched her retrieve her clothing.

"Aye. We will." His eyes had dilated again, and a thrill of anticipation shot through her. But not only that, he wasn't leaving yet. Gavin still wanted her.

She dressed quickly, and he gave her a small kiss before she dashed out the door toward her chamber.

Stepping in and closing the door, she sighed. Her night with Gavin had been amazing, and she'd not even panicked about being closed in, about someone sneaking into her room, or that he would leave her.

"Look at ye in the same gown as yesterday." Isobel's voice tsked in a teasing tone. The sound came from her bed. She laughed. "I ken where ye've been."

"I thought ye were staying at Camelot."

"I am, but I still needed to be certain ye are dressed properly. I cannae have Miss Clarke thinking I'm no' doing my job."

"Well, let's order a basin and get me washed up and ready. I have a busy day."

The ladies hurried through the tasks, and before long, the morning had sped by. She'd missed Gavin as the group had broken their fasts, and instead of going on the tour with the rest of their party, she returned to her room to await the time to meet Magnus in the lobby. She prayed that Stewart had journeyed out with the others because she didn't want to deal with him today.

At two, she stood in the lobby, waiting for Magnus. By the time he arrived ten minutes late, her heart had been beating like the rain during a thunderstorm. Thankfully, Stewart was not with him.

Magnus offered her his arm, "I'm looking forward to meeting this brother of yours."

"I am too. I think ye two will get along well. Ye have so much in common."

The show was on.

～

The morning had been frustrating. Well, except for waking to find Kate in his bed and claiming her body once again. He'd merely been a man with a woman who called to some primal part of him. After that, he'd become the constable and all business once more.

Upon leaving his room, he'd darted straight to the main desk to ask directions to the local watchman's office. The clerk gave him easy instructions, and he set off.

When he reached the address, a good half hour away, he strode in, confident that the man in charge would be happy to answer questions for him.

"Good day sir, I'm Constable Gavin Davidson from the Glasgow City Police Force."

"I'm Nigel. What brings ye here, Constable?" The man didn't share his title and looked suspicious of Gavin's motives.

Nigel looked to be in his early fifties, and Gavin just barely made out gray that was beginning to claim his shock of dark-red hair. He had pale skin but rosy cheeks that gave him the appearance of a jovial man who laughed often. He also wore a kilt, which instantly put Gavin at ease. He had a respect for men who tried to recover Scotland's identity after the English rules of proscription had been overturned. He always felt a calling to honor his ancestors and those who fought for the Scots independence.

"I have some questions about William Douglas." He leaned onto the counter.

"Is he in some sort of trouble?" The man's cheery disposition disappeared.

"No' yet, but I'm investigating him for some crimes, and was hoping ye might have time to give me some information on him."

"Will has his problems, but he's a good man. I don't think I can help ye." Nigel crossed his arms and stood taller.

Gavin recognized instantly that the lawman held some kind of loyalty to William and was resistant to his investigation. Pressing wouldn't help and might lead to problems later on, so he played along.

"Good to ken. I'll remember that," he said casually and smiled. "I'm also looking into a lass named Kate. I'm afraid she may be in some trouble. Do ye ken anything about her?"

"Och. I hate to hear Kate's gotten herself into something."

"Ye ken her then? I'd like to keep these men away from her, but she doesnae seem to want to listen." Gavin shook his head.

"Kate's a sweet one, kind of keeps to herself, and comes and goes. I haven't seen her around in a long time."

"Do ye think William might have information on her?" Gavin queried.

"What kind of trouble did ye say she was in?" Nigel's eyebrows knit together, and the lines on his forehead deepened.

"There's a couple of men from Glasgow that I'm investigating for murder and endangering children. I believe she's garnered their attention."

"Nae, she'd never be involved with anyone who harmed children. She brought two to live at Camelot no' too long ago because they were in some sort of trouble. I dinnae ken all the details, though."

"I dinnae think she would harm anyone. I'm worried the men might harm her."

"I'm happy to help with anyone willing to tangle with that

bunch, but I cannae give ye any more information on them." Nigel's face went blank.

"I can appreciate that."

Perhaps William was some kind of informant for the officer, but whatever the reason, it was clear the watchman wasn't going to help Gavin with that line of questioning.

"Ye should tell Will, though. He looks out for his own," Nigel insisted.

"And is Kate one of his?" he held his breath, even though he already thought he knew the answer.

"Aye. Since she was a wee thing."

"Thanks for yer time. If ye think of anything else ye can share, I'm staying at the Aberdeen Imperial Inn."

"Absolutely."

Gavin strolled from the watchman's office and clenched his fists. He wanted something to punch. No, someone. If he saw William right now, he'd let the man have years of pent-up rage and hurt.

As he headed back to the hotel, he stopped for a bite to eat since he'd skipped breaking his fast. He'd not gone for his run this morning either, and he was jumpy, like something bad was about to happen, and he wouldn't be able to stop it.

After eating, he made it back to the Aberdeen Imperial Inn, went to his chamber, and washed up before heading back outside to a spot he'd staked out earlier. It was shaded from the sight of the hotel exit but afforded him a nice view of those entering and exiting.

When Kate and Magnus exited the building, they headed in the opposite direction. He easily followed them on a fifteen-minute walk to a restaurant. Luckily, it had outdoor seating, and the pair of them were shown to a table where a man was already sitting.

He tensed. Had she taken Magnus to meet William?

It had been years since he'd seen the William, but he saw nothing resembling the boy from his youth on the newcomer's face as he drew Kate in for a hug. His body tensed at the familiar contact, but then the man released her and shook hands with Magnus.

Upon getting closer, he realized the man was too young to be his target. Who was he? Not the nine-year-old Joseph Reid, but perhaps a man claiming to be him.

Gavin moved closer but had to keep enough of a distance so that he wouldn't be seen. Kate laughed, and the men continually talked. With each moment that went by, increased dread knifed his gut and twisted.

Whatever Kate was up to was more dangerous than she could ever know. It was imperative that he find out who she truly was and keep a close eye on her.

Magnus Fordice was not a man to be toyed with.

CHAPTER 20

The midday sun bathed the day with a warm light. A whisper of a breeze kissed the air and set Kate's nerves at ease. As she and Magnus strolled toward the restaurant, they spoke of what they liked about the different cities they'd visited, influential figures they both "knew," and about the theater scene.

When they approached their destination, relief reached her. Callum waited for them at the outdoor seating. With his dark, wavy hair, bold, blue eyes, and strong build, he stood out among the crowd. Dressed for the part, he looked every inch a wealthy, sophisticated merchant with a taste for the finer things. No one would know he was a whisky smuggler with a penchant for finding trouble and always making others laugh.

Callum's twin, Cole, was the serious, brooding type, but Callum had a mischievous streak. And although she'd bonded with both of them over the years when she'd stayed at Camelot, Callum was the one who could change his persona like her. Only a year younger than her, he retained a boyish charm that most men lost during the gangly growing phase. His mind was quick, and he had a clever tongue to match it with a talent for worming his way out of treacherous situations.

Her plan was going to work.

The smell of fresh-baked bread mingled with the scent of spices as they navigated through the tables of many patrons who were out to drink in the temperate and peaceful weather.

The setting was perfect, as she'd known it would be. Magnus looked like a strutting peacock. He was enjoying the attention.

Callum stood to greet them and pulled her in for a long warm hug. "Allison, I'm pleased ye were able to come into the city."

"I as well, brother." She smiled, then turned to her mark.

"Joseph, allow me to introduce ye. This is Magnus Fordice." She gave her best smile. "Magnus, this is my brother, Joseph Reid."

"Such a pleasure to meet ye. Please sit, I've ordered their best wine." Callum winked, his charisma on full display.

"Of course," Magnus said, thrilled by the attention Callum was bestowing upon him. She was happy to witness him employing some of the tricks she'd taught him.

She'd written to Callum with a detailed report only a couple of days ago to give him all the information he'd need to make Magnus's pride swell as he thought they were flattering him. First up were the people in high places that he'd like to meet.

"Magnus has never met the Sutherland family. They would be so fortunate to make his acquaintance. Do ye think we can arrange some time together next time we're all available and in the area?"

"Oh, aye. I was just there, and Donnie was looking for some connections in the Glasgow area." She had to hand it to Callum for using a shortened version of Donald Sutherland's name to make it look as if they were well-acquainted, despite none of them ever having met the man.

She could almost see Magnus drooling over the thought of having the Sutherlands as close friends and business allies.

They conversed for a while as the food was brought, the wine was consumed, and Callum charmed Magnus. She'd slowly sipped on one glass of the expensive wine and paced herself, but Callum and Magnus were almost through their third when Callum baited the hook.

"I'm disheartened to say I may not be coming back to Aberdeen for some time. We may have to put off that meeting."

"Why's that?" Magnus questioned, his cheeks flushed from the spirits.

"My deal fell through, and I'll not be able to purchase the building I was hoping for. Without it, and it being so hard to find property for sale on the west end of town, I'll have to wait for another opportunity."

Magnus took a long sip on his wine.

"Oh, Joseph. I hate to hear that. I do love coming to Aberdeen." Kate tossed in a sigh for good measure.

"I have a building at 4008 Skene Street. Is that far enough west? I'm willing to sell it." Magnus looked eager to part with the parcel.

"Aye. I've seen Skene Street. I'd need to go by to check the condition, but I'm intrigued." Callum gave another casual wink.

"I have to warn you, the tenants are giving me lots of trouble, and I'm in the process of evicting some of them."

"That's easy enough to deal with." Callum waved a hand in the air as if dismissing the inhabitants like a swarm of flies.

"I think ye'd be doing me a favor by taking it." Magnus laughed.

Callum rubbed his chin. "Ye might make this trip worth it, after all. Do ye mind if I investigate it this afternoon?"

"Nae. Be my guest," Magnus insisted.

Kate wanted to sing. Magnus was in.

The men began discussing prices and locations, and she finally allowed herself to relax and have a bit more of the wine to celebrate.

Magnus was finishing his last glass when Callum said, "I have to leave early Friday morning for Inverness. If the building is to my liking, can ye settle tomorrow? I ken it's soon, but that way, I'll have my men start on it, and I can come back in a couple of months to check on progress. Then, mayhap I can convince Donnie to come down, and ye can join us for a few days."

"I can do that. But I'm not certain I can have the paperwork prepared in time."

"Not to worry. I have a man here who can work miracles. He can handle all the details."

Magnus looked skeptical, but he had no way to know that Kate had had everything they needed ready to sign a month ago and a fake office space rented in an exclusive area of the city, waiting for Will's accountant to seal the deal.

"He's Donnie's numbers man as well, competent and thorough." Callum leaned in. "And he won't work for just anybody. I pay out of the pocket to keep him on retainer."

"Aye, then. If ye like the property, I can settle tomorrow."

They finished out the plans for meeting the next day. After standing to go, Callum drew her in for another warm hug, then gave Magnus a firm handshake.

As she and her mark strolled back to the inn, she breathed a sigh of relief. One more step down. Camelot was almost saved.

⁓

G avin watched from his hiding place as the three people he'd been studying for more than two hours stood and began saying goodbye. Magnus had seemed pleased with whatever conversation they were having, and he'd had more wine than Gavin thought the man had been capable of drinking.

Kate and Magnus headed back toward the inn, but he focused on the well-dressed man who they'd dined with. He strolled off in the opposite direction. Gavin waited until he wouldn't be seen, then covertly trailed the dark-haired stranger.

Five minutes later, his mood darkened further as he found himself still following the man onto Skene Street. He'd seen the name before, in his notes. This was the street where William Douglas lived. As the dark-haired man approached 4008 Skene Street, another man looking just like him exited the building and greeted him. The newcomer's clothing didn't look as if it had come from the finest tailor, and his brow wrinkled as he took in Kate's dining partner's attire.

Twins, Gavin thought. Cole and Callum Campbell were listed in his research as possibly being smugglers in an illicit whisky operation. He'd bet that Magnus had no idea who he'd been dining with. The pair headed into the building.

This was where the Camelot Crew lived. What the hell was Kate up to? The more he dug, the more questions he had. But the thought that solidified in his head was that when Magnus found out what she was about, Kate was going to be his next target.

Gavin made himself more comfortable by settling onto a bench at a park across the street. He settled in to watch from the spot that just barely afforded him a view of the entrance to William Douglas's building. It was late in the afternoon before he saw the face that had haunted him for years.

The one who had left him for dead in a field near the orphanage.

William's shoulder-length black hair was a touch lighter than Gavin's pitch hair, but he could still remember that William's eyes were a deeper blue. They'd almost looked like brothers when they were younger, a lifetime ago.

Once, they'd been friends.

The sun was descending, and although he knew he'd miss the evening meal with Kate, he followed William at a comfortable distance as he walked through one neighborhood after another, heading into businesses, staying a while, then going on to the next. As he made his way down the streets, most people ignored him or moved to the side and let him pass without speaking.

William had been a bit of a loner as a child, but it seemed to have worsened over the years. Except with the people who lived at Camelot. Those criminals gave him undying allegiance; apparently, so did the local watchmen. Gavin shook his head.

His thoughts turned to Kate, and he wondered how they'd met, then not for the first time, how William had ended up here with an apartment full of derelicts and children that should be in good homes.

He shuddered as he imagined what a child in that place went through.

It was late in the evening when William made his way back home. As he stepped onto the landing before heading into his building, he turned and glanced to where Gavin stood. He had a thin smile on his face and his head almost imperceptibly dipped. Was it possible the man had seen him?

William's intense study remained in the shadows for what seemed like an eternity before he broke the connection and disappeared inside.

By the time Gavin made it back to the hotel, the party from the Stonehavens' had long since gone to bed. He tried

Kate's door, but unlike the broken one at the Stonehaven estate, it was locked.

He made it to his bed, weary and with a bolder in his belly, despite only eating the small meal this morning.

Gavin rubbed the rough skin where he'd been burned by the fire, a reminder that he had to be prepared at all times. Tomorrow, he would rise early to run.

He had the awful premonition that something unimaginable was coming, and he wasn't going to be fast enough to stop it.

CHAPTER 21

*L*ight filtered through the open window and let Kate know that the day was beginning. She'd lain awake for what felt like hours. Sleep had been elusive as she'd thought about what could go wrong today and . . . what could go right.

Anything to keep her mind off Gavin's absence.

He'd disappeared yesterday and not returned. Was he already preparing to say goodbye, or had he left already? And why was she letting it get to her? She was planning on retreating as soon as her plan was complete, and it was safe to do so.

She rose and pulled on her gown, then paced the room. She'd imagined her doorknob jiggled during the dark hours of last eve, but it must have been her imagination. She'd been hoping Gavin would come for her, but no knock sounded, and she'd convinced herself that she must have heard something else in the hall.

One more day, and she'd be on her way somewhere where no one could find her. She'd need to disappear once all was done. Magnus and his sons would come looking for retribution, but there would be nothing they could do.

Yesterday had been the hardest part.

Now, if today went as planned, she'd soon be on her way to collect the remainder of her things at the Stonehavens' and then she'd make an excuse to leave. This version of Allison Reid would disappear as if she never existed.

If Gavin hadn't left, Kate could stay with him until he was done with her. She'd risk going to Glasgow to spend more time with him, but the idea that he'd want her after he knew what she was capable of was laughable.

Perhaps it was better if she didn't see him again.

Her silly eyes watered at the thought.

It felt like another hour of pacing and worrying passed before a light rapping came at the door. She rushed to the portal and swung it wide. Disappointment returned as Isobel strolled in.

"I thought ye'd still be in bed." Isobel strode in.

"Nae. I couldnae sleep." She rubbed her arms and hugged herself.

"Are we still going back to the Stonehaven estate tomorrow?"

"Aye. We'll return with everyone else."

Kate had figured that would give Will's man enough time to shutter the fake office and get the paperwork filed in the proper places. She couldn't let Magnus know anything was amiss until everything had been registered and it was too late for him to stop the process.

"And after a day, I'll need to leave, but ye stay close to Miss Clarke, and if anyone asks, ye dinnae ken where I went. Ye were only filling in after Flora left, and ye didnae ken me before."

She'd never thought of Isobel being in danger by association, but it was best if she claimed not to know her.

"All the servants think that already, so ye have nothing to worry about. As far as the world outside of Camelot kens, we'd never met until last week."

"Good girl. Keep it that way," Kate instructed.

"Aye."

"Now, help me dress, please. I have work to do this morning."

A little while later, Kate strolled into the dining room. As she sat between Magnus and Irene Bartrom, she talked about anything except the coming deal. She'd left all the business talk to Callum yesterday, even though she'd planned the specifics. She didn't want to appear to be any part of the negotiations, just as a man of Magnus's stature would think. To him, she was a woman, only something to be placed out for viewing and bed play.

He was going to be livid with rage when he discovered the truth. And she guessed Gavin was correct; Magnus was probably capable of taking a human life. It was why she would have to be long gone before then.

Their party was done with the meal by the time Gavin strolled in. He hadn't left. Relief flooded her as his stare met hers, then took in the people at her side. He looked disappointed but also a little bit agitated. He was forced to sit at the opposite end of the table, where Mr. Clarke pulled him into some conversation.

Her companions rose, and she followed. It was time for her and Magnus to head to their appointment.

Mr. Clarke kept talking to Gavin, oblivious to the rest of the patrons dispersing. It was probably best that she didn't have to come up with some lie about where she was going. If Gavin asked in front of Magnus, he might expose her ruse, and she couldn't risk it, so she rushed ahead, thinking to avoid him.

She'd have to seek out Gavin upon her return. Then it would be time to celebrate, and she could spend the rest of the day giving him all her attention.

She took Magnus's arm, and they strolled from the hotel. The twenty-minute walk was a blur as they spoke about travel and the latest news. They were suddenly close to the location she'd chosen for Will's man to set up an office that would appear official.

"What was that street number again?" she asked, purposely pretending as if she knew nothing of the area that they were in.

"Just ahead, number 205."

"Does Stewart usually accompany ye on yer deals?"

"He typically does, but . . ." Magnus was interrupted when a group of children ran by and bumped into them.

"Miscreants," Magnus blurted as the lads continued on. He turned back around. "Ah, here we are." He pulled the door open and ushered her inside.

It only took a moment to locate the office. Once they entered, it was to find Callum and Will's businessman already in place.

Time seemed to slow down as they all sat around a large desk, discussing the specifics of how the transaction worked. Will's man was well-versed in the process, but this was one area she had no expertise in, so she sat back and let the words wash over her as the deal was made.

Magnus believed that he was getting a large sum of money for the property, but a nominal amount would reach his account in actuality. She was thankful to Will's man for figuring this part of the plan out. Apparently, something had to exchange hands to make the transaction seem legitimate if Magnus challenged it later on.

She'd amassed a decent sum of money over the years, and she'd easily offered up her entire savings for the plan. Camelot was worth it.

What felt like an eternity later, every paper was signed, and the deed transferred.

"It was a pleasure working with you all," Will's man said as he stood and opened the door for them.

"I think we might develop a strong partnership," Callum boasted as he patted Magnus on the back.

"I'm looking forward to our next meeting," Magnus returned, as his cheeks puffed with a smile.

But Kate knew Magnus would most likely never see Callum or his look-a-like Cole again. By the time that the Fordices learned of their treachery, she would be gone to France, and her accomplice, along with his twin, would be off on a whisky smuggling mission. There would be no one in Aberdeen who could explain how Camelot had been left in an irrevocable trust to a minor boy.

Kate smiled. "Brother, we'll have to reach out to the Sutherlands. Perhaps they will even invite all of us to Dunrobin Castle for a stay. I ken the spring is a beautiful time there."

She'd never seen the famed stronghold of the Sutherlands, but she'd heard stories, and although the deal was signed, she had to keep up appearances until she could safely vanish.

"What a splendid idea. Magnus, would ye be interested in planning something for the spring?" Callum asked.

"I would enjoy that."

Callum pushed the door and held it for them all to exit. Clouds had swallowed the sun, and although the light was abundant the skies were darkening with the threat of rain.

"Great. I will reach out and make the arrangements. Sister, can ye accompany me on my next bit of business?" Callum glanced at her, then back at Magnus. "Do ye mind if I steal her for a while before we have to say our goodbyes? I fear my travel will keep me from home for some time."

"No. I understand deep familial bonds." Magnus reached out with his hand. "I look forward to our next meeting."

"I do as well," Callum replied as they shook.

They turned to head in the direction of Camelot as Magnus began his trek back to the hotel.

She could barely contain her excitement. With the help of Callum and Will's man, she'd pulled it off. Their home was safe, and all would be well.

As they strolled down the street, ominous thunder boomed as it announced a pending storm.

~

Gavin stayed perched in the doorway of a building almost a full block from the door that Magnus and Kate had entered. They'd been in there for about two hours before they finally appeared again, along with one of the dark-haired twins from yesterday. Gavin had almost lost patience and determined he might have to enter the building to learn if they were still there.

The twin and Magnus shook hands, then the group parted. Gavin's curiosity was piqued further as Kate left with the man from Camelot, and Magnus moved in the direction of the inn and toward where he'd positioned himself behind a column. He turned to determine if he could exit and rush away before Magnus reached him or if he'd have to stay hidden until the man passed.

He'd wanted to follow Kate, but that wouldn't be possible until Magnus had moved his position. After he glanced in the other direction, Gavin's breath caught as Stewart came into view along with another man, one he'd not questioned yet, but observed in Glasgow.

It was Thomas Fordice, the younger son, the one whose proclivities had driven him on this quest for justice.

Gavin stayed hidden as the group met up, so close that he could hear the conversation.

"Thomas, you made it. How are you feeling?" Magnus's voice was airy and pleased.

"Much better."

"I wasn't expecting you for a few more days."

"I healed after Mother insisted that we go to the Glasgow Weaver Inn. She said the broth there heals any ailment, and I think she's correct," Thomas replied.

Magnus gave a hearty bark of laughter. "Yes. She swears by that place but keeps it a secret. She said if everyone knew, we'd never be able to get a room."

"Mother is back at the Aberdeen Imperial Inn. I thought I'd bring Thomas to witness the deal, but it seems we're not in time." Stewart cut in.

"You just missed the Reids. That's them turning the corner now."

Gavin couldn't look, but he imagined Magnus pointing to Kate and the twin farther down the street.

"Who was that lady? She looks familiar," Thomas said.

"That's Allison Reid. She's quite the beauty."

"Aye, she is." There was a longing in Stewart's voice that set Gavin's nerves on edge.

"Stewart, perhaps ye should court her. I do like her family," Magnus continued.

"Did ye say, Allison Reid? What was the man's name?" Thomas's voice quaked with what seemed like alarm.

"That's her brother, Joseph."

"Nae. Where are they going?"

Was it anger that had crept into Thomas's tone?

"I didn't ask," Magnus said.

"I didn't get a good look at her that day, but I think . . ." Thomas paused as though he was trying to piece things together. "She's the one who caused the problems."

Doubt crept into Magnus's tone. "What do ye mean?"

"She may be the one who saw me with the children and took them away." After another pause, Thomas hissed, "I'm certain of it now."

"What are you two on about?" Stewart sounded confused.

"Surely not. She wouldn't have anything to do with that band of misfits."

What the hell was going on? What had Kate seen? Thomas sounded as if he wanted to challenge Kate to a duel.

"Let's follow them to see where they go. Stewart, go check on your mother and let her know we'll be back shortly," Magnus ordered.

It appeared as if Stewart might lack knowledge of his brother's and father's activities.

Boots pounded on the pavement as the two men took off to trail Kate and the twin as Stewart kept going toward the inn. Gavin emerged from his spot and shadowed the pair as they beat down the sidewalks. They were so intent on following Kate that he wasn't worried about being seen; still, he kept a discreet pace behind them.

When they finally stopped, he noticed the park looked familiar. It was the one where he'd watched Kate yesterday. But this time instead of heading into the building, Kate had stopped, and she was down on her knees hugging two younger children, a girl and a boy, who had just been running around with a group of others.

The girl looked to almost be of teenage years, and the boy still a young child, possibly ten years at most. Instinct told him they were the real Allison and Joseph Reid.

His eyes flicked back to the men who had followed her. Magnus and Thomas both had red faces as waves of fury seemed to emanate from them. He could no longer hear what they were saying, but he could tell all the rage was directed at Kate.

He imagined if the twin weren't there and several other men hadn't joined the crowd outside, the Fordices would pounce and do something dreadful to Kate.

William stepped into the park, and Gavin's blood turned from ice-cold worry to full-on inferno in a heartbeat. Kate released her grip on the children and stood to face William. Gavin was luckily off to a spot that afforded him a view of the sides of both their faces.

Kate smiled at Will, but there was something sad in her eyes. She handed him the stack of papers she'd been carrying since leaving the other building. William took them but looked confused, then his face darkened. He said something that had Kate glancing down at the ground, ashamed—but only for a moment before she pointed to the two children, then threw some challenging words of her own back at William.

William's gaze darted around the park. The King of the Streets turned back to Kate. Gavin wished he could hear what was being said, but William motioned, and the crowd dispersed. Kate followed them as they headed into 4008 Skene Street.

Staying in his spot, Gavin watched as the Fordice men argued for a little while, then headed back toward the inn. Until he knew what had happened exactly, he'd have to be certain Kate stayed well away from them because if there was ever a man capable of murder, it was the older Fordice. Even from across the park, Gavin could read the ill intent radiating from Magnus's eyes.

What had Kate done?

Gavin moved to the spot he'd taken before and waited for Kate to reemerge. When she did, hours later, it was with Isobel and both twins, who escorted the ladies back to the inn. There, the men turned and left as Kate and the maid entered.

He hurried inside to make certain he reached Kate before the Fordice men. The lobby was empty, so he rushed upstairs just as the door to the lasses' chamber shut. He had his hand on the knob before they could latch the door.

He pushed it in.

"I need ye to come with me, Kate."

Both ladies' eyes were wide with surprise. He didn't care. Kate had lied to him too many times, and now she was in danger for it. She was about to tell him everything.

"Isobel, will ye please inform the other guests that Miss Reid is not feeling well and won't be at the evening meal, then have food and wine sent to my room?"

Isobel said, "Aye, I think 'tis a good idea."

The lass looked at Kate as if she knew of the danger facing her as well. Isobel's eyes were pink and slightly puffy, as if she'd been crying recently. His gaze shot to meet Kate's, and he was surprised to find wariness there, but her shoulders were tall and proud.

Isobel took Kate in a fierce embrace, which seemed to shock her, but then Kate slowly wrapped her arms around the lass and returned the hug.

"Everything is going to be all right," Kate reassured Isobel.

"Yes. It will," Isobel replied, pulling back. She glanced at him and smiled, then rushed from the room.

"Come." Gavin held the door and peeked out into the hall. It was empty. "Lock the door," he instructed.

When he finally had her safe and secured away in his room, the tension released from his shoulders, but the fury at her actions returned.

"Tell me what ye've been doing," he demanded.

"Touring the city." She met his gaze straight on and blinked twice.

Fury exploded in his head. He clenched and unclenched his fists as his mind ventured down the path of wondering what she'd done to make herself the target of a murderer.

She was not leaving this room until she told him everything.

She wasn't going anywhere until he knew she was safe.

CHAPTER 22

*K*ate's body trembled. The rush from completing her mission had dissipated with Will's anger and subsequent lecture about her putting herself in harm's way. She'd somehow earned Gavin's ire as well.

The rain had yet to start, but the cold had moved in ahead of it, and it seeped into her bones. This was supposed to be a joyous day, and all these men kept ruining it.

Gavin paced as she strode over to the window to push it open and inhale the cool air. What did he know? Waves of anger wafted from him like plumes of smoke from a chimney, one that harbored the hottest of fires.

She took another calming breath, then turned and ambled to his table to sit. She'd faced Will's rage. She could face down Gavin's, although he might toss her in jail once he learned what she'd done. She no longer cared.

Her family was safe.

Everything had been set in motion, and Camelot now belonged to Joseph Reid. Those children would be loved and cared for at Camelot, and they could now use the proceeds from renting out the other rooms to finance the education of all the children.

"Are ye angry with me?" She had finally had enough of his pacing and had to start the conversation.

"Kate." He sat at the chair opposite her and ran his fingers through his hair. "Honestly, I dinnae ken what I am right now."

She pursed her lips and averted her gaze.

"I need ye to start with what ye were doing with Magnus and one of those twins yesterday and today."

She almost said Callum, but she wasn't going to implicate anyone even if Gavin had guessed where they'd come from. "I was securing the future of two children." She opted for part of the truth, then stuck her chin in the air and glanced away.

He slammed a fist down on the table. The thud jarred her, and she flinched. When she glanced back at him, he'd pinned her with such anger that she wished to go back and endure more of Will's verbal lashing.

"I want the whole truth, and we're not leaving here until I have it all."

She gulped.

"Ye have figured out that I ken Will. I'm sorry ye have a problem with him, but he's a good man." Although she didn't want to defend him at the moment, she was loyal.

Gavin only nodded, then stared, waiting for her to continue. She caved to his dark scrutiny.

"I dropped two children on his doorstep several months ago."

She knew Gavin viewed the world in terms of right and wrong, but perhaps he would have some sympathy if she explained everything.

"Allison and Joseph Reid?"

She nodded. "I took them from a bad situation. Ye ken I'm no' Allie, that I'm just Kate." A lump stuck in her throat, and she blocked back tears at admitting who she was. A weight settled on her chest.

"I pretended to be her so that I could ensure that she and her brother were always looked after." She dug her fingernails into her palms to halt the tears that pricked at the back of her eyes.

"And how did ye do that?" Gavin leaned back in the chair and crossed his arms.

"By tricking Magnus into giving the deed to a building to Joseph."

Gavin's eyes shut and he buried his head behind his fingers as he shook back and forth. He was disappointed. He dropped his hands and glowered at her.

"Do ye ken what he'll do to ye when he finds out?" Gavin hissed as his anger returned.

"I plan on being gone. He won't ken until 'tis too late."

"Ye are wrong. He already kens." Gavin's abrasive tone was accusing, and she wasn't certain if he was directing his fury at her for being a criminal or for being careless.

Chills erupted on her neck. "Nae. He cannae ken yet."

"He followed ye back to William's place today."

The blood drained from her face, and a wave of dizziness swamped her. A knock sounded at the door, and she jumped. Her hands began to tremble.

Gavin calmly stood and strode toward the exit. Fear invaded as she imagined Magnus behind the door, then clarity struck. It wouldn't matter what happened to her—the children and Camelot were safe. She sat taller.

Two young men dashed in with trays of food and wine. Relief rushed in as a glass was set in front of her and filled with wine. She reached for the liquid, realizing she'd not had anything to drink since early in the morning. Her mouth and lips were parched with thirst.

The ruby liquid filled her mouth and throat as Gavin closed the door behind the hotel staff.

"Why would he follow me? Were ye following me?" When they'd left the building, everything had been fine.

"Aye. Of course, I followed, and if I hadn't, I wouldn't ken that Thomas Fordice appeared after yer meeting and had some foul things to say about ye."

"Nae. He can't be here."

Fear spiked in her chest. Her acquaintance at the Fordice home was supposed to continue putting small doses of the laxative medication in his drink through today. He couldn't be here.

"Well, he is. How do ye ken Thomas?" Gavin took a long sip of wine and studied her.

"We've never really met," she spoke the truth.

"Then how did he recognize ye today?"

She inhaled and shut her eyes. The horrid scene played in her mind yet again.

When she glanced back at Gavin, genuine curiosity glittered back at her. His irritation with her had dissipated, and she realized Gavin might be the only thing keeping her safe until she could get away. He was a man of the law, and although she'd kidnapped two children, it had been for their safety. Surely, he would recognize that.

"I caught him in the act of molesting children, and I took them away from him," she admitted.

Storms erupted in Gavin's eyes. His rage reemerged, hotter and more intense than it had been before.

Perhaps she'd been wrong to give him the truth.

G avin's nerves fired with wrath as the weight of her words struck him. Thomas was a monster. Then, astonishment set in as Kate's confession hit home. She had been the answer all along, the one who held the evidence to get Thomas off the street and away from innocent children.

Kate was the witness he needed.

And now, she'd put herself at risk by prodding the beast that was Magnus Fordice.

"Ye have to come back to Glasgow with me."

Panic filled her gaze, and she stood. "Nae. I'm no' going anywhere." She stood and sprinted toward the door, but he sprung up to catch her, afraid that if she made it through the exit, he'd never see her again.

"Where are ye going?"

She began to pull it open, but the lock stopped her, then he flattened his hand on it so that she couldn't unlatch and pull it in.

"Are ye going to put me in prison?" Fear colored Kate's question.

"For what?"

She spun in the space between him and the door to face him. He as so close, he could smell her intoxicating scent.

"Take yer pick. Stealing the kids, forging documents, impersonating people." Now defeat sizzled in her hazel gaze.

It was true—she'd done some unethical things, but they no longer seemed black and white to him. Her whole purpose had been to protect others in the only way she knew how. This wasn't like every other case he'd worked. It wasn't a matter of her misdeeds because, through them, he'd found the answer to put away the true evil.

"Nae," he soothed.

She glanced away.

"I want ye to turn king's evidence on Thomas Fordice. That's why I came to the house party. To locate a servant who would speak out against the Fordices. I have found no one willing to do so."

Fear was evident in her eyes. "I can't." She shook her head. "I have to get far away. They'll kill me before I have the chance."

"Nae. Ye can stay with me. I'll protect ye." He reached out to trace her cheek.

"Ye won't say that when ye ken who I am."

"And who is that, Kate?"

"I'm the daughter of a whore." Her voice shook as she tilted her chin high. Despite the defiance in the words, her pretty lip quivered. Kate's face was ashen, and she appeared wobbly on her feet.

She leaned into the door as if defeat had won.

"Ye cannae help who ye were born to." He took her trembling fingers and pulled her over to the bed to sit next to him on the mattress.

She continued as her eyes began to water, "I told ye what she did to me when we moved to Aberdeen."

He nodded, holding onto her hand as he studied the pain in her frightened stare. He wanted to comfort her and tell her she didn't have to relive the painful memories. He understood ghosts from the past that never went away, but he had to know why she kept everyone at a distance. And he didn't want her to do the same with him.

"Once we arrived, she found us a place to stay with a man I didnae ken. He locked me in a room, and they only opened the door to give me scraps from the table. I was so scared that for days, I lied about my hunger. When he let me out of the room, I told them the truth. I was so hungry my belly ached and that I felt sick and I wanted to go home."

She paled, and the hand he wasn't holding had subconsciously rested on her stomach. Kate took a deep breath and continue, "Afterward, my mom took me for a walk to a bakery. She purchased a loaf of bread for me, then instructed me to wait on a bench and eat it as she went into another shop."

"I devoured it as I sat and waited. Hours passed. She never came back." Kate's lip quavered.

He closed his eyes, remembering being left by his parents. At least they'd left him at a home where they had assumed that he'd be cared for. "Hell, how old were ye?"

"Almost ten."

"That is so unfair."

She glanced away and stared at something on the floor. "She left because I told her the truth. If I'd kept my mouth shut or told her I was happy, she wouldnae have left me."

A sudden clarity rocked him. This was how she'd learned to lie so easily. It was her way of coping with what had been done to her. She used her deceptions to protect herself.

He cupped her chin in his hand to turn her gaze back to his. He was stunned by the moisture that clouded her eyes, but she took a deep breath and didn't let the tears fall.

She squared her shoulders and said, "My own mother didnae want me."

"*I* want ye."

She blinked a few times and met his scrutiny straight on. Confusion mingled with her multicolored eyes.

"Nae. Ye're just saying that. When ye realize what I am, ye'll leave."

"Kate, I will always want ye to stay with me." He traced his thumb on her cheek, and she turned into the touch.

He released her hand and pulled the pins from her hair. He didn't think he had the words to comfort her, so he wanted to show her what she meant to him. When her hair fell free, he stared directly into her eyes and said, "I won't leave ye."

His mouth closed on hers, and the intensity of the embrace bowled him over. This wasn't like the kisses they'd shared in the past—yes, the passion was still there, but there was so much more. It was like they were one now, and they completed each other.

He let their contact sweep him away as the scent of warm, spiced oranges and gardenias invaded his senses. He'd never desired like this—as if his whole body were on fire with energy that craved not to be set free but to be captured and held by the lady in his arms.

She softened, and her arms closed around him. The same need pulsated back at him as her fingers tightened on his leg. She seemed to hunger for him the way he did her as if she were the drink of life, and he'd not truly been whole until he'd found sanctuary in her arms.

This was the real Kate, unfiltered, unedited, and as honest as the golden setting sun. He craved her like the trees did the life-giving rays of that fiery mass. He drew her to standing and unbuttoned her gown.

He didn't want to return to a world without her in it.

CHAPTER 23

*A*s rain pounded on the pavement outside, Gavin peeled the last of Kate's clothes from her body. She shivered as his dark gaze focused on her with an intensity that melted her core. She stood unclothed before him, but her heart was also unadorned with her usual defenses. He regarded her as if she were more than the refuse that had been left out on the streets, and his interest made her feel cherished and wanted.

She'd told him the truth, and so far, he'd not deserted her. Only time would tell, but for now, she was going to bask in the desire in his eyes, soak it up and bathe in its power as long as she could.

As he watched her, she leaned back on the bed to observe him undressing. Fire erupted in her center as his erection popped free from his breeches and showed the evidence of his appetite for her. Hunger overwhelmed her as he moved onto the bed, crawled toward her, and leaned down to place searing kisses on her neck.

She tilted her head to give him better access.

"Tell me ye'll come home with me, Kate," he whispered in her ear, then nibbled at her lobe.

A sigh escaped her throat as her body and her heart filled with emotions and sensations that sent her spiraling into bliss. His hot breath scorched her as he said, "I want ye to come with me."

He bit down again, and need—intense, raw, and naked—racked her senses.

"I will never leave ye, Kate."

So much emotion washed over her that a tear bubbled over and fell down her cheek. The thought that he wanted her to return to his special place with him stunned her.

"Yes." Her breathy reply was all she could muster in the face of the overwhelming feelings assailing her. He wanted her in a way no one else ever had, and it left her bare and exposed and needy.

"Say it again, Kate. Say ye'll come to stay with me." His rough hand slid down her taut belly, leaving a feverish wake of sensation as his fingers found the nub at her center.

She gasped, then her tremulous reply burst from her lips, "Yes. I'll go with ye."

He drew back, and his gaze pinned her with a thirst that parched her. His head dipped as his lips landed on hers, and his tongue delved into her mouth and began a dance with hers. She met the strokes with a heated fervor that washed away everything else but this moment with him.

One finger entered her as his thumb stroked her core. She arched into every inch of him that she could reach. With each pulse and stroke, he heaved her further into the sweet abyss of just being.

She was close to reaching her peak when he pulled free of her mouth and her passage. He lay prone on the bead and drew her up to straddle him. As she sank onto his penis, she threw her head back as he filled her more completely than ever. She gasped at the pressure, and he groaned as his mouth fell open.

He stilled and studied her to see what she would do. She'd

not known this position was possible, but it gave her a power she'd not held before. She wiggled her hips from side to side, and his eyes fluttered with the pleasure she was giving him. The sight and feel only increased her desire.

She made the move several more times before switching and finding a rhythm of moving up and back that hit deep inside her, while stroking the sensitive area at the apex of her passage. Pure bliss rocked her as she gazed down at Gavin. His hands clasped onto the flesh of her rear and encouraged her onward. He appeared enthralled by her movements, captivated by her, and his words echoed in her head. "I will never leave ye, Kate."

And she knew in that instant that she loved him.

With everything in her, everything she'd ever held back from anyone else.

She'd never allowed herself to love another, but he'd broken through her barriers and reached the part of her she'd hidden away all those years ago. He had become her world, and she was lost in the exploration of her new home . . . Gavin. She'd never had a place of her own, or at least, one where she felt comfortable enough to stay.

He'd said the words to her that no one else had ever thought to say. The ones that drove away all her fears and made her feel wanted, desired, loved. Moans of pure bliss escaped as her body began to convulse around him. As waves of ecstasy wrapped her in deep oblivion, the only thing she was certain of was that her soul had found its match.

Gavin was captivated as Kate climaxed above him. She was sensual and mesmerizing as bliss claimed her, and she stilled. The muscles in her sheath contracted around him. He fought his own need to climax, wanting to continue to revel in the clenching of her completion.

The real Kate was now irrevocably his. And he knew he'd never get enough of her. He would always want her by his side. She'd opened to him in a way he was certain she'd never done with another, and the feeling was heady as if he'd been given a drug that he knew he would crave for the rest of his life.

He was addicted to Kate.

Staying buried deep within her, he coiled an arm around her waist and flipped so that now he was on top and in control of their movements. It dawned on him that in the game they'd been playing, she'd been in control the whole time. Kate had easily and thoroughly won him over.

He thrust in and out of her in slow, measured movements, letting her slick passage massage his cock and drive him so far into oblivion that he couldn't tell where she began, and he ended.

His last thought before pleasure exploded in every part of his body was that she'd agreed to come home with him. She was completely and utterly his, and he would have her by his side the rest of his days.

Perhaps they had both won.

His seed filled her as the ripples of ecstasy assailed him.

When he finally collapsed on top of her, he was spent and sated and fulfilled, but somehow, he knew it would never be enough. She was now the center of his world.

She would always be his mission from here on out. Keeping her safe with him and letting her know that she was cared for and that he'd never leave. She deserved that.

Rolling over, he drew her into the space between his arm and chest. "I cannae wait until ye see my home. Ye're going to love it."

"I'm sure I will as long as ye are there."

They talked into the wee hours of the night about his ideas for farming, the city of Glasgow, and how the events might play out in court with the Fordices. By the time she fell asleep, he was certain their life together was going to be perfect.

He drifted off, thinking that tomorrow, they would return to the Stonehaven estate, collect their belongings, then head toward Glasgow. He didn't want to try to apprehend the Fordice men with Kate close by. She was now in too much danger to let them anywhere near her.

When they reached Glasgow, he would discuss the best way to bring the criminals in with a proper force supporting his efforts. After all, the Fordices would have to return to Glasgow soon. It was their home as well.

CHAPTER 24

*V*oices and laughter from the street filtered through the open window, rousing Kate from a deep, dreamless sleep. She blinked and stretched, her body deliciously sated and rested. Rays of gold sunlight peered through, shortening the shadows of the room. The rain had stopped, and it appeared a beautiful day was on the horizon.

Fresh wood and bergamot enveloped her, the powerful male fragrance that made every nerve in her body snap to life. She burrowed into the covers to inhale the scent. She was still in Gavin's room. A smile crept onto her face as she turned to look at him.

Gavin's spot on the bed was empty.

Her heart thudded in her chest as a wave of nausea invaded. Where was he?

Had he left her?

She took a deep breath. She told herself the fear that gripped her was irrational. He'd said he wouldn't leave, and Gavin didn't lie. As she rose, and with trembling fingers pulled on her chemise, she noted that his trunk was still in the room.

Heartbeat slowing, she padded over to the desk where a methodically scrolled note lay dead center.

Dinnae leave the room. I'll be back shortly.

G.

She held the paper to her chest, sighed, and let the anxiety go. He was coming back.

A few minutes later, she heard voices in the hall and the key in the lock, and then the door swung open.

Gavin strode through with two of the hotel staff plodding in behind him. One held a tray of food and the other a basin to wash with. They set the items down, and Gavin gave both of them a coin before they turned and left the room.

"Good morning," she said, rushing up to him and throwing her arms around him. He smelled of the outdoors and exercise. "Have ye been out running?"

"Aye," was all he said before his mouth landed on hers in a fierce, possessive kiss.

"I almost didnae find yer note."

"I'm glad ye did. I was worried ye would leave the room before I got back. We have much to discuss. Let me sponge off, and we can break our fast."

Kate plopped into one of the chairs and watched as Gavin stripped from his shirt and sponged off his chest and upper extremities. The sinew of his muscles bulged and glided as he reached to cleanse his body.

Once done, he drew on a fresh shirt and joined her at the table. Kate spread a generous dollop of preserves on a warm roll as Gavin took a sip of the hot tea. Popping the bread in her mouth, Kate savored the mix of flavors.

"I saw all the Fordices below," Gavin began.

She shivered.

"Is Magnus's wife here as well?"

Kate hoped she was. Perhaps the woman's presence might do something to curb her husband's anger with Kate. She'd woken during the night, terrified that she'd been discovered and cornered by the men but had easily slipped back into sleep in Gavin's arms.

"Aye. They are breaking their fast. Mrs. Fordice has some shopping she wishes to do before they head back to the estate."

"That's good, at least."

"Magnus said they would spend the rest of the day here in Aberdeen before heading back tomorrow morning. Then he asked if I'd see ye. I told him no."

Kate finished chewing and swallowed. "We should head there immediately and gather our things to leave."

"I agree, but I have some business I need to see to here first."

Disappointment crept in along with that ever-present unreasonable fear that he was going to leave her. She hated that her mind went there before waiting for a rational explanation.

"I thought we would go together," she confessed.

Argh, now she sounded desperate. He'd said he wanted her to come to live with him, not that he cared for her in any way. But for now, he needed her, and that was enough to beat back the absurd panic.

"I won't be long. Ye and Miss Ferguson should leave soon, and I'll follow as soon as my business is done."

"Can I ask what ye are doing?"

"Just visiting a person from my past. I'll let ye ken how it goes when I arrive back at the Stonehavens' estate."

She nodded, but worry beat at her. He'd never indicated he knew someone in Aberdeen.

"Once ye arrive at the Stonehavens', get yer things packed. We can leave for Glasgow tomorrow morning," he reassured.

"I'm looking forward to seeing yer home," she confessed.

The thought of the carriage ride without him felt daunting. He'd been able to distract and calm her on the journey here. After his soothing description, she had not been able to stop thinking about how beautiful his home and land must be. Now she would have the opportunity to see it.

"I've already spoken with Isobel, who is preparing yer things this morning. She'll help ye dress in here. I dinnae want ye to go to yer room and risk being seen by the Fordices."

"Thank ye." Relief overwhelmed her at the small gestures he was taking to keep her safe. The steps might only be to protect his case, but she could hope that it meant he also truly cared for her.

"I'll see ye safely off, then take care of my business and follow close behind."

She nodded as she ate another bite of the roll.

"I'll be on a horse, so I'll make good time." He took her hand; the reassuring motion was sincere and calming.

What was wrong with her this morning?

But she knew the answer: for the first time since her mother had discarded her, she'd truly opened her heart to someone. She'd spent years running. Anytime she'd gotten close to another person at Camelot, she would leave for long enough to close her emotions off. Now, she was truly and utterly tied to Gavin in a way that left her vulnerable.

She loved him, and it scared her to the depth of her soul.

The room closed in and became stifling despite the open window. "I need to tell Lady Stonehaven I'll be on my way."

"Nae need. I've had Isobel deliver the message that ye are no feeling well and will head out on yer own this morning." His thumb glided back and forth over the flesh of her hand.

He'd carefully planned everything, but somehow, she was still terrified he was going to disappear and leave a gaping hole in her chest. Damn her mother for putting this fear in her.

They finished the meal, and he stood.

"We have a good half an hour before Isobel arrives." He gave a mischievous smile that said he was not yet sated.

Then he took her in his arms, guided her to the bed, and slowly entered her body. His eyes, his moves, his words, all made her feel cherished and wanted. Her worries faded as she let go and climaxed with him.

A short while later, Isobel was at the door. She dressed Kate as Gavin explored the hotel to be certain the Fordices wouldn't see her leave. Then, he returned and escorted her down a posterior set of stairs she'd not even realized was in the hotel. Her carriage waited in the back.

"Be safe," he told her as his fingers tightened on her hand.

"I'll be all right, just hurry." She stood tall, remembering the hard part of her mission was done, and all she had to do now was collect her belongings, and she'd be going home with Gavin. She let glee and excitement course through her.

"I may even catch up to ye, but I promise I'll be there by the evening meal. My visit shouldnae take long."

With the reassurance, he helped her, then Isobel up into the box. Her lungs began to close in straight away. The horses jerked to a start, and she craned her head around to watch him as she left. He remained in the same position, observing the carriage retreat. She didn't turn back around to face Isobel until Gavin was no longer visible.

Relief filled Gavin's heart as he watched Kate and Isobel head out of the city to safety. Knowing she was out of reach of Magnus and Thomas allowed him the peace of mind to finally confront William Douglas. But now, he wasn't doing it solely for work. In all honesty, he needed the past events cleared from his head so that he could separate them from Kate's association with the man.

She deserved to have all Gavin's affections without them being colored by a previous prejudice.

By the time that all the preparations had been made, and she was on her way, it was nearly noon, and the sun was high in the sky. The temperature was pleasant, and he was thankful that the ladies would have an easy ride back. The rest of their party wouldn't be leaving for a couple more hours, so he had plenty of time to run his errand without having to worry. The gap even allotted time for Kate to escape the carriage's confines for a few moments if she needed to on the journey.

"Be safe," were the last words he'd said to her.

"I'll wait for ye." Kate smiled, and warmth invaded his heart.

"Ye willnae have to wait long." He'd reassured her, and he'd meant it. He'd had his trunk loaded along with hers and had arranged for a swift horse to carry him back, hopefully arriving before any of the other guests.

After seeing Kate and Isobel safely off, Gavin made his way to Skene Street. It was time to face his demons and inform William Douglas that Kate was now his responsibility. He could no longer live with the questions haunting him or the thought that the man might come for her and steal her away.

Kate was his.

At the apartment entrance, he knocked on the door, then straightened his back and clenched his fists, prepared for whatever attack William or his crew might pursue.

The door swung in. A lass with a mass of red curls peered at him through striking green eyes.

"Can I help ye?" the girl about the age of fifteen asked.

"I'm here to see William."

The lass nodded and drew the door in to admit him. "Come in. I'll get him."

Gavin stepped through the threshold and closed the exit. Expecting to find a din of filth and neglected, mistreated children, he was quite surprised to find the opposite. All heads turned his way, assessed him, then most returned their attention to their tasks.

He scanned the room, looking for any indications of abuse . . . nothing alerted him.

Other than the redhead, who according to his meticulous notes must be Greer Harkness, there were five kids present. A man who looked like the person who had pretended to be Kate's brother for her deception sat working with a young boy on reading. It was one of the twins, Cole or Callum Campbell, but he couldn't say which. He imagined the lad was the real Joseph Reid.

The twin was the only one whose mistrusting gaze covertly returned to keep an eye on him.

A young lass, most likely Joseph's genuine sister, Allison, was playing with a child of about one, and another young boy was rifling around the kitchen area as if he'd been cleaning after a meal. All were properly groomed and appeared to be well-fed.

The apartment seemed at first glance to be meticulously kept and the occupants well-adjusted. Perhaps he'd been wrong about William Douglas. He hoped for Kate's sake he was because if the man were ill-treating a child, he wouldn't be able to overlook it.

The redhead returned. "He'll be right along."

Gavin nodded but did not attempt to move farther into the room. He'd need to get William on neutral ground for their conversation. Here, if things went wrong, the twin and the lad in the kitchen would side with William. The odds came down to him against three, and Gavin might lose should an altercation break out.

A few seconds later, the man he'd once called friend emerged at the entrance to what he guessed was a bedroom. William stilled. His sharp blue eyes took Gavin in and sized him up in one swift appraisal.

"Gavin," his voice declared without an ounce of hesitation

as if he'd known Gavin was in town and expected him to make an appearance.

Gavin had anticipated the sound of William's voice to be that of his youth, but he didn't recognize the deep, vibrating tenor of the man who had moved away and never looked back.

"William," he returned.

After an uncomfortable pause, the King of the Streets began, "We should have a drink. Let me get my shoes."

Gavin nodded.

The young lass looked up from the babe she'd been entertaining. "Ye're the one Isobel told us about. The one Kate fancies."

If he were capable of blushing, he would have then. He never let strangers in on his personal life, but he guessed this was what Kate had of a family. Still, it was nice to have the reassurance that she truly had feelings for him. He smiled at the lass but said nothing.

"Ye better be nice to her. She saved my brother and me and brought us here." Allison tilted her head toward the boy reading with the twin, who still eyed Gavin with trepidation but also an unveiled curiosity.

"Are ye well cared for?"

"Aye. Better than we ever were at home." Allison smiled.

"Ye're from Glasgow?"

She nodded. "But we're never going back. There are bad people there."

He hoped it wouldn't come to needing them to return to speak out against Thomas Fordice. He thought Kate's testimony would be enough, and the children wouldn't have to get involved at all.

William returned, dragging Gavin's attention away from the child.

"There's a public house nearby. We'll have privacy there."

Gavin gave a slight dip of the head and followed William

from the apartment and down the steps out into the clear, blue day. They walked in silence about two blocks to the east, then hooked a left onto Mount Street. It briefly crossed his mind that his old friend might be leading him toward a trap. William continued to a dingy age-worn sign that read, the Luck Lantern Arms.

William opened the door and held it for Gavin. When William entered, he called to a server as he led Gavin to a table in the corner. "Helen, two whiskys, please."

Gavin occasionally enjoyed a strong drink, but he got the impression by the lass's puzzled face that William typically didn't. Perhaps seeing a ghost from his past was haunting him.

William claimed a chair with his back to the wall, giving him a full view of the public house and leaving Gavin to take the seat that left him exposed to the rest of the room.

"Are ye here to talk about Kate or that hell house?" William didn't ask about where he'd been or what Gavin had been doing.

Somehow, he recognized that his childhood friend had kept abreast of his comings and goings, or at least looked into his life when he'd discovered Kate's involvement with him. Either way, William wasn't going into the conversation blind, which was what Gavin had anticipated.

Somehow that made it easier.

"Both," he confessed.

Helen sat two generous glasses of whisky before them. William took a large gulp, then winced as the burn hit his throat. Gavin picked up his and did the same.

"Let's tackle the past first. What's there to say? I've attempted to put it behind me," William said.

The King of the Streets shrugged his shoulders, but his gaze darkened and became cold as he leaned back in the chair, looking like a powerful predator in need of prey.

Despite his words, William had most definitely not forgotten the horrors he'd faced in that place.

"What happened that night?"

William's eyebrows knit together. "Ye dinnae remember?"

Gavin didn't know there was anything to remember. He'd gone to bed that night and woke in the field as the house burned in the distance. He rubbed the scar on his head.

"Do ye no' ken how ye got that?"

Gavin shook his head. "All I remember is ye and Drostan dropping me in a field and running off to save yerselves."

"That's not how it happened." William's head moved side to side in slow disagreement.

William studied him, puzzled, as if he couldn't understand Gavin's absence of memories—recollections Gavin hadn't known he was supposed to possess until William's words had them surging back.

"Ye're going to make me say it." Disgust clung to the small lines at the edges of William's lips. "I've never talked to anyone about this." The words came out almost like a growl, a possessive beast not wanting to share the morsels of knowledge clinging to its teeth.

William's eyes roamed the pub, looking to be certain no one could overhear their conversation.

"Why didn't ye save my brother?" Tears stung at the back of Gavin's eyes.

"We tried. Hell, ye really were hit that hard in the head."

Gavin pursed his lips.

"Let's start with the scar." William upended and finished his whisky. The glass trembled in his hand, but Gavin got the impression the quaver was from reliving that awful time and not a normal occurrence.

Gavin downed the remainder of his drink.

"Helen," William bellowed. She must have looked their way because he held up the glass and then two fingers.

"Do ye remember what old MacDougal did to young boys?"

Gavin dipped his head in acknowledgment. Aye, he did. It was why he'd focused his investigations on stopping men like him.

A vision of the man, who had seemed like a giant to young children, now played in his head. He'd been the *schoolmaster* at the orphanage, but they'd been taught nothing but pain at that place. With piercing blue eyes that were so light they almost looked like ice, a full head of gray hair, and the build of a farmer, the man had cut an ominous picture.

And even though some people believed the qualities made him look distinguished, Gavin knew of the horrors that others had faced at his hands, especially William, who had been the man's favorite. Gavin fought off the shudder that snaked down his spine.

"He came for me that night. He dragged me down the stairs, but I fought him. Ye and Drostan woke and came to check on me." William's gaze glazed over, and he averted his eyes as he swallowed.

A memory flashed in Gavin's head, the three of them making a pact never to let it happen again. Gavin was a year older than William and had developed sooner. Drostan had been a year his senior. Only William had fit the perverted man's ideal of a young lad.

MacDougal had never touched him or Drostan. For a moment, pity crept in, and he remembered the helplessness that had consumed them all and eaten away until the three of them had seen no other choice but to defend William at all costs.

Helen appeared with more glasses. She took the empty ones away, and Gavin immediately reached for the next.

"Ye got to the bottom of the stairs just behind us, and ye told him to stop. MacDougal struck ye with something. It was pretty dark, and I dinnae ken what it was, but it gave ye that." William pointed to the jagged line on Gavin's temple.

The memory floated to the surface and clawed at Gavin.

"Ye fell and couldn't get up. We didnae ken it until a few minutes later, but in the scuffle a lamp was tipped over. It landed on the floor near the curtains and must not have caught right away.

"MacDougal pulled me into the room." William swallowed. "All ye need to ken is by the time Drostan got to the room and broke in the door, there was a struggle. The old man pulled out a gun to threaten Drostan, but he charged anyway. MacDougal fired and hit him in the side, and then he set the weapon on his desk as he attacked Drostan on the ground with his fists. I picked up the pistol and checked it, and then I called out to MacDougal. When he stood, I fired." William's eyes were cold and held no remorse for the man who had tortured him.

"That's when ye crawled into the room, blood gushing down yer face. Ye helped me pick up Drostan, but by the time we were back in the hall, the front of the house was engulfed in flames. We couldn't reach the steps. The fire was too hot."

Gavin remembered now, glancing down at his arm. That was when he'd been burned. He'd tried to run past the fire, but it blazed so hotly that he'd barely been able to get near the only set of steps in the house. His shirt sleeve had caught, and William had stripped his own shirt off to throw it over the spot and stifle the flame.

He'd helped William get Drostan out.

"Take him and go get help," Gavin had instructed.

"We'll come back for ye," William had said.

Then, Gavin had gone for the ladder in the stables in hopes that he could get to one of the second-story windows. He'd become dizzy and must have momentarily lost consciousness, but then woke to find William and Drostan retreating into the night.

"Drostan nearly bled out before I found a physician. When I returned, ye were gone, and there was nothing left."

Gavin had spent too long hating William and Drostan for things that had been beyond their control, injustices the three of them had faced at the hands of others. It was time to put that hurt aside and focus on the future.

He nodded to let William know it was enough, then took a gulp of the whisky. "Tell me about Kate."

William's stare turned darker. "First, I must ask, what are yer intentions?"

"I'm going to marry her," Gavin said.

He'd not known the truth of it until that moment. Gavin had grown to relish the little games they played, how she teased, and the way she made him feel whole again.

William nodded, and the corner of his lip turned up in what could almost be a smile but wasn't quite.

"That might work." William rubbed his temple.

"What do ye mean?" Doubt crept in.

"She has a habit of running off when someone tries to get close to her. Has she tried to run away from ye yet?"

She'd retreated on several occasions, and he'd bet that if she'd not had that crazy plan of hers to see through, she'd have been gone a long time ago. Gavin let out a sigh. Had she lied? Would she run away from seeing Thomas in prison? Would she run away from Gavin?

Helen appeared and placed more glasses in front of them. "Why?"

"Flora thinks that it's because of what her mother did. She thinks Kate doesn't let herself get close to others and takes off before they can leave or disappoint her."

"I'm not going to leave her."

"Marriage might work then. Did she agree?" William questioned.

"I havenae asked her yet," he admitted as fear sank in.

"Well, ye better get to it quick. From what I've heard, she's grown rather attached to ye, and that means if ye give her the chance, she's going to run."

Gavin picked up the third glass of whisky and downed the serving in one large gulp.

"Does she still sleep with the club?" William broke into the unease that was settling into his bones.

Gavin blinked at the unexpected question. "Aye."

"When I found her, I was saving Callum and Cole from a man who was going to sell them into servitude. She was locked in a closet, and I wouldn't have even discovered her had she not been making this awful noise like she couldnae breathe."

A tinge of guilt settled in his gut. He'd not even asked Kate what had happened to her after her mother deserted her.

William continued, "I finally got out of her that she'd been living with a woman who had forced her to pretend to be her starving child so that people would give her food and money. When Kate finally told the truth to a man who caught them in the lie, the woman told Kate she didn't want her anymore because she was too honest. She thinks the lady sold her because that night, a man rolled her up in her covers and took her from her bed. He'd been planning to hawk her, along with Callum and Cole."

"That's awful. I'm glad ye were there for her." Gavin had misjudged William. Perhaps because of what he'd gone through as a child, he was even more intent on protecting those who were left behind.

"She went weeks with barely sleeping before I gave her the club and promised no one was coming for her. I told her she had my permission to clobber anyone who came near her, and Callum and Cole set up fake people for her to practice on. They were especially keen to protect her."

He could visualize a little Kate swinging the club to learn to defend herself.

"Over the years, she's disappeared frequently, but every time she came home, she had the club with her. She never went anywhere without it."

"It's my job to keep her safe now," Gavin stated.

"I'm glad she found ye."

Gavin nodded and tossed some coins on the table. He needed to get going so that he would make it to the Stonehavens' estate at a decent hour.

He almost stood, but curiosity stopped him. "What happened between ye and Drostan?"

William's gaze fogged over as his regard focused on something over Gavin's shoulder. The silence dragged on.

He'd almost decided an answer was not forthcoming when William said, "That story would take three more rounds of whisky. And fair warning, I never drink, so that would get ugly. I'm not going to do that to you or myself right now." William pushed the untouched glass in front of him away.

"I'm glad we spoke." Gavin was surprised that he meant it.

"Ye should get back to Kate. I'm afraid I had harsh words for her yesterday when I learned what she'd done. She should never have put herself in danger like that."

"I agree." Gavin stood.

"It was good to see ye," William said, not moving. The gulf between them had shortened, but they were a long way from being friends again. "Take good care of her."

"I will," he said as he turned and hurried toward the door.

CHAPTER 25

*A*s the carriage bounced along, Kate inhaled deep, calming breaths and shut her eyes to envision Gavin's home. She'd be joining him there with the open fields and the gurgling stream. She imagined them sharing a meal on a blanket by the water, then him slowly making love to her. The thoughts were enough to keep her drifting in and out of a peaceful consciousness until they drew up in front of the Stonehaven estate.

"I'm going to be leaving, so we'll need to get upstairs and pack," she said to Isobel as they came to a stop.

The lass had fallen asleep five minutes into their journey and slept the whole way, so she'd not had a chance to share her plans with Isobel. She had envied Isobel's comfort with the carriage ride.

"I guessed by Will's anger yesterday and yer peaceful look, that whatever yer plan was, ye completed it." Isobel smiled.

"Aye, but I'll tell ye nae more because I don't want ye to have to lie. If anyone asks, tell them I'm gone, and ye dinnae ken where I went." Kate had thought about telling Isobel everything, but the girl couldn't lie to save her life. It was best she didn't know.

"Can ye have the trunks sent up straight away?" she asked the coachman. Then, Kate gave her attention back to Isobel. "I'm going to have a cup of tea, then I'll meet ye in my chamber so we can prepare Flora's things to be sent to her."

"I think she wanted ye to have them."

"Nonsense. Now that Lord Dunbridge and her are getting married, she will want them. He bought most of it for her. They'll be at the same inn we just left this week, so we can have them sent there."

"Are ye certain?"

"Actually, a better idea is if ye are going to England, take them with ye. Ye will need some new things."

Isobel blushed.

"I'm happy ye'll have Flora nearby."

"Me too. That made the decision much easier," Isobel smiled.

They stepped into the reception area of the house. They'd made good time, and the late meal would still be a few hours away, so she asked the butler who had greeted them at the door to have a light refreshment prepared, and she headed toward the drawing room.

"I'll see ye in my chamber in about an hour."

Isobel rushed off farther down the hall.

The rest of the afternoon sped by with tea, then packing and separating her items from Flora's. She kept aside what she would need for tonight and in the morning to pull together before she and Gavin left tomorrow. After they were done, Isobel excused herself and said she'd be back to prepare her for the meal in a little while.

Kate began to pace. They'd been back for a couple of hours, and there was no sign of Gavin. She'd expected him long before now. Her gut began to twist with concern, so she made her way downstairs to head out to the terrace for some fresh air.

Miss Clarke, Lord Perry, and the Stonehavens had

returned and were relaxing in the drawing room. The company diverted her attention and eased the worry that had crept in. Although knowing the Fordices were not due back tonight and she planned to be at the evening meal, she took the time to pull Lady Stonehaven aside.

"I have truly treasured yer hospitality, but my brother wishes for me to join him in Inverness."

"Dear, it's been such a pleasure to host ye." Lady Stonehaven drew her in for an embrace.

The surprising gesture warmed Kate, and she regretted all the lies she'd told that had landed her here. They'd been necessary, but because of her deceptions, she'd never again see her or Mrs. Bartrom. She'd grown quite fond of the older women.

Releasing her, Lady Stonehaven drew back and asked, "When do ye plan on leaving?"

"As soon as I can," she said, purposely being vague because she and Gavin hadn't discussed a time.

"I'm sorry we weren't able to meet yer brother."

"Perhaps another time. When will ye return to Scotland?"

"I believe we will continue to make this an annual affair, and ye are welcome to join us again next year."

"I'd like that," Kate said.

"I enjoy this casual atmosphere, away from society, where we can just be ourselves. Did ye ken that before I met Lord Stonehaven, I was a singer and a merchant's daughter? Imagine the stir that used to create in London." Lady Stonehaven laughed.

"I'm sure that was a difficult adjustment."

"It was. Over the years, the ton has warmed to me, but only because I started following all their blasted rules, and with lots of time and James's influence, they began to forget." A sly, mischievous smile slipped onto Lady Stonehaven's lips.

"There is something to be said for being comfortable in many worlds." Kate understood that all too well.

"Irene and I had something we wished to discuss with ye, but it can wait until after dinner. She should be back within the hour."

"That sounds lovely," Kate said.

"I need to prepare for the meal. Will ye excuse me, dear?"

"Aye." Kate bowed her head as Lady Stonehaven headed back to her chamber.

Miss Clarke and Lord Perry joined Kate

"I appreciated the trip into Aberdeen. Thank you for planning it," Miss Clarke said.

Although terse upon first meeting, Miss Clarke had grown on her. She'd been cruel to Flora, and there was nothing to excuse it, but the English lass wasn't all that bad. It had been jealousy and fear that had driven her earlier actions.

"Ye're welcome. I always savor my visits there."

"It's a shame the constable was called away," Lord Perry ruminated. "I heard ye say ye were leaving, so ye may miss him."

Kate blinked. Nae, he was coming back. He should be here any minute—he should have been here hours ago. Her lungs suddenly wouldn't fill.

"I thought he was returning this afternoon." Her voice sounded thin and hollow.

"He appeared in the inn lobby before we left." Miss Clarke took a sip of the tea she held.

"The clerk gave him a letter that had been delivered. Once he read it, he mumbled something about the watchman needing to see him, and he rushed from the hotel. The way he was moving, I think he's possibly halfway to Glasgow by now." Lord Perry laughed.

Kate plastered a fake smile on her face as she fought the sickness in her gut. It was all she could do before her suddenly wobbly legs gave out on her.

Miss Clarke continued, "He didn't even say goodbye. I was shocked."

Kate was bewildered as well. More than that, she had a pain deep in her chest, as her heart was breaking in two.

He'd left.

"Did he send a letter?" Kate managed as bile rose in her throat.

"No. Nothing. I'm sorry." Lord Perry seemed to be picking up on her distress.

"Oh, I didn't realize the time. I must get ready for dinner," Miss Clarke said.

She was thankful for Miss Clarke's declaration. It gave her justification to excuse herself as well. If she stayed here longer, she'd end up a blubbering mess on the floor. She was a good actress, but she didn't think she could hide the pain consuming her.

Gavin had left.

Kate nodded in agreement and somehow absently followed Miss Clarke from the room and up the stairs, where they parted, and she fled for the isolation of her chamber. Something stabbed at the back of her eyes—tears. She fled down the hall before they became noticeable.

It couldn't be true. He'd promised. He was going to be here by the evening meal. Despite the oath, she remembered her mother leaving her on a bench, then the lady who had taken her in only to sell her to the highest bidder when she refused to lie.

The truth had always been her enemy. And she'd set it loose on Gavin. She should have known better.

She shut her door, and her limp legs carried her to the bed where she collapsed and gave in to the panic. Utter devastation claimed her. She'd been deserted again. He'd not even sent word to her, knowing she would have to leave in the morning before the Fordices returned.

Her life probably depended on her escaping in the morning.

Isobel strolled in that blasted door that wouldn't lock.

"What's wrong?"

She felt that urge to flee. Isobel wanted to console her, but she couldn't take comfort in anyone's arms right now.

They always left.

Every one of them.

She continuously ended up alone.

"I'm no' going to dinner," she muttered.

"Let me ken what's happened, Kate," Isobel pleaded.

"Nae. I need ye to go." She had to bite her lip, hoping to convey some semblance of being in control of her emotions, although her lungs were collapsing, and she couldn't breathe. She rushed over to the window, but the air refused to sate her starving body.

She wrapped her arms around herself and fought off the next round of tears. Isobel didn't need to witness this.

Kate spoke without looking back at her, "And ye dinnae have to return to dress me in the morning. I'll be gone by then."

She would leave at first light. No amount of distance was going to stop the grief that had clamped onto her soul and torn into it with its vicious teeth.

"Kate, let me help. Talk to me."

"Nae, Isobel. I need to do this alone. Please go." She had to shut it back off, turn all these emotions away, and squash them.

All these feelings were going to rip her to shreds. She had to survive the next little while, and then she could follow her original plan. France would be perfect.

The door shut behind Isobel, and she let her grief pour out.

She cried, gut-wrenching, heart-rendering sobs until her

eyes were dry and her body was weak from fatigue. And still, she knew before the night was done, she would weep more. The pain was coming in waves now. She'd pull herself together long enough to stand, and then she'd collapse on the bed again.

Another hour and a half later, Gavin still had not appeared. Some part of her had still hoped it wasn't true, that he'd not lied to her. The evening meal was probably near its end when she heard noises in the hall. She took a deep breath, hoping beyond any dreams she ever could have that it would be Gavin.

The knob on her door began to turn. She stood and rushed toward the door. When it swung in, the stone-cold faces of Magnus and Thomas Fordice came into view.

∾

G avin sped toward the Stonehaven estate as fast as he could on a horse that had taken him a goodly amount of time to find. Someone had paid the stable master with whom he'd rented his planned steed a fortune to take the beast before he got back. He'd had to travel to three different stables before he had found another one.

The sun had already set, but thankfully this time of year, a light glow emanated most of the evening, and he could still see to make his way back.

The afternoon had not gone to plan. He was supposed to be dining with Kate right now, then taking her up to his chamber to make love to her and ask her to marry him. At least he still had that to look forward to. Perhaps not the meal, but the rest of it.

After his visit with William, he'd stopped at the hotel to have a light repast before starting the journey back to Kate. When he walked in, it was to find a note had been sent from Nigel, the local watchman. The words had chilled him to the bone, and he'd set off on the thirty-minute walk to consult with the man straight away.

I have news on your men from Glasgow. Come see me. Nigel

He'd rushed over, only to be told that Nigel was out seeing to a domestic dispute and should return soon. The man at the counter had no idea what Nigel's news was, so Gavin was forced to wait. He wanted to see Kate, but at least he knew she was safe and back at the Stonehavens' estate.

An hour and a half later, Nigel strolled in. "Ah, ye received my message."

"I did, but I'm in a hurry. What did ye discover?"

"Yer two men came by this morning, and I think ye're correct."

"How's that?"

"The older one had murder in his eyes, and he was asking about Kate. I saw right from the start he was out of his mind with rage, so I told him I didnae ken Kate."

"Were they satisfied?"

"Nae. They made me take a full report and gave me a crazy story about Kate pretending to be some child and swindling them out of a building. Said she even faked an office somewhere with characters who filed all the transaction forms."

Gavin knew the man was on Kate's side, but he wasn't going to interrupt and tell him that the Fordices had been speaking the truth. What Kate had done was wrong. He couldn't believe he was excusing her actions, but her motives were in the right place.

Nigel continued, "Apparently when they went back this morning, the office had been closed up as if no one had been using it for months."

"Did ye tell William?"

"No' yet, but I will. I don't think they're going to stop until they kill her. I've seen some sick things, but what was in that man's eyes even scared me."

"There was just the two of them?" Gavin was still uncertain if Stewart knew anything of his brother and father's actions.

"Aye. Magnus and Thomas Fordice," Nigel said.

"She's agreed to turn king's evidence on Thomas. He's the one I was telling ye about. Magnus is his father, and I suspect he is capable of murder."

Nigel shook his head.

"Please let William know they're looking for her and that I'll keep Kate safe. I need to get back to her now."

"Will do. Take good care of her."

Gavin stopped with his hand on the knob. He turned. "Thank ye for letting me ken."

"Of course," Nigel answered and tipped his head.

Now, he focused on his steed and the road before him. As the horse galloped down the path, he knew the hour was growing late. Kate was already most likely finishing up the evening meal. He'd promised her he'd be there before dinner, but the delays had been unavoidable.

When he reached the house, he would take her hand and sweep her up the stairs to his room. She would be by his side every night from here on out. He would make love to her slowly tonight and let her know what she meant to him. Then he would take her home.

CHAPTER 26

*T*he blood drained from Kate's face. Magnus's mouth was twisted into a menacing snarl, but what terrified her was the coldness in his eyes. Thomas stood there with a knowing smirk as if he were excited about what his father might do to her.

"Get out," she ordered.

But the men moved into the room and shut the door behind them. She thought to scream, but everyone else was at dinner. It would do no good. She pivoted and rushed toward the bed for her club.

Her fingers clenched around the solid weight of it, but before she could swing it around, Thomas was on her and clutched onto the wrist of the hand that held it. He raised her arm above her head so she couldn't strike.

Magnus darted forward and pried the weapon from her fingers, throwing it. An ominous thud reverberated in the space as it hit the floor on the opposite side of the room. She wouldn't be able to reach it.

Fearing it would still not bring assistance, she bellowed anyway, "Help!"

As she did, Thomas's fist struck the side of her cheek.

Pain exploded in her head, and she thought she might fall over, but Magnus grabbed her from behind in a tight squeeze that left her arms useless at her sides.

"The rag," he roared at Thomas, who reached into a sack she'd not noticed before.

She blinked the pain away and inhaled sharply to yell out again. Before she could, Thomas threw one hand over her mouth as he rummaged through a sack that he'd slung over his chest. He pulled out a fabric of some sort and began stuffing it in her mouth.

She screamed again, but her words came out jumbled, and she struggled harder with Magnus. It was no use. She didn't have the strength to overpower both men. Her entire body trembled with terror.

"Give me her hands," Thomas said, and she felt her eyes widen as she tried to protest.

Nausea claimed her as bile rose from her belly, and she remembered the way her mother had trussed her up and packaged her in that crate so long ago. Panic became tangible. The air in the room thickened.

Magnus's grip loosened long enough to move and secure her forearms. As he held them in front of her, her already dry eyes watered again as the helplessness of her situation saturated her nerves. She went limp.

Thomas wound twine around her wrists, tugging tightly, burning her skin. She shook her head back and forth and made another escape attempt, kicking out. That wasn't successful, so she tried to bring her knee into Thomas's groin. He twisted to the side in time to render her blow useless.

"Bitch," he called out and punched her in her belly.

She wanted to double over with the pain, but Magnus still had her pinned from behind.

Tying the rope off in several organized knots, Thomas backed. "Done," he boasted.

Then, he reached back into the bag and pulled out a strip of cloth that he wrapped around her head to keep the gag in her mouth. Magnus eased his grip. When Thomas had it secured, Magnus pushed her to sit on the bed.

"Find a bonnet in her things. It will hide the material."

Fear beat through her veins, and she heard her heart's erratic rhythm pounding in her ears.

Thomas rifled through her trunks as Magnus turned his attention on her. "So, ye are no' Allison Reid. Ye are just plain Kate from Aberdeen."

He couldn't have any idea how hard the blow of those words struck her. Of all the things that had gone wrong today, that was the sum of it. She was just Kate. And no one wanted Kate. Not even Gavin. If he had, he would've been here like he'd promised. He wouldn't have gone back to Glasgow without her.

"Ye may have my building, but ye'll never take another thing from a Fordice again," Magnus taunted, a sinister smile lighting his face.

"Here," Thomas said as he handed Magnus the bonnet.

The older man tied it in place, then jerked her from the bed, his talons digging into the meat of her upper arm and dragging her across the room. "Get the door, Thomas."

The men led her down the hall toward the back of the house, away from the other guests. She attempted to dig in her heels and then to go limp, but it was no use. One man was on each side of her, holding her arms and hauling her along.

Thomas pushed open the door to the dwindling light. She breathed in deeply through her nose. It felt as if the air was finally reaching her lungs. A full moon shone high in the sky. There was still light. Someone would see them.

Hope sparked.

They dragged her along toward the stables, and she realized the reason for the bonnet. If anyone from the house saw them from behind, they wouldn't notice the bindings around her head, and it would appear as if two men were simply out walking a lady.

She continued to struggle, but her limbs were weakening, and with each yank, the rope at her wrists tightened and dug into her skin, burning her raw flesh.

When they reached the stables, she glanced around, looking for anyone who could help, but there was no one about. The men hauled her to a wagon near the rear of the building. Thomas hopped into it then heaved her up behind him.

Magnus climbed in. "This is what happens when ye cross a Fordice." They grabbed both her arms and forced her down. Wood scraped across her ankles as the world tilted, and she landed harshly on her back.

It was dark down here, and she looked to see how to escape, only to discover slats pinned in her on all sides. The smell of freshly shaved wood filled her nostrils as she fought for breath. Her entire body went numb with fright.

They'd put her in a coffin.

Her body shook uncontrollably. She attempted to sit up, but before she could, they put another plank on top, and the world became dark. Her breathing grew even more labored as full-on panic struck her like a bolt of lightning.

She struggled anew, kicking at the covering. It jolted a little, and a shaft of light broke through where the wood was askew. She tried again, but then pressure was placed on it, and she couldn't get it to budge. The covering was moved back over the center, and despite her efforts, she couldn't shift it again.

Magnus's voice reached her through the wood. "Take Eddie and go get her trunks. It has to look like she left on her own."

She stilled. An odd awareness washed over her. It didn't matter where they took her or what they did to her; no one would come looking. She left all the time. Everyone expected it of her.

Hammering began on the wood as Magnus sealed her in.

She was going to die.

~

G avin handed the reigns to a lad at the front of the house and barked instructions on its care. He'd have to arrange to have the animal returned tomorrow, but for now, all he wanted to do was get inside and find Kate.

He rushed through the front door without waiting for the butler and charged toward the drawing room. He scanned the area. The Bartroms, Stonehavens, Miss Clarke, Lord Perry, and Mr. Clarke were all present, but no Kate.

He collected his breath and strode up to Lady Stonehaven. "Good evening," he said, feeling like he couldn't just blurt out his question.

"Constable Davidson, so glad you made it. We expected you some time ago."

"I had some unavoidable delays."

"Shall I have a meal prepared for you? The kitchen staff probably still has everything out."

"Nae, thank ye. Was K . . .. Miss Reid at the meal?" he queried.

"I'm sorry, Constable. I believe ye have missed her. As soon as we arrived, her brother sent word that he wanted her in Inverness with him."

That didn't make sense. His mind searched for something he'd missed. They'd decided to leave for Glasgow in the morning . . . together. Lady Stonehaven was mistaken.

"Are ye certain?" He couldn't believe it.

Lady Stonehaven looked perplexed. "Well, I thought she was going to wait until the morning, but she hasn't been down, and I overheard her maid tell Miss Clarke that she was free to help her with a task because Miss Reid was leaving."

He had a heavy feeling in his belly, and his heart began to pound loudly. He swam in disorientation as everything in the room blurred and his lungs became tight. Lady Stonehaven's perfume, normally the scent of understated roses, seemed over-applied and gnawing as his senses heightened and expanded.

"Will ye excuse me? I'm tired from the long day." He turned, not waiting for a response, and plodded for the stairs. Afraid of what he'd find when he opened Kate's door, his feet trudged on like a soldier headed into his first battle. But he had to see her, had to know she was there—that she was safe, and she hadn't left him as William had warned.

After bounding up the stairs, then cutting through the hall, he arrived at Kate's door. Twisting the knob, he pushed in. A quick scan of the room told him she had fled. Stepping in, he drew it closed behind him as he took in the evidence of her betrayal. Her trunks were missing, and no items rested on the dressing table. The room was empty.

Kate had lied to him.

She was gone.

Pain beat at his chest, suffocating him, as he fought a wail that wanted to bubble up to the surface and scream out for her. His throat hurt as he struggled to take his next breath.

How had he fallen for her lies?

Now, not only had she left him, but he wouldn't have a case against Thomas Fordice. He wanted to scream with frustration, with regret, with devastation. She had played him as easily as she had the Fordice men. Kate had been the one in control all along. Had he imagined the desire in her eyes? He'd believed she could love him in return.

He sat on the bed and could still smell the trace of spiced oranges and gardenias, now scents that would forever be tainted in his mind. A smell that would haunt him.

He ran his hands through his hair, surprised that they trembled, with what?

Anger, grief, loss.

He stood, turned, and punched the mattress several times, then snatched a pillow from the bed. Bringing it to his nose, he inhaled and fought the ache that knifed at the back of his eyes.

Pushing away his anguish, he squared his shoulders. He had a mission. He'd track her down. She might not want to go home with him or marry him, but he could lock her away until Thomas answered for his crimes.

That little boy deserved justice.

Taking a deep breath, he drifted toward Kate's still open window to get a breath of air before collecting his thoughts and beginning his search. She only had a few hours start, but he'd bet she'd lied about Inverness being her destination.

The night was calm, and a gentle breeze wafted over his skin. He would find her, he reassured himself.

As he turned to leave, his gaze caught on something he'd missed near the corner of the room. The object was out of place, thrown askew like it had been tossed aside. He blinked.

Kate's club.

William's statement came back to him. "She never went anywhere without it." His mind raced back to seeing her that first night with it by her side on the bed. If William was correct, then something was deadly wrong.

His rage and grief turned icy in his veins. Fear clamped its claws around his heart and blocked out everything else. Where was Kate?

He rushed to his room, unlocked it, and pushed through the terror. He tossed Kate's club on his bed, then rummaged through his trunk. He grabbed the pistol he kept in the hidden pocket, checked it, then fastened it to his side.

Only moments later, he tore back into the drawing-room. Uncaring of following any decorum, he raced to the Stonehavens, who sat conversing with the Bartroms. "Who was the last person with Kate?"

They all looked at him, stunned. "I mean, Miss Reid. I'll explain her name later. When was the last time anyone saw her?"

"About an hour before the meal," Lady Stonehaven said.

Lord Stonehaven's face was pale. "Does this have anything to do with . . .?" He didn't finish the question as his regard drifted to the Bartroms. He pursed his lips.

"Aye. It might. Are the Fordices still in Aberdeen?"

"Magnus and Thomas returned today, but Mrs. Fordice and Stewart stayed behind," Lord Stonehaven stated as he stood.

"Were they at the meal?" Gavin questioned.

"No." Lady Stonehaven shook her head.

"Do you think she's in danger?" Lord Stonehaven stood. A determination and strength Gavin had not seen before emerged.

"Aye. I do. I'll explain everything later, but for now, we need to find them and Kate."

"But who's Kate?"

"Miss Reid is Kate. She is a witness against Thomas Fordice. The deception of her name was necessary to keep her safe." Technically, this was not a lie, but he found it odd how easily the words slipped from his mouth to protect her.

The truth had turned into varying shades and no longer lived only in black and white.

Mr. Bartrom chimed in, "I stepped outside for a smoke before dinner, and I saw the Fordices take a wagon down the path that led into the woods behind the pond."

Sweat broke out on his temple as time slowed. A scream lodged in his throat. That was hours ago.

Whatever had happened to Kate, with all his running, he would never be fast enough.

CHAPTER 27

*K*ate drifted in and out of consciousness.

The coffin she was in was hastily built or of poor quality because somehow air continued to reach her. She tilted toward a slight breeze and somehow made out a glow in the dark space. A knot in the wood had marred the perfection of the smooth, flat surface.

The wagon, which had been plodding along down a bumpy, possibly deserted road had come to a stop, and she heard men's voices but could not make out the jumbled words.

She floated back into a vision of her mother closing her in the chest all those years ago. She remembered how she'd thought she would die, that no one would ever pull her from the confines of her prison. She was back in that moment, but she was in the present, too. The worlds jumbled together, and she lost consciousness again.

The box shifted and jolted her from her haze. They were removing her from the wagon. When it tilted, and the bottom hit the ground, her knees buckled, hitting the plank that had been placed on top to close her in. Thank heavens, at least her head hadn't been on that end.

Although her hands were bound, she was able to reach up and tug at the strip of cloth around her face. She drew it down, then yanked the stuffing from her mouth. She was slightly more comfortable, but her mouth was dry and had an awful taste.

She didn't call out. There was no use because the voices were that of Magnus and Thomas, possibly one other man, so screaming for help would do no good until they were gone.

She drifted back to sleep.

A feeling of weightlessness, then a thud, jarred her from her slumber. It appeared as if they'd tossed her into a hole, but she couldn't guess how deep.

A thunk and swish sounded from the surface of her box. Dirt, she thought, and she could practically feel the weight of it as more was shoveled on top.

A new tear drifted down her cheek, and she turned into the knot for air, hoping to make it a little while longer. The air in the small space was already thin, and she'd been having trouble filling her lungs.

She'd never look upon Gavin again, smell him, feel his arms around her. She let a daydream intrude, one where they were together and at his home. Where he truly cared for her, and he would never leave. A place where he loved her as she did him.

Perhaps this was a fitting way to go. She'd just disappear.

She thought of Camelot. No one would ever know what had happened to her, and they'd always be expecting her to return one day. But at least all the children had a home and were safe. William would see to their care, and they would all be fine without her.

No one needed Kate.

As the ground continued to be heaped on top of her and the sounds of the voices faded, silent tears streamed down her face.

G avin sprinted to the stables, thankful that the evening sky still held enough light to see easily. As he'd taken off, Lord Stonehaven had begun barking orders to assist in finding Kate, Magnus, and Thomas. Lord Stonehaven, Mr. and Mrs. Bartrom, Mr. Clarke, and Lord Perry followed him. But with his training, Gavin was leagues ahead. Lady Stonehaven and Miss Clarke stayed behind to search the house for any clues.

Stepping inside the building, which had plenty of room to house the carriages as well as the horses, he noticed the steed he'd planned to use to get back earlier. Magnus must have persuaded the stableman to lend it to him instead.

Familiar voices from the far end of the structure reached his ears. Gavin sneaked down the corridor.

"Eddie, if ye say anything, ye are next," Magnus's voice threatened.

"I promise, sir," the voice quavered. It was Eddie's, the carriage driver he'd interviewed last week.

Gavin stepped from around the corner and took in the three men. They all had scuffed shoes and patches of dirt on their persons. Gavin's gaze turned to the shovels pulled from the wagon and laid up against its side.

The men froze when they noticed him.

"Where is she?" The steely gravel in his bellowed question scratched his raw throat as rage took the place of fear.

"Who?" Magnus Fordice stood tall.

Nigel had been right. There was a coldness in his eyes that chilled Gavin to the quick of his bones. He had no qualms ending a life if it suited him, and by his dismissive posture, he knew the man had already taken matters into his own hands.

Panic mingled with fury as he bounded closer.

"Kate. Miss Reid. Whatever ye want to call her." Gavin

took another pace forward. He didn't have time for games. He had to get to Kate. "If ye have harmed her, ye will pray for a swift death."

Eddie separated himself from the men, inching to Gavin's left. He was the one who cracked.

"They made me do it," Eddie sobbed. "I didnae ken there was a lady in there."

"Shut up, Eddie," Thomas bellowed.

"What did they do, Eddie? I'll keep ye safe," Gavin cajoled.

"Dinnae say a word." Magnus stepped toward him. "Ye are in my employ, and dinnae have to answer any questions."

Eddie was nearly beside Gavin now. "They made me help. It was a coffin."

Dread captured Gavin, clenching around his heart.

"Stop," bellowed Magnus, and he drew a gun from somewhere in his waistband. He aimed it at Eddie.

"Duck," Gavin shouted at the coachman as he wrenched out his pistol, aimed at Magnus's shoulder, and pulled the trigger a hair before the arse could engage his.

The bullet pierced Magnus's shoulder, and his shot fired up into the air. Magnus wavered. He grabbed his newly limp arm. Agony etched on his face, he stumbled, then plopped onto the ground.

Thomas lunged, knocking square into Gavin's chest, and jolting him backwards. The gun slipped from Gavin's hand, but he kept his footing. Thomas drew back and threw a punch. Gavin dodged and came up with a hook that hit Thomas at the bottom of his jaw. The man howled in pain and retreated.

Gavin landed one more blow, then Mr. Clarke and Lord Perry swooped in and pulled Thomas away, easily restraining the man.

Magnus was still bleeding on the ground, but Lord Stonehaven and Mr. Bartrom stood watch over him. At the moment, Gavin didn't care about his case, didn't care what happened to these men. He needed to get to Kate.

Was she alive when they buried her? How long would she have air? If she'd panicked because of the small space, she would have less.

Bile rose and burned his throat. "Where is she?" he roared at the men.

"I ken," Eddie volunteered. "I'll take ye."

"I'll help." Mr. Clarke grabbed the shovels as Eddie pushed open the large stable door, then seated himself back in the wagon.

"Was she all right when they buried her?"

"I dinnae ken," Eddie answered. "There was nae sound."

Anguish like he'd never known erupted in his chest.

He was going to be too late.

CHAPTER 28

*K*ate opened her eyes, but all was still dark. No more air reached her through the knot on the side of the wood, and no light showed in. How long had she been in here? It felt like days but could have only been minutes.

Voices filtered in again, and for a moment, hope returned until she recognized one of them as Gavin's.

She was imagining things.

He'd left her.

Just like her mom had.

She began to sob again, and what little air remained wouldn't fill her lungs.

Then, everything went blank.

*E*ddie drove the cart back to the location where Magnus had done the unthinkable.

Shadows grew around them as they traveled through the dense forest that circled back behind the pond he'd been running around in the morning. It was secluded back here, and the route was not traveled often.

The wagon came to a halt. They grabbed the shovels and followed Eddie down an overgrown path. A few paces in, they came to a recently disturbed mound of earth. A shudder wracked him as he thought of Kate buried beneath the dark soil. If the coachman had not volunteered to take them to Kate, they might not have ever found her.

They began chipping away at the spot.

The cool night was thick with humidity and sweat dripped down Gavin's temple. His heart raced, and with each plunge of the spade into the disturbed dirt, it pounded louder in his chest.

How long had she been in there? He threw a shovel full of earth to the side. The scent of worms, muck, and decay suffocated him with dread.

Would she have enough air? He dug into the ground again. The *che* of the instrument plunging into the loam was followed by the *shhh* of tossing it aside.

The questions tormented him and kept repeating over and over in his mind with each load of soil he moved.

Che.

Shhh.

Che.

Shhh.

Mr. Clarke and Eddie dug right along beside him. Tears streamed down Eddie's face. Gavin knew he had been an unwilling participant in the Fordices' plan. Magnus had probably planned to put the man below the ground as well when they got back to Glasgow.

"It's no' deep. We've almost got it." Eddie insisted, but the fact that Kate was buried under the earth at all was too far.

Che.

Shhh.

Gavin had failed to keep her safe . . . and now he might be too late.

His chest felt as if a tree had fallen on it and pinned him to the moist dirt—the smell of which invaded his nostrils and clung to the evening air. There was still a little light, despite the dense forest around them, but if they didn't make progress soon, they would need some lanterns.

Che.

Shhh.

They didn't have the luxury of time to retrieve the lanterns. He needed to get Kate out now. He remembered her reaction to the carriage and the closet. The space she was in now was much smaller. She'd probably been inconsolable, and her panic would have diminished her air supply too quickly.

Che.

Shhh.

Gavin's shovel hit wood.

Thank heavens they'd only buried her about two feet below the surface. Magnus probably thought no one would ever discover her back in this desolate spot, and no one ever would have, had it not been for the silly club she carried around.

When he got her out, when they were married, that club would have a place of honor beside their bed.

"Kate," he called out as they unearthed more of the sarcophagus.

There was no reply. Pain pounded in his chest.

Mr. Clarke and Eddie increased their pace along with him.

Che.

Shhh.

The others had stayed back to secure the Fordices so they couldn't escape. Those men better hope she was alive because if she'd been harmed, he would bury both of them alive and insert a pipe to give them enough air to draw out their suffering.

"Kate," he shouted, but it might have come out more like a wail. Still no reply.

They'd pulled enough dirt away now, but the top was sealed shut. "All on this side," he ordered. "We'll have to pry it open."

They positioned the spades just under the lid, then pushed them down together. The leverage was enough to pull the nails free from that section. The wood creaked and opened up to reveal Kate's limp body.

"Hold it back." He pointed to the cover, and the men understood. He needed it out of the way to retrieve her without scraping one of the nails across her sensitive flesh.

She didn't stir.

Reaching in, he collected her still-warm body in his arms and heaved her up into his chest, liberating her from the prison. He took two steps back and collapsed onto the ground with her cradled near. Her hands were bound, but it appeared as if she'd been able to remove the cloth that had been secured around her mouth.

Trails of salt marred her cheeks. His heart ached for the torment she must have endured in the wooden crate. He wouldn't call it any other name because she was alive.

She had to be.

Gavin placed his head on her chest, and the world around him quieted as he concentrated. Nothing.

He readjusted and covered his opposite ear with a hand. The steady but slow rhythm of her heart reached him.

"She's alive." Relief rushed through him, and his eyes stung.

Still, he put his cheek to her nose to check that she was breathing. A slight intake and exhalation of air were detectable.

"She's breathing." The reassuring words were more for

himself than to inform the men with him. Gavin pulled at the strings on the bonnet to loosen it from her head. He tossed it aside. "Do either of ye have a knife?"

"I do," Mr. Clarke said. He reached down to a strap at his ankle, unfastened it, and handed Gavin the dirk.

Gavin took it and went to work on the rope binding her wrists together. When it fell free, red marks were visible where the twine had rubbed against her soft flesh. Next, he cut the material that had been tied around her head but now lay like a loose scarf around her neck.

When he had the offending remnants of her ordeal removed, he caressed her face with his fingers. "Kate," he whispered, an ache scratching the inside of his throat.

Her limp body didn't respond. "Kate," he said louder and gently shook her. He looked up at the other men as helplessness engulfed him. "Why won't she wake?"

"Let's get her back to the house. We can send for a physician," Archie said calmly. "She's going to be all right."

Gavin nodded, and he let the men help him up, but he couldn't let go of Kate—didn't know if he would ever let go of her again. It had been bad enough when he'd thought she'd left him, but the desolation he'd felt at nearly losing her was too much to bear.

He paid no heed to the short journey back to the house as he cradled Kate in his arms.

"I have ye now," he assured her. "Ye're safe. We're out in the open with the whole sky above us. Ye can breathe now. Come back to me, Kate."

When the wagon stopped, he found Eddie had driven them straight up to the house so he wouldn't have to walk too far. "Eddie, I'll need ye to testify against them. If ye help lock them away, they will never be able to threaten ye again."

"Aye. I will. I have a daughter her age." Eddie nodded at Kate. "And what those bastards did was heartless. They should never be allowed out. I promise I didnae ken what they were going to have me do until we got out there, and then I thought they were going to kill me."

"I ken," Gavin said as Mr. Clarke helped him down, and he proceeded toward the house.

He carried Kate straight through to the drawing room where a group of the guests waited for news, but he didn't notice the faces of who was there because his sole focus had become the woman in his arms.

In the light, a swollen red patch became visible under her left eye. A burst of rage intruded on his grief. If he'd seen either of the Fordice men at that moment, he would have killed them.

"I sent a man to fetch the physician." Mr. Clarke appeared at his side.

"Is she breathing?" Mrs. Bartrom asked.

"Aye." He nodded.

Isobel ran in with tears in her eyes. "Is she all right?" She stopped in front of him and raised a hand to caress Kate's cheek as if she too needed to feel that Kate was still warm.

He wanted to say yes—needed to say yes—but he wasn't certain. It was as if she'd gone into a sleep and didn't want to wake up.

"I dinnae ken," he admitted as a new wave of anguish wracked him.

Mr. Bartrom had been pacing the room. His face paled as he analyzed Kate's limp form in Gavin's arms. "We have the bastards secured, and Lord Perry is taking a turn keeping watch."

"Here, come sit." Lady Stonehaven indicated the sofa in the center of the room.

He shook his head and glanced over toward the large, windowed doors. They were open. "Outside. She likes the air."

Threading through the furniture and the crush of people who moved back to let him pass, he exited the room. He noticed a gentle breeze as he stepped back out into the cooling night.

He passed over the terrace and moved down the steps into the yard, heading for a bench on the outskirts of the garden. The others stayed back, sensing that he needed the time with her.

Sitting, he propped Kate up farther in his arms, so that her head was at his chest level. He placed kisses on her forehead.

"Wake up, Kate. I'm here. Ye can wake up now. It's safe. I'm no' going to let anything happen to ye ever again. I'm so sorry I wasn't here before," he choked out.

Placing his ear back to her chest, he was encouraged that her heartbeat was strong and steady. "Kate, ye have to wake up now." He took in a deep breath and let it out slowly. "The box is gone. Magnus and Thomas are gone. We're sitting outside in the refreshing night air. The stars are shining down on ye, and they might fade if ye dinnae wake up."

She stirred, and her head tilted closer into his chest as if seeking his warmth.

He kept her nestled near with one arm and reached with the other to trace his fingers over the soft flesh of her cheek. Her lips curved in a smile. He dipped and put his mouth on hers, the gentlest of embraces, before straightening and studying her placid face.

Kate opened her eyes, closed them again. Her lids fluttered once more, and then she kept them open. They were alert and questioning.

"How are ye feeling?" he asked as he continued to caress her cheek.

"My head hurts. I . . ." She blinked a few times.

He massaged her temple. "We've sent for a physician."

Her expression was blank.

"Ye dinnae have to worry about them anymore."

She frowned. "Who?"

"Magnus and Thomas."

She stiffened at the names and blinked one more time before the confusion disappeared from her stare. Fear mingled with the hazel of her eyes.

"They cannae hurt ye now. Ye are safe," he insisted.

A drop of moisture tore down her cheek. "I thought ye'd left. I didnae think ye were coming back."

"Oh, Kate. Ye willnae get rid of me that easily." He wiped away her tear and kissed her. "I was detained in Aberdeen, but I got here as fast as I could."

She smiled and snuggled closer to him, and then her lids flickered again.

"Magnus and Thomas are here," Kate blurted. She stiffened as if she'd only now remembered.

"It's all right. They're being watched. Ye're safe."

He wanted to get her mind off it. "Let me tell ye about my afternoon."

She smiled. "I'd like that."

He went over everything he'd done since seeing her off in her carriage earlier in the day, hoping her mind would focus on something other than the trauma she'd endured. When the physician arrived, Gavin carried her up to his room for the man to examine her.

It might be proper to take her to her chamber, but that was where the monsters had found her. He didn't want Kate to have to relive those moments. Gavin refused to take his eyes off of her. He didn't care what anyone else thought at this point, and they didn't question him.

Kate was safe, and he wouldn't be letting her out of his sights for some time to come.

CHAPTER 29

ate was perched on Gavin's bed, sitting upright with the mass of pillows that he had insisted she recline upon. The physician had left, and Isobel darted in with a bevy of servants, carrying a water basin, food, and wine.

"I didnae ken what ye would need, so I brought it all." Isobel gave a worried smile.

"Thank ye," Kate said.

Isobel ran in and hugged her.

When she pulled back, Isobel looked at Gavin. "Take care of her, and if she requires anything, ring for me."

A short time later, Gavin helped her undress to her chemise, then sponged her off, taking care with the raw rope burns on her wrists. They would heal, but she didn't imagine she would ever shake the fear she'd known as the dirt had been tossed on top of the box that she'd been buried in.

She might have nightmares for years to come.

After returning the cloth to the basin, he pulled the pins from her hair. His fingers delved into her tresses and massaged her head as he leaned forward and seemed to inhale her.

"Are ye hungry?" he asked when he was done.

"Nae, but I'd like some wine." Her body was parched from all the crying she'd done. And although her trembling had settled, her nerves were still on fire. Perhaps along with Gavin's presence, a glass might help to calm that.

"How did ye ken I'd no' left? I overheard them say that they were going to make it look as if I had."

"I thought ye had for a bit, but I found yer club. William told me ye never went anywhere without it."

As they sat on the bed, Gavin then opened up about his time at the orphanage and knowing William and Drostan. She'd not known that her brother had had such a relationship with the King of the Docks. There must be more to that story, but it was for William or Drostan to tell.

They had another glass of wine and continued to talk late into the wee hours of the morning. By the time they lay in bed, they were both mentally and physically exhausted. She closed her eyes and burrowed down into Gavin's supportive arms as a deep, dreamless sleep claimed her.

~

Gavin woke with Kate's arm draped over his chest. The soft, warm weight was reassuring. He was not going to run this morning. He wasn't ready to leave her side. The physician had said she would suffer no lasting effects from her ordeal, but although he knew that to be the case physically, it might be sometime before her mental state recovered.

His mind drifted to his home and how he could make the plan more spacious for her, possibly opening up some walls to add more windows. He would do whatever she needed.

They'd talked late into the night and he'd held her as she told him what had happened with Magnus and Stewart and how terrified she'd been.

Kate stirred.

"Good morning, beautiful."

"Yes, it is. I didnae think I would make it to this day." Her voice quavered. "I didnae think I would see ye again."

"We will have many more, and ye're never getting rid of me now. By the way, I told everyone yer name was Kate."

She stiffened, and he turned to wrap his arms around her and draw her in.

"They all think ye were a planned part of my investigation of the Fordices."

Still, she bit her lip.

"They see ye as a hero, Kate." He made it a point to let her know that the rest of the guests truly respected the real Kate. "I'm sorry that we cannae leave yet. I'll send word today, but we need to wait until I have some men present to help transport the arses back to Glasgow."

"As long as I'm here with ye, I'm fine. I'm no' certain I wish to climb right back up into a carriage anyway."

"When we do return, we can go slow and take as many breaks as ye need. Also, I can think of many ways to distract ye on the journey."

He kissed her, savoring the touch and feel of her, deepening the embraces and intensity until they'd made love and lay sated beneath the covers.

A little while later, they sat at the table, breaking their fast and answering the other guests' questions. He leaned in and whispered, "Dinnae go anywhere. I'll be back shortly."

Then he looked at Mr. Clarke on his other side. "Stay here with her until I get back. I need to pen a quick letter to get transport here for Magnus and Thomas."

"I won't let her out of my sight."

"Thank ye."

He hurried to Lord Stonehaven's study, wrote the request, then gave it to the butler to send on its way.

Rushing back to the room, he sat and reached for Kate's

hand, holding on for reassurance. The chatter continued for a while longer, and when their bellies were full, he drew Kate outside.

"Walk with me," he said as he led her toward the labyrinth.

As they entered the tangled web of branches, she asked, "Are ye trying to get me alone?"

"Always," he replied.

He had memorized the maze, and when they were almost to the center, he asked, "Do ye remember what Lord Stonehaven said the day we walked this path?"

"A little, but I have to admit I was distracted by yer presence." She smiled up at him.

"He said that this was 'more than a mere maze. It's a labyrinth that is built to guide you to your purpose.'"

"I remember that."

Gavin was nervous for some reason. Perhaps that was one of the reasons he'd brought her here. She couldn't run from him without him finding her.

"Lord Stonehaven also told us, 'It has been said that a labyrinth 'represents a journey' and 'helps us find our way to our center.'"

"He did." Kate nodded as he led her to the bench in the middle and encouraged her to sit.

He knelt in front of her.

"I kenned the moment I laid eyes on ye that I would be lucky to find a woman like ye. Like the real Kate. I've learned over the past couple weeks that ye are the center of me, what I've been looking for my whole life."

She blushed, a pretty shade of rose.

"I'll never leave ye, and I hope I can persuade ye to settle down and make a life with me. Marry me, Kate. I love ye."

"Yes," she said as her eyes watered with happiness.

His heart was filled to bursting.

"I love ye too." Her hand reached down and caressed his

cheek, then her fingers threaded into his hair and captured the back of his neck to lock his gaze with hers. "Ye have found yer way so deep into my heart that I dinnae ken where I end and ye start. I have nae intention of ever leaving yer side."

He kissed her then, knowing their journey had only just begun.

EPILOGUE

OUTSIDE GLASGOW

*A*pril 1812

The afternoon was sunny but cool. Kate had been in the house most of the day yesterday, cleaning and preparing for a visit from Will, Callum, and Cole, who were bringing Allison and Joseph to give a short statement against Thomas Fordice.

She would also be testifying, but the group of them had agreed that the children could as long as Thomas wasn't present. By all the correspondence she received, they were thriving at Camelot, and all the other residents loved them, which was a good thing since Joseph was now the titleholder of the building.

Magnus had already received the news that he would be spending the rest of his life in prison for the murder of his previous coachman and the attempted murder of Kate. However, Gavin believed he was possibly guilty of more that they hadn't uncovered. Eddie and Gavin had both testified against him, but when Kate had stood before the judge and made her statement, tears were seen throughout.

Reliving the incident had been difficult, but Gavin had been there to hold her when it was over. She'd never outgrown her fear of enclosed places, but her husband's accommodations had made it bearable. And when they had to go anywhere by carriage, he was there to comfort her and guide her through the anxiety.

After further investigation, it was found that neither Mrs. Fordice nor Stewart had known of or been part of Magnus and Thomas's actions. Once the pair discovered their family's deeds, they shunned them, not even showing for Magnus's trial.

Kate and Gavin had come up with their own routine. Gavin was still a constable. He'd never stop pursuing justice for those harmed by others, but he'd cut back on his hours to spend a little more time with her, and he'd been doing research on the garden that he wanted to plant. A small one, just for him and her, to bring him enjoyment.

Her husband had also apparently visited with Will, and they'd reconciled the friendship that had formed when they were wee lads on this very land. She briefly wondered how Will would react to seeing the place and the changes Gavin had made.

Kate had found a position as well. Three days a week, she rode with Gavin into the city to work at the new Glasgow School for the Arts that Mr. and Mrs. Bartrom had opened. They'd been hoping to expand into Scotland for some time and had seen her skills as the opportunity they'd been waiting for. They'd been adamant that she take the lead in their endeavor to teach and groom the newest talent in the area.

She found great joy in the work and sharing her skills with others.

On days when she was at home but Gavin was in the city,

Eddie's wife would come by to visit along with a whole host of others she'd recently met. They had discovered that Eddie and his family lived not far from them, and their presence had been welcoming as they'd introduced her to several of the locals. It felt odd to have friends and let people close to her, but at the same time, she savored the fact that she wouldn't have to uproot herself and leave ever again.

She was at peace here.

As she kicked her shoes off to step into the stream for a brief feel of the cool water, she tilted her head up to the sun and let the wind blow across her face.

Gavin's voice came from behind her, "Ye're a lovely sight."

She turned to face him and couldn't contain the smile that broke across her face. "As are ye, husband. How was yer day?"

"Perfect, now that I get to spend the rest of it with ye."

"I was waiting on ye." She pointed to a blanket sprawled neatly on the ground. A basket and a bottle of wine with two glasses sat nearby.

"I never told ye what I thought about the first time I saw ye."

She stepped out of the water, rushing toward him to claim a kiss. "In the drawing room?"

"Nae. It was at a stream similar to ours. Ye were on yer way to the Stonehavens' estate, and I had been out riding."

"What did ye think?" She was in front of him, near the blanket now.

He took her hand. "That I wanted a woman like ye. One who could be wholly herself and not care what the rest of the world thought of her."

"That wasn't me until recently."

"It was, but ye always hid it. I also thought a lass like ye would never be able to handle my dark side." A smirk lit his lips.

She laughed. "Ye didnae ken my past was shadier than yers."

"My soul must have recognized then that we were a match."

"Funny how fate works," she returned.

"Ye ken what else I thought about?" He glanced down at the picnic dinner she'd readied for his arrival home.

"What's that, husband?"

He wrapped his arms around her and pulled her with him to the blanket. His warm body pressed to hers as his mouth claimed her lips in a passionate embrace. When he drew back, his eyes locked on hers—the blue of them shined with amusement and desire as his pupils dilated.

"Making love to ye here."

"Then I am here to make all yer dreams come true."

Thank you for reading TO SAVE A HIGHLAND SINNER! Please consider leaving a review. I read them all. I love hearing from readers and reviews help me when I'm plotting my next book.

More Wicked Highland Misfits coming soon!
Sign up for my newsletter to see a behind the scenes look at my writing life, get exclusive content, and stay up to date on my latest releases.

https://mailchi.mp/c964d580bc9a/loriannbaileynewsletter

ABOUT THE AUTHOR

Lori Ann Bailey is a best-selling author and winner of the National Readers' Choice Award and Holt Medallion for Best First Book and Best Historical, Lori writes hunky highland heroes and strong-willed independent lasses finding their perfect matches in the Highlands of historic Scotland.

She's lived in Mississippi, Ohio, Manhattan, Pennsylvania, and London, but chose to settle in Vienna, VA with her husband and four children. When not writing or reading, Lori enjoys time with her real-life hero and kids or spending time walking or drinking wine with her friends.

facebook.com/LoriAnnBaileyauthor